Dawn Light

– BEYOND THE PALE –

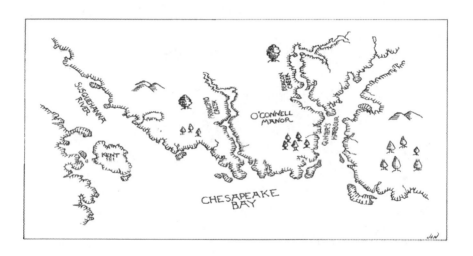

Map of Northern Reaches of Chesapeake Bay

Also by Harv Nowland

Dawn Light on the Chesapeake

Dark Shadows at Dawn Light

Dawn Light

— BEYOND THE PALE —

HARV NOWLAND

WestBow
P R E S S

Scriptural quotations are taken from the **King James Version** of the Bible, which has passed out of copyright and is freely reproducible in most of the world, except for the United Kingdom.

Graphics by Justin L. Nowland

WestBow Press books may be ordered through booksellers or by contacting:

WestBow Press
A Division of Thomas Nelson
1663 Liberty Drive
Bloomington, IN 47403
www.westbowpress.com
1-(866) 928-1240

ISBN: 978-1-4497-0116-1 (sc)
ISBN: 978-1-4497-0117-8 (e)

Library of Congress Control Number: 2010924404

Printed in the United States of America

WestBow Press rev. date: 03/29/10

Contents

Acknowledgements

In the first book of this series, *Dawn Light on the Chesapeake*, I had purposed to write about the people whose family name I bear. The opening chapter in that first book actually occurred as written. However, as I continued to write it seemed awkward to use my family name of Nowland, so I substituted the name O'Connell.

Even if you didn't read the first novel, if you should ever find yourself near North East, Maryland, I invite you to stop at the St. Mary Anne's Episcopal Church. The church was built in the early 1700s and the graveyard that surrounds the church is one of the oldest in Maryland. It contains graves that date back to the 1600s and hold the remains of several of my kinfolk, as well as some Susquehanna Indians. The markers of my Nowland ancestors are found close to the east side of the present church building.

Once again, I thank our grandson Justin L. Nowland for producing creative ink drawings for my books. All that Justin had to work with was my description of something and he would come up with the finished, excellent artwork.

I express my loving gratitude to my best friend, my wife Bobbie. Without her patient encouragement this book would not exist. She continues to gladden my heart with her loving belief in me. And through the way Bobbie lives her life, she continually demonstrates how I am to keep my eyes on our Lord, Jesus Christ.

Introduction

In the first book of this series, *Dawn Light on the Chesapeake*, we found young Sean O'Connell in Dublin Ireland and in desperate need of deliverance from a slothful life of pretense.

An unexpected letter from Colonial Maryland provided a startling source of redemption for Sean's life and he journeyed to the New World to find that he had become both a land holder and slave owner.

He is shocked when on his day of arrival in the New World an attempt is made on his life and he is continually astonished as he encounters all manner of unexpected intrigue and deception.

In the land of his new home, Sean struggled with his role as master of the manor. Colonial Maryland presented him with the cultural clashes and brutality of slavery as unforeseen challenges.

However, Sean also came upon true friendship, the astonishing hand of God in his life, and the love of a woman. His life was changed forever. In fact, when last seen, Sean and his betrothed, Julia Wells stood together quietly looking out upon the Chesapeake Bay.

Looking toward the bay Julia said, "Whether Dawn Light remains with us or not, the day is bright, so very bright, because we will be together."

Pausing, she turns, looks up at him and says, "Most importantly Sean, our future is eternally bright with God."

Gazing into her striking green eyes Sean says: "I agree, because with you and the Lord God, the days ahead promise to be so very exciting and brighter still—brighter and better than ever I've dared imagine."

In the second book, *Dark Shadows at Dawn Light*, Sean continued to resist the cultural clashes and brutality of slavery and his role as master of the manor. Nevertheless, with the love of Julia Wells and their wedding just a few weeks away, images of a bright future fill their hearts.

Still, Sean's dreams—both those that had been fulfilled as well as those yet to be realized—began to unravel.

It is a fortunate truth that God, in His wisdom, allows us only imagined glimpses of the future. For, indeed, bright days did lie ahead for Sean and Julia, but those days also brought with them some *Dark Shadows at Dawn Light*.

This third book, *Dawn Light: Beyond the Pale* finds Sean O'Connell struggling as he faces a future without his wife Julia. But what does it mean to be *beyond the pale*?

A "pale" is a pointed wooden stake. And the paling fence was once significant as an area enclosed by a fence of pales. The figurative meaning is that "the enfolded area is safe". Therefore, to be *beyond the pale* is to be outside a safe area that one might consider as home.

Pales were enforced in various European countries for political reasons, notably in France where the *Pale of Calais* was formed as early as 1360. And in Ireland there was the *Pale of Dublin*.

The first printed reference to the phrase *beyond the pale* is found in John Harington's 1657 lyric poem *The History of Polindor and Flostella*.

In that work, the character Ortheris ventures forth, "Both Dove-like roved forth beyond the pale to planted Myrtle-walk," and his recklessness meets with tragedy—attacked by armed men with "many a dire killing thrust".

The message of John Harrington's poem is clear. If there is a *pale*, you should stay inside it. Sean O'Connell dared to venture *beyond the pale*.

———— Chapter One ————

Wilderness Bound

Common wisdom reveals that each of us has had some form of adversity or tragedy in our past. Even so, we must be cautious not to persist in reflecting on earlier misfortunes, lest they destroy our lives presently. Instead, it is very important to recognize current blessings, of which each of us has a portion; and by embracing those blessings we have the prospect of a splendid future.

"I'll care for him as I know Julia would," Cynthia said as she hugged Sean just before he left. "And I'll tell Nathan of you and his mother every day of his life until you return for him."

The promise that his mother-in-law Cynthia had whispered in his ear would keep calling to him through the years, yet the sorrow of losing his dear wife Julia and everything that had meaning in his life weighed heavily on Sean O'Connell.

When Sean's wife died the dreams, visions and pledges that he and Julia had made were gone forever. Yet, through lengthening weeks, memories of his wife continued to flood his mind.

Oh, dear Julia, he thought, *I know I've disappointed you in many ways. But, I swear on my life that I'll fulfill my pledge to our son. I left Dawn Light behind me, but it was because I was forced to. I couldn't take young Nathan with me just now. Oh God, you have such strange ways of directing us in your paths.*

Sean left Gunter's Harbor in 1718 after he had lost his family's Dawn Light manor—the home, land and possessions—and in the process he had illegally freed his slaves. He thought he could simply ride off and begin anew by putting more and more distance between himself and his losses. However, he found that he was unsuccessful in trying to imagine a future without his wife who had died to the fever—and now he had left his son behind also.

As Sean entered the thickets leading into the woodland forming the beginning of the great forests that showed the way to the western wilderness, another figure had fallen in silently behind him, staying in the shadows at a distance safe enough to observe without being seen.

"Until you return for him," Cynthia had said. Of course Sean meant every word of his pledge to return his son too, yet he had no idea what he would face or the time that might pass before his dreams became reality and he could fulfill his promise to Nathan—and Julia.

He came upon a clear shallow stream, dismounted and allowed the horse to drink. Unsaddling the horse he took a small packet from the saddle, sat down, unfolded the cloth and ate the ham and corn cakes that the Murphy's house slave Missy had given him.

He finished the food, but was in no hurry to go on. After drinking from the stream, he tethered the horse loosely and lay down on a patch of moss next to a large oak. He awoke to the hoot of an owl, sat upright with a start and in the bright moonlight saw that his horse stood close by sleeping. He thought the horse seemed to have made a wise choice, so he took the blanket from the saddle, lay back down and fell fast asleep until the nickering horse wakened him just after daybreak.

Sitting up, he stretched and when he stood his back ached from the root of the oak tree that he had rolled upon. He went to the stream, splashed cold water on his face and wished that he hadn't eaten all of the food Missy had packed. Saddling the horse he thought he caught a glimpse of movement from the corner of his eye, but when he turned to look he saw nothing so he mounted and rode on.

As he wove his way through the dense growth of trees the air was warm. The sound of songs from a variety of birds made the day pleasant and when the sun was almost at its zenith he came to a clearing. Two men and a woman were hoeing a patch of vegetables and stopped to watch Sean as he approached them from the forest.

"Good day to you and God bless those of your home," Sean called to them as he drew near.

The men looked at one another, but the woman called out. "And a fine day it is. But, who are you—trespassing on our land without permission?"

"Aye," one of the men shouted as though it had been his idea to ask. "Who are you and by what right do you claim to be on our land?"

Sean dismounted in the hope that he wouldn't appear to be a threat and led his horse walking toward the three.

"I mean no harm and I've come to see Francis Hough—a Quaker like yourselves, is what I'm thinking."

"Hough the Quaker is it?" replied the other man. "And, why should we not think it's some rogue of a highwayman that you are?"

"I understand and you're right of course. In these times we must be cautious, and I've nothing to prove myself for who I am. But, my name's Sean O'Connell and Francis Hough is concealing my slaves."

"Oh—hiding your slaves he is, then you're one of those who hold slaves," the woman sneered. "Well then, we've nothing more to say than for you to turn back and get yourself from our land."

"I assure you that I have freed my slaves and I only want to meet with Hough. We are friends, and as you can see I have come unarmed and have no shackles—I have neither rope nor chain, so I'm not well prepared to recover slaves as you can imagine."

Again, the men looked at one another not knowing quite how to respond, when suddenly the woman screamed and pointed past Sean toward the edge of the forest.

Sean turned and saw a savage, and even from a distance Sean was confident that it was the same Indian who had helped Ezekiel and the captain a few years back when they had been beaten by thieves. Sean turned his horse about and began to walk the horse slowly toward the motionless Indian.

Drawing closer, Sean had no doubt that it was the same man. Around his neck he wore the ornamental device that lay upon his chest, a large knife was in a leather belt tied around his waist and. yes he was certain now, because in his hand the Indian held a weapon that Sean would not soon forget—the club with a sharpened bone attached to the business end.

Sean dismounted and continued walking toward the man, dropping the horse's reins as an indication that he meant no harm. The Indian casually removed a wooden plug from the gourd that hung across his body. He drank from the gourd and then held the open gourd out, offering it to Sean, who accepted it and drank as his response of goodwill.

"I know who you are," Sean said. "You are the man who helped my friends two years ago. I greet you in their names, Captain Murphy and Jonathan Shore."

The man nodded his head affirmatively, but stood silently gazing beyond Sean. When Sean looked behind him, he saw the men and the woman running back towards what was undoubtedly their house.

Continuing, Sean asked, "Why have you been following me? I know you've been trailing behind me since I left Gunter's Harbour."

Before he could respond, shouts filled the air and Sean turned to see a group of men running toward them. All were bearing farm tools, mostly shovels and hoes, and trailing behind the group Sean recognized Francis Hough.

Suddenly, the men veered away from Sean and when he looked back he saw the Indian slipping quickly into the forest. The men stopped at the edge of the field, unwilling to follow the Indian into the dense thicket. Hough had slowed to a walk, then stopped and bent over with his hands on his knees. Finally he dropped to the ground and Sean could see that he was exhausted.

"Francis Hough, how good it is to see you, my friend," Sean shouted. "But, I'd ask you to call off your friends, because the savage is a friendly sort who has helped us before. Do you not recall—it's the same savage that we told you may have saved the life of Captain Murphy?"

"No way . . . to know . . . such as . . . this," Hough was struggling to breathe and speaking was difficult.

"Yes, of course. I know how we often say that it's difficult to tell one Indian from another. But this is a friendly one who means me—or the rest of you—no harm and of that I am certain."

Sean turned to look for some sign of the Indian but he was nowhere to be seen.

"Come," said Hough, "Let's get back to my house, because I have much to tell you."

Sean reached down to Hough's extended arms and pulled him to his feet. He then offered his horse, but Hough waved him off and chose to walk instead.

As they drew near Hough's home, Sean saw a familiar face trying to stay hidden as he peeped around the corner of the building.

"Obadiah!" Sean shouted. "Come here you little scallywag."

"Mas'Shawn be here. He be here now," Obadiah yelled to no one in particular as he ran toward Sean. Obadiah, the child of Sean's slaves Samson and Kezie, was their only child that had survived the fever

Sean jumped down from his horse as Samson, Kezie and Ezekiel came from the back of the house. He knelt down and Obadiah ran to him and threw his arms around Sean's neck, bowling Sean over backwards. All were laughing as they excitedly talked for several minutes and then Francis Hough spoke.

"Into the house with you Sean, we've been expecting you, and my wife has gathered some dried meat and some victuals for your journey."

"That's most generous of you and your wife Francis. I was by no means calling on you for such kindness. I only wanted to see what plan you might have devised for the Blacks."

"This will be known by me and no others," Hough said as they walked through the low door of the house. "I've already assembled a small group of trusted acquaintances who agree to help me place the slaves safely to the north. Of course, you can always contact me to inquire of their well-being. But for now it's best that you not know where they'll go. I assure you that they'll be safe. Please ask me no more."

"I'll count on you for that, friend. I'm thinking that you'll help them settle somewhere in Pennsylvania—perhaps with another Quaker family, where hopefully they'll be able to remain free and . . ." Hough held his hand up to silence Sean.

"But as you've said," continued Sean, "I'll ask no more."

"Agreed, and a wise decision we've both made," Hough nodded. "I'll send them now to our neighbors and you can take some food at out table and then be off with the provisions my wife will give you."

"And, I shall make inquiries of you later when I'm able," said Sean. "Now please, if you will, help me slip out of here without so much as a farewell to Samson and Ezekiel. I request that you make that possible and that you ask me no more as well. It seems best for all that we know not of one another's whereabouts—at least for now."

An hour later, Sean was riding west by northwest across patches of cleared ground where the Quakers were trying to grow crops for the winter. The sun was sinking low as he entered the forest again and the darkness quickly surrounded Sean, so when he came upon a small clearing next to a creek he chose to stop for the night.

Not wanting to make the same mistake he had made the day before, Sean decided to save the meal Mrs. Hough had given him until morning, because he was always hungry at the start of a new day. He secured the horse to a small pine next to the creek where there was grass and prepared a pallet with his blanket and some limbs from a young pine tree and then slept a deep sleep.

Sean awoke before dawn and opened the cloth packet that Mrs. Hough had given him. He found salt pork, what appeared to be dried venison, some fried corn cakes, and small red objects somewhat larger than a berry. He bit into one of the small objects and immediately spit it from his mouth. He was unimpressed with his first-ever taste of a hard, bitter crabapple. Mrs. Hough had failed to tell him that crabapples were not intended for the major portion of anyone's meal—at least not until they would become soft and reddish brown in late fall. Even then they provided a very sour offering, but something that could be quite tasty with a meal of meat.

He went to the stream and knelt to splash his face with the cold water, then cupped his hand to take a drink. As he stood, he sensed movement and heard a slight noise behind him. Startled, he turned and there was the savage, squatting with a drinking gourd in his hand.

"You frightened me. Have you come for water?" Sean asked.

The Indian simply stretched his arm that was holding a gourd toward the creek.

"Take the water you need," Sean suggested somewhat agitated because of the way he felt the Indian had slipped up on him.

Standing, the Indian went to the creek and filled his gourd.

"Are you hungry?" Sean asked. "Do you want something to eat?" he said as he imitated chewing something while at the same time rubbing his stomach.

"Eat now," the Indian offered, but he turned and went back into the forest from where Sean assumed he had first appeared. He returned momentarily with the carcass of a small animal that had been skinned.

Holding the carcass in front of him the Indian said, "Fire—eat."

Sean smiled and said, "See here now, I am Sean—how are you called?"

"*Nokona*—I am called Nokona. You are one with Black slaves. I see you many times."

Many times? thought Sean. *It sounds as though he has been spying on me—but for what reason?*

"Where?" Sean asked. "Where have you seen me, and why—and how many times have you seen me?"

"Nokona know your village. I go many times find my people. Dutch kill many *Honniasont*."[1]

"*Hosanot*? I have heard the name. What does it mean?"

"No," insisted the Indian. "*Honniasont* we are called—we are the people. Some say *Honniasont* bad—no can trust. They lie. We are the *people*. We are *Minqua—Honniasont*."

"I am sure you are," Sean said somewhat puzzled "Shall I call you Nokona?"

"I *am* Nokona," he replied and appeared surprised that Sean would even ask. It was as though he expected that Sean should know he was who he was—Nokona.

Sean wanted to ask more questions but instead, he offered his hand to the Indian as a non-menacing gesture.

Without hesitating, the Indian grasped Sean's forearm with a strong grip, said something that Sean did not understand, then handed him his gourd and said, "Sean, drink."

They built a fire and the Indian skewered the small animal with a stick and roasted it. As they ate, Sean fascinated by the man, asked questions about the device he wore about his neck. It was a dark piece of leather that had some type of figure inscribed on the surface.

Nokona's responses made little sense to Sean, but he did manage to understand that there were other Indians, perhaps from the same tribe, who did not wear the badge and Nokona said they were also called Minqua.

They fell silent for a time and then Sean asked, "Do you know a man called Pack?"

"Pack friend. Pack die—no live."

"I didn't know he was dead," Sean replied. "Pack told me that you were looking for the bones of your family. Is this true?"

"*Susquehanock* kill family—the people. Look to find family—find bones. They no sleep until find bones—spirit no rest until death dance."

"Well then," Sean replied, "Did you find their bones?"

Nokona reached to the badge on his chest, turned it over and let Sean see two small bones that were laced firmly to the back of the badge. Sean could only assume that Nokona had found his family members—at least some of them.

"Do you have more friends of your tribe?" Sean asked.

Nokona looked at Sean and then looked into the fire without saying anything, and Sean wondered if the Indian didn't understand the question, or just didn't want to respond. After a brief time the Indian stood and walked into the forest.

Sean waited to see if he would return and when he did not, Sean rolled his belongings into his blanket, saddled the horse and once again headed through the forest northwestward.

—— CHAPTER TWO ——

Dangerous Living

Sean traveled for five days and took his time crossing the many small streams and creeks that ran to the west or to the south. The forest had few clearings and there was little change in the hilly terrain, so there was not much to see except an occasional deer or an inquisitive turkey. On one occasion he chose a rock that was light enough to throw but heavy enough that it might kill a turkey if he were able to hit it and he placed the rock in his saddlebag.

That afternoon he saw a turkey and dismounted, quietly reached into the saddlebag for the rock, crouched down and carefully waited for the bird to come close. When the turkey was within 20 feet, Sean stood and was easily able to throw the rock in a deadly fashion—however the tree that he hit with the rock remained alive and well, as did the turkey.

Sean wished that he had been wise enough to arm himself properly. Of course, Fian O'Niall, a member of the crew from Captain Murphy's ship had given Sean his own well-sharpened short sword. Actually, it was more a long knife than a true sword. Nevertheless, Fian assured Sean that it would be dependable for fighting as well as for carving meat.

"A fine weapon it is and good for carving meat—no matter where you might be findin' the meat," Fian grinned.

"It'll serve you well, same as it's served me," Fian had said. And Sean often wondered what sort of meat—or whose—Fian had carved.

Sean's past days of solitude were producing neither thoughts for his future life nor relief from the heartache of leaving young Nathan behind. He tried to envision some sort of plan that might become obvious to him—something he would be able to recognize if it should ever be revealed to him.

However, he remembered how his dreams of becoming a tobacco farmer, then a printer, and finally a ship builder had all diminished and then collapsed. Sean was beginning to doubt himself and wondered if he would ever again be successful, happy, or even be able to provide a meager livelihood for himself and his son Nathan.

He had wrapped one of Julia's favorite poetry books in his blanket, thinking that the verses from her book might somehow ease his pain. The first few days he had tried to read the poetry when he stopped for the night. However, the words seemed dull and meaningless without the voice of Julia to tint the verse properly, and he soon gave up the practice.

I wish I had asked the Tubbs for a Bible, he reflected. *Oh, how I wish I had a Bible to read. But then, I might as well hope to find a ship's canon here in the forest as to wish for a Bible. And what would the Tubbs then do for a Bible if I had theirs? What might those Tubbs cousins be doing these days—and I wonder what lies on the other side of this hill I'm approaching?*

Unable to concentrate, Sean's mind wandered as he rode along. He found himself whistling— tunes he had heard many years ago in the pubs of Dublin. This led his mind to drift again. *Strange how there's so little music in the colonies compared to Ireland—at least in Gunter's Harbour. I wonder why that should be.* With that notion he stopped whistling.

He rode on for several hours and then stopped, dismounted and allowed the horse to rest awhile at a spring that bubbled up from a small outcropping of rocks. Sean noticed a cluster of trees that appeared suitable as a place to rest, so he sat down with his face in the sun, leaned back and watched the drifting white clouds, then closed his eyes and was soon dreaming. However, his reverie was shattered by a woman's scream.

"Shut that rancid mouth you ugly squaw," a man's voice exploded—a barrage of obscenities followed his shouts.

Sean jumped to his feet and listened, trying to establish the direction from which the voice had come.

"You'll do as I say or you'll die!" the man demanded.

The sound of the man's voice was drawing nearer and Sean was able to determine the bearing of the noise. Without hesitation he headed toward the continuing obscenities. Sean drew the short sword as he ran and just then two horses with riders came into view, a woman, naked from the waist up, was in the lead on a saddle-less horse and she was followed by a man. Sean quickly hid himself behind a large pine.

"Just as I say squaw, as I say—do like I say or you'll die," the man shouted again and with that he almost knocked the woman from her horse with a blow from a coiled rope.

They came within a few yards of where he had hidden and Sean stepped out in front of the lead horse and grabbed its bridle.

"You'd best step back now or you'll taste my rope too," the man shouted at Sean, adding curses for emphasis.

Sean slapped the rump of the woman's horse and it veered to the left, just as the man was pulling a pistol from his belt. Pointing the gun at Sean to fire, his angry face changed to shocked disbelief and then pain as he tried to shout out. He fell from the horse and landed flat on his face.

Sean saw a familiar looking object in the man's back and then saw Nokona step from behind some large bushes. Nokona's war club had found its mark in the man's back.

Sean went to the man, pulled the weapon from his back, rolled him over and saw the glazed eyes of a dead man staring at nothing. Sean had never seen the man before. When he looked up, Nokona was leading the woman's horse back toward them and he could now see that she was an Indian.

Sean handed the club to the Indian and in turn Nokona wiped the blood from the club on the man's clothing.

"You've been following me again," Sean said as he looked at Nokona. He wanted to be angry, but knew that once again his life had been spared because of this inscrutable Indian.

"No," Nokona said accompanying the statement with a vertical wave of his arm. "Want find Minqua woman. Nokona know this man bad—he take her," he said pointing to the woman

He didn't know whether to believe him or not, but Sean was satisfied that he was alive because of the Indian. Whatever the reason may have been that caused him to show up so unexpectedly, it had certainly been good fortune for Sean.

Sean took the dead man's pistol, powder and shot, and a small hatchet with carvings on the handle that made Sean think it might have once belonged to an Indian.

Nokona saw Sean investigating the carvings and said, "Tuscarora."

"What did you say?" Sean asked.

"Tuscarora. Man have Tuscarora hatchet," Nokona replied.

Sean divided the food in the man's saddlebags among them and then pointed to the body in a gesture that he meant as an offering for the Indians to take whatever else they might want.

The Indians looked at one another in a way that indicated they wanted nothing that belonged to him. Then they lifted the man's body and carried it into the forest. They did not return for a long time and Sean was about to start again on his journey when they came back. The woman had clothed her upper body and she had several small birds in her hands. Sean had often seen the birds on the Dawn Light manor, but had never eaten a bobwhite quail before. Tonight he would.

The woman prepared a fire and Nokona disappeared again. Sean took the saddles from the horses and was about to tether them to separate trees. However, the woman saw what he was about to do and motioned for him to refrain.

She then took several lengths of leather strapping from the dead man's saddlebags and tied the straps just above the front hooves of the horses, binding their front legs loosely together. This hobbled them and allowed them to move about slowly and eat and drink wherever they chose. A rather simple method used by the Indians to keep the horses from running off, but Sean marveled at what he considered a rather ingenious practice.

The birds were beginning to cook and Sean thought they had a delicious aroma. Nokona must have thought so too, because before long he returned. Sean wondered where he might have gone, but thought better of asking.

The birds tasted even more pleasant than they had smelled. While they ate, the Indians spoke quietly in short sentences with long pauses between. There seemed to be some sort of bond between them. Sean found himself thinking, *She's rather beautiful for a savage—they are inferior in so many ways, but this woman has a pleasant face and seems to have kind ways. Perhaps she's his wife, but who could be sure—some of their behavior is almost like the ways of animals.*

He was about to try entering their conversation when they abruptly arose and walked off together into the darkening forest. They didn't return that night and Sean refused to think about where they had gone or consider what they might be doing.

Sean laid on his back gazing up at the stars as the fire slowly turned to embers. He thought, *this savage seems determined to have a part in my life. Or, is it God's hand at work? Is God seeing to it that my life is being spared through this savage? How I long to ask someone—men like my friends Ben Dixon or the Tubbs cousins—or dear Julia. I may be able to question Ben and the cousins at some time, but never again will I be able to ask my dear wife.*

He awoke in the morning and almost expected to see the Indians around a cooking fire. But they were not there—neither were the other two horses. They had come back quietly during the night and had taken the horses—the man's saddle lay on the ground but the saddlebags were gone.

Strange ways they have, thought Sean. *But maybe they're not so strange as they are simply different than mine.*

Sean grinned when he saw that the Indians had left two of the small cooked birds on a rock next to the dead fire. He brushed the flies away and hungrily ate both birds. They were cold, but some of the taste he had enjoyed last night lingered. As he saddled his horse he also noticed that the woman had left the straps on his horse's front legs.

I believe I'll try that Indian woman's way of keeping my horse tonight, he thought and soon he was on his way to his unknown destination.

The skies had begun to cloud over as he rode along and before long the heavens erupted with a strong wind accompanied by displays of violent lighting. Some of it was striking very near to Sean. *It's almost as though it were searching for me,* he thought when a bright bolt of lightning startled him as it ripped into a tree and the top half toppled to the ground.

He was reminded of a violent storm he had once gone through on a voyage destined for Bermuda with Captain Murphy aboard the *Southern Swallow.* They had been forced to turn back to Gunter's Harbour because of the storm's ferocity—and this storm reminded him too much of that prior experience and was making him as nervous as he had been aboard ship in that storm.

That last particularly fierce lightning bolt that brought the tree down frightened his horse too, and when Sean saw a rock ledge that jutted from the side of a low lying hill he decided to seek shelter under the rock.

It was barely high enough for the animal, but the horse didn't seem to mind having to bow his head in order to stay under the limited shelter. Sean was glad to be protected from the rain that had pelted down upon them in the driving wind. They remained there until the fiery display yielded and passed on its journey to display it powers elsewhere.

As rapidly as the storm had raised its rage the sky now began to clear quickly and the warm sun was causing steam to rise around them. Sean removed the saddle from the horse and decided to take off most of his own wet clothing as well. Finding a suitable bush, he vigorously shook its branches to eliminate the moisture and hung his outer garments there to dry in the sun.

He wanted to start a fire, but could find nothing dry enough to burn, so he busied himself going through his belonging to see if there were other items he needed to dry. Julia's book of poetry was wet, so he opened it and laid it on a flat rock that was already beginning to warm. His blanket had protected much of what had been rolled inside even though the blanket itself was soaked—so he spread the blanket out to dry.

As he was stretching the blanket over a bush that was in full sun, he thought he heard voices. He stood still and listened. Yes, he could hear voices speaking lowly and it seemed they were drawing closer.

Sean wasn't that familiar with firearms and didn't know if the powder would be dry enough to fire a shot if needed. He was squatting down fumbling with the unfamiliar pistol then suddenly looked up in surprise as he saw Nokona and the woman leading their horses toward him.

Sean stood with the pistol still in his hand and Nokona stopped and placed his hand on the woman's arm to prevent her from moving forward. Realizing how he must look, Sean smiled, laid the pistol on the ground and the Indians dropped the horses' reins and continued toward him.

"No find men," Nokona said.

"What? What men didn't you find? Where did you go?"

Nokona looked at the woman then back at Sean and pointed to the woman, saying, "*Lomasi*, 'pretty flower'—Lomasi—Nokona's sister."

"Sister—she's your sister?" Sean asked taken aback. "She's your sister and her name means 'pretty flower'?"

"Lomasi—she Lomasi" Nokona repeated, again amazed at the ignorance of white men who always seemed surprised that Indians had been given names.

"And your name, Nokona—what does your name mean?"

"The people say Nokona is *Wanderer*."

"I see," said Sean.

And he really did see now—he understood. *This is the man who never stopped wandering because he was looking for members of his family. And in his wandering he came to the aid of me and my friends and even saved our lives.*

"I see," Sean repeated. "You are Nokona the Wanderer and bless you for having that name. Now then, so this is Lomasi," he said looking directly at the woman as a cautious smile came to her face.

Nokona said something to Lomasi and she stretched her arm toward Sean. Remembering how Nokona had grasped his forearm, Sean carefully did the same to the outstretched arm of the woman.

"Nokona, Lomasi—friends," Sean said, and this time a full blossoming smile came to her face.

Sean thought, *ah then it's for this reason she's called Lomasi, the pretty flower, and as pretty as a flower she is—prettier than I've seen in awhile.*

For whatever reason, Sean felt his face flush.

Realizing that he was standing there in damp underclothes, he went to the shrub where he had placed his clothes. They were still soggy, but he felt better about putting on wet clothes than he did marching about in his underclothing, even though it certainly didn't seem to bother the Indians. Looking at an almost naked Nokona, Sean wondered if the savages didn't have the right idea after all, especially when the weather was fair and even when it rained.

Nokona wore a breechcloth that was looped outside of the front of his leather belt, drawn between the legs and then tucked into the belt in the back. It appeared to have been cut from a blanket and then decorated with bird feathers that had been sewn on. He wore leather footwear made of deer hide and decorated with the quills of porcupine. They had high cuffs that came above the ankle and were securely tied with strips of deer hide. Nokona's head was shaved except for a single lock of hair on the crown of his head that was known as a scalp lock. Of course, he wore the badge that identified him as Black Minqua.

Lomasi wore a deerskin skirt that wrapped around her waist and was held in place with a sturdy leather belt. She wore deer hide footwear similar to Nokona's but much more decorative. Hers also had high cuffs and these were adorned with quills that were dyed red. She wore leggings that were tied just above the knee. Sometimes she wore a short tunic, a sort of jacket that came just below her waist—and sometimes she wore nothing above her skirt. On some days she wore her hair in a simple flowing style, while on other occasions Sean had seen her hair in a long single braid.

The woman had gone back to the horses and was removing a small deer from the back of her horse. Without hesitation she took a knife from her belt and began to dress the animal. It appeared that the Indians would be staying long enough to prepare a meal.

It did not take the woman long to find enough dry wood to build a fire and although there was a considerable amount of smoke at first it was mostly steam and soon a hot fire was roasting the deer. It wasn't much larger than a small dog. Sean first wondered how they had managed to kill it and then he imagined that it was probably a helpless fawn.

The sun had gone down before the carcass was ready to eat. Lomasi had gathered some type of herb from the forest. It was a leafy plant and Sean especially enjoyed the pleasant taste it produced when he chewed a leaf with a mouthful of venison.

"Good," Sean indicated to the Indians as he rubbed his stomach, "Very good. Thank you for the food."

Nokona and Lomasi looked at one another, not sure what Sean meant.

Sean continued, "You said you couldn't find something. What were you looking for?" he asked Nokona.

"Man bad—take Lomasi. Look find family. No find."

There seemed to be no way for Sean to determine just what had gone on. He assumed that they thought they could find others from their family, or perhaps other men who were taking slaves, but Sean could not be sure. The limits placed on their lack of understanding one another's language presented some real barriers.

Sean smiled to himself, because he was thinking: *I recall the problems I first had trying to understand that black rascal Samson. The language obstruction always existed to some extent between us, but we managed to understand one another eventually—at least I think we did. I wonder if I'll be able to expect a similar language breakthrough with these members of the Honniasont—these Minqua Indians. But then, why should I expect to, or even want to?*

They fell silent as the fire waned and before long, as if by signal, the three arose. Lomasi bound the legs of the horses as she had done previously and then she and Nokona went off into the forest just as they had done the night before.

Sean lay down for the night, but unlike the previous evening he did wonder about them. He wondered how long Nokona had been separated from his sister and tried to imagine what they might be saying. He thought of his Julia and remembered the long nights with her. Then, strangely, he began to have notions of Lomasi—pleasant impressions that lingered for a long time before he finally fell asleep.

CHAPTER THREE

Horrible Encounter

Just before daybreak Sean heard the Indians and today they made no attempt to be quiet. Lomasi was coaxing flame from the embers of the fire and Sean was finding it difficult to keep his eyes from her, especially because she had chosen not to wear her tunic. Just then, Nokona stepped into the clearing with a larger gourd, one that Sean hadn't seen before.

Assuming its use he asked, "Is there water nearby?"

"Big water—many waters gather," Nokona responded.

They ate some small animals that Lomasi cooked over the fire. Sean seldom asked what they were eating, because even though the food didn't always suit what he might have chosen for a meal, but he was grateful for something to eat that he had no need to catch or prepare.

Sean was eager to see the 'big water—many streams gather,' that Nokona mentioned.

"Where is the 'big water?" Sean asked. "Is it near?"

The Indian pointed to the west and Sean wondered: *Might this be the large Susquehanna River that empties into the Chesapeake Bay near Gunter's Harbour, or nothing more than just a smaller tributary.*

"Will you show me the way?" Sean asked. "I want to see the big water."

Nokona called to his sister and said something in their dialect. She turned around as he spoke and then in an unconcerned manner she returned to what had been occupying her.

They left the horses at the campsite, began walking, and in less than a half mile Sean could hear the sound of rushing water. They continued to the edge of a prominent hill and looked down at the river. Sean thought, *big water, indeed—this must be the Susquehanna.*

The mighty river had eroded the side of the hill where they stood and as Sean looked to the north, he could see a rather large creek entering the river from the east.

Pointing northward to the creek, he said, "Small river, what is the small river—and what is the island—is that an island?"

Nokona seemed puzzled but he looked to the north, then pointed and said, "Pequehan – Shawanee people—bad whites, some good whites."

Sean had no idea what any of Nokona's gibberish meant—something about bad and good whites could have meant anything or nothing.

"The water—what is the water called?" Sean tried again.

"Pequehan water—Pequehan," was the only response.

Whatever it was called, it didn't seem far off, and the land appeared to slope downward as far as he could tell and he was determined to discover more about this Pequehan water.

They went down to the river and Sean filled the water gourd that Lomasi had given him. Then they climbed back to the top of the hill and headed back.

When Sean saddled his horse he was rather surprised that the Indians seemed reluctant to leave the area. Actually he had hoped that they might accompany him, at least for a while. After all, in this short time he had learned to depend somewhat on Nokona's help, and he certainly appreciated Lomasi—and her abilities—often finding that he was not far from her as she went about her activities.

He mounted the horse and waved his arm in farewell to them, but was pleased that they climbed on their horses too and begin to follow. Then after a brief time Nokona took the lead and they rode to the north. They crossed several small creeks and one that was quite large, which Sean thought might be the Pequehan. However, Nokona took them east several hundred yards and they crossed that creek scarcely getting the horses' flanks wet, then turned back north by northwest and before long they stopped again at what Sean was now certain must be the Pequehan.

Nokona and Lomasi dismounted, but they seemed somewhat apprehensive, casting their eyes about as they spoke in low tones to one another.

Noticing that Sean seemed puzzled by their caution, Nokona said, "White men maybe here. Pequehan here."

"Yes," replied Sean as he pointed to the creek, "I took this river to be the Pequehan just as you said."

"Yes Pequehan water," replied Nokona. "Pequehan people here."

As Sean dismounted he dropped the reins and let his horse graze freely. *I'll never understand these Indians,* Sean thought. *Is the river the Pequehan or are the people Pequehan—I'll never understand.*

"*Vous êtes qui? Hallo—Vous êtes qui?*" a strange voice called out.

Sean looked across the wide creek and saw a white man standing there holding a pistol at his side and two Indians were behind him. Sean had no idea what the man had said.

"Sean O'Connell I am," he shouted back to them. "And these Indians are guiding me."

The man looked at the Indians, spoke a few words to the men behind him then called out, "You are not from the Philadelphia? You are not come for to tell us to no live here—that the people called the Swiss own this land?"

"I know nothing of such things," Sean replied. "I'm simply traveling—searching for a place to live."

The man shouted with an apparent sense of relief, "I am Francois Benoit. I to make the trades with the Shawnee[2] Indians. Go back to the east and you to see a place to do the crossing. We meet there—*oui?*"

Sean looked at Nokona and when he nodded affirmatively, Sean shouted out, "Yes, then we'll meet you there."

They came to the place Benoit had suggested and Benoit stood on the other bank waving them toward his side. They led the horses across the creek where some large flat rocks had broken from a ledge on the bank. Sean's horse slipped, reared back and Sean was knocked into the water and Lomasi giggled as Sean came up sputtering. Arriving on the other side Benoit gave Sean his hand.

"I come to trade with Indians. They to give us animal skins and meat and we trade to them the blanket and . . ." Benoit looked about as if to see if someone was listening. "And we sometimes give to them the gun—but only if they make the pledge they shoot to the English."

He paused and then broke into a raucous laugh. "I make the funny tale—no?"

Nokona looked at Lomasi and then at Sean, to see if he was laughing. Sean didn't laugh.

"Ah, *excusez-moi*—then you are the English?" Benoit asked in a tone of mock apology.

Sean grinned, "Not on your life, Benoit. I'm Irish as can be—Sean O'Connell and running from the English at that."

"So," Benoit laughed, "we may to be the friends, no?"

"That we shall see, Benoit—that we shall see. We've only now just met. And, as we Irish often say of the English, 'A sly rogue is often in good dress.' We'll see Benoit."

"I to agree with the manner to speak you have. Sean O'Connell, to you I think we could be the friends. But, as you say—we shall see."

Benoit led Sean and the Indians toward a small settlement where he had a crude cabin that doubled as a home and trading store. He pointed to three smaller, well-constructed cabins about fifty yards away from his.

"These they are the Swiss men," he said. "They are called Mennonites. I know they are not of the faith—not Catholics. And you, Sean O'Connell, you have the Catholic faith?"

"This is something between me and God, Benoit. But, about these Mennonites as you call them, why do you not favor them?"

"They want to take the Indians' land to make the farms. William Penn he thinks to sell the land to these Swiss men, but Indians say not to do this thing."

"Then, do they fight the Indians?" Sean asked.

Benoit laughed, "*Merci*—no they do not to fight. They say they have the spirit of—how you say, the peace—peaceful—*oui* peaceful, because Penn robs the Indians and gives to the Mennonite."

"I know something of this, Benoit. I lost my land to the English in much the same way the Indians have. And what is their tribe—the Indians of this land? Are they Minqua?"

"No, no—not as your friends here, they have no *des decorations* on the breast. They are Shawanah—they call to themselves, Shawnee.

"I see," said Sean, not fully understanding. "Then, what do you trade with these Indians?"

"I have tell you before—they give to me sometimes the meat, the deerskins, the beaver and bear hides, and they give to me the gourd containers—but I give them not so much for these."

Sean thought, *Yes, and I'm sure you don't give them much of a good trade for anything.*

Then he asked, "And what do they receive in trade as a good barter?"

"The good barter?—oh yes—*Je comprends.* They are children—the child wants the shiny gift. I trade to them brass and copper pieces, glass beads—they like very much—scraps of bright cloth, blankets, iron tools and salt. And—sometimes I give the gun—if they make to me good trades and promise to shoot the Englishman—maybe Penn, *es-tu d'accord?*"

Before Sean could respond, Benoit insisted that Sean come to his cabin to see his supply of trading goods.

As they walked to the cabin, Benoit said, "You have the very nice pistol. I see that you have the Indian hatchet, *oui?*"

Suspecting that Benoit recognized the arms, Sean said, "They belonged to a man I met in the forest—he no longer needed them, because he was dead."

"Ah, *merci*, then you kill to the man?"

"No," replied Sean truthfully, "He was killed by another, but I took the man's weapons and his horses."

"This I have thought," admitted Benoit. "The horses your Indians have were that man's. He wanted to trade the woman to me, but I have no use for the Indian woman. He must be the bad man, *oui?*"

Sean did not feel comfortable talking more about this matter, because he was unable to tell if Benoit was telling the truth or if the dead man had been his cohort.

They spent considerable time at the trading cabin and Sean wondered how a man like this Benoit could sleep at night with a good conscience—because, except for some of the blankets, most of what he used as trade articles looked like items someone had discarded.

He gave Benoit a portion of a silver coin for three woolen blankets then rolled them and tied them with a leather thong that Benoit offered him.

"Well, I must leave," said Sean. "My friends wait for me."

"*Oui*, yes—of course. But, let me say to you this. I leave at daybreak to go north. You will travel with me, *oui*? I pay for to help me take the flat boat and the horses to pull from the riverside. You will come? We can be there in three or maybe four days if it no rain."

"I thank you for the offer," Sean replied, "But I wish to travel alone and seek my own way with my Indian companions."

However, Sean was unaware that Nokona and Lomasi had already left the area.

Another matter of which no one in this Pequea community was aware was that William Penn had recently died. And, even though Benoit had suggested in jest that Sean may have come with bad news from Philadelphia, in fact three men had been sent from Philadelphia to inform the Mennonites that Penn had died—and to make them aware that perhaps this would make their land rights at Pequea somewhat tenuous.

Nevertheless, the three messengers would never reach Pequea. Unfortunately, they had been ambushed, killed and scalped by a band of Shawnee led by Kaweequa—also known as Six Toes, because of the extra toe on one of his feet.

In 1711, Kaweequa's father Opessa had voluntarily abandoned both his role as chief of the Pequehan clan of the Shawnee and his tribe, and then sought a home among the Delaware. Although Opessa's oldest son Kaweequa fought for the right to become chief, tribal leaders never recognized him as worthy. He thought it was because his father had abandoned the position and the tribe, but many Shawnee elders said that he was bad medicine because of his six- toed foot. So Six Toes, Kaweequa, became the renegade leader of a small band of outcast warriors.

Sean walked about the area and managed to meet some of the people Benoit had referred to as Swiss men—the Mennonites. He met Johann Anton and his sons Henry and George, and a man named Hans Weaver who seemed to have no family present with him.

They were very hesitant about conversing with him. However, it did not matter to Sean, because he had difficulty understanding them anyway—although he felt certain that they had at least a rudimentary command of English that they did not care to use with him.

Sean wondered: *Will I ever again meet anyone with whom I can have a proper conversation where each of us can easily understand the other?*

He continued searching, expecting to find Nokona and Lomasi. He did come across their saddle-less horses tied to a tree in an obscure area just outside of the cleared land and considered calling out to Nokona, but hesitated doing so lest he should bring more attention to himself than he wished.

The two Tuscarora[3] Indians who had been with Benoit made a clumsy attempt of concealing the fact that they were following Sean around the compound. He assumed they had been ordered to do so for the purpose of reporting his whereabouts to Benoit.

Sean was getting hungry as the sun began to set over the Susquehanna. He went to his horse and led him away some distance from the cabins of Benoit and the Mennonites, but opposite from where the Indian horses were tethered.

He removed the saddle and took some dried meat from the saddlebag. Then, placing his blanket on the ground he lay upon it and began chewing the hard meat and drinking water to help soften it so he could swallow. Before long he was asleep. He hadn't notice that he didn't plug the spout of his drinking gourd and it was leaking water on his blanket—and he also failed to observe that he was still being watched by one of the Tuscarora.

The nickering of his horse wakened Sean and the full moon illuminated the surroundings almost as if it were day. Sean heard a faint rustling and then he saw a figure running silently away. *It's one of Benoit's Indians headed toward his cabin,* he thought. *No reason to delay, he'll soon be giving an account of my whereabouts to Benoit.*

Sean quickly saddled his horse and began to ride northward, avoiding the cleared area and staying close to the forest edge until he was well away from the small Pequea community.

He had been using the North Star as his point of reference, just as Captain Murphy had taught him. However, the forest was becoming so dense that it became increasingly more difficult to read the starry sky. He had no sense of the time and thought it would be daylight soon. But he rode for almost two hours before dawn approached and he stopped at a small but swiftly running stream.

This looks as likely a spot to rest awhile as any, he reflected. He dismounted, and walked about the area. It provided an almost unobstructed view in all directions—all but the narrow, heavily forested path he had chosen to bring him to his present position.

Through a small break in the trees he could see a hill in the distance and considered whether it might be not be a more ideal location from which to establish where he was before deciding on his further travel.

So he rode on and before long he was at the base of the hill and thought he could hear a low roar. The sound was confirmed as he came to a clearing at the hill's crest and saw the Susquehanna below. A small island jutted up from the center of the river forming rushing rapids on either side.

Removing the saddle, he bound the horse's forelegs and then set about looking for some limbs with which he could build a small shelter. In his search, he startled a rabbit. The animal ran about thirty feet then froze under a seedling pine. Without so much as a second thought, Sean drew his short sword and threw it toward the animal.

He laughed when the pommel of the sword struck the rabbit, stunning it, and he said aloud, "Sean, me boy, you've become a savage yourself, but don't think you'll be such a clever hunter every time."

He dispatched the rabbit quickly and needed only to find some wood and tinder to build a fire for his breakfast.

Sean began to think, *Yes, this might be the place I've been looking for. There's water available within a hundred yards, animals for the taking of food and certainly enough trees to build any size structure I might be willing to undertake. Yes, this might be the place.*

With visions like that swimming through his mind he decided he should build more than just a temporary shelter. And that consideration repeated itself throughout the day—*Yes, this might be the place.*

In the early afternoon he decided to use the hatchet he had taken from the man that had captured Lomasi and put it to good use cutting saplings for a more stable shelter than he had at first proposed. Arming himself with the sword and pistol, he set off seeking the perfect tree limbs for his dwelling.

He was about to cut his first sapling when he heard something below him toward the foot of the hill. He thought it might have been voices but couldn't be sure, so he hid and before long 15 or 20 Indians came into view, quietly following one another at a fast pace and headed toward the river.

He could not see them clearly and wondered if Nokona and Lomasi might be with them. He wondered if they had found more of their family— or perhaps other members of their tribe. So he followed the Indians at a distance, stopping whenever they did.

When they reached the river they followed it downstream and just as the sun was beginning to disappear in the forest on the western bank of the river, Sean heard a familiar voice—so did the Indians.

It was Benoit and the two Tuscarora. Benoit was screaming in French, but Sean couldn't tell if he was shouting at the Indians, the two horses that struggled against the current pulling the flat boat upstream, or perhaps he was shrieking and cursing all of them.

It was becoming obvious that the Indians Sean had been following were now planning to do violence to Benoit—of that he was certain. Unfortunately, while he hesitated trying to determine the safest way to warn Benoit—they attacked.

In horror, Sean could only watch helplessly as they took the life of Benoit. Strangely, they forced both Tuscarora to run between the attacking Indians as they struck at the Tuscarora with clubs and hatchets over and over again until they were dead. Finally, they scalped the three men.

Sean could not believe how quickly the men's lives had been taken. Then he watched as they killed Benoit's animals, built a fire, then butchered and ate one of the horses.

Sean was afraid to move, not wanting to be seen by the marauding Indians. But it was dark now so he decided to slip away just as flames leapt skyward. He looked back to see that the Indians had taken what they wanted of Benoit's trade goods, then set fire to the remainder of the contents of the small barge and pushed it away from the bank until the current carried it southward.

Sean could hear the Indians intoning some strange chants accompanied by blood curdling, high-pitched yelps as he stumbled his way through the dark forest, hoping he would soon be safe. He had no way of knowing that he had just avoided what would have been a catastrophic meeting with the cruel Six Toes, Kaweequa the renegade Shawnee and his band of outcast warriors.

Sean stumbled through the dark forest, running into limbs and spider webs and falling as he stepped into depressions. He was exhausted as he finally staggered up the hill to what he had earlier thought: *might be the place*. He gave water to the horse, stopping to listen for several minutes every time he thought he heard a sound in the forest.

Was this a mistake? He wondered? *Should I have stayed at Dawn Light to claim what was rightfully mine? Leaving Nathan was difficult—but I had no choice. Maybe I should abandon this quest to find a new life for Nathan and me and simply return to face the authorities. I might have better fortune with the devious and scheming English than among these cruel savages. Still there are those like Nokona and Lomasi—ah, Lomasi, such a fair one she is. Those dark eyes must hold secrets—deep secrets—even as an unfathomable pool doesn't disclose what it hides in the depths.*

Then he wrapped himself in his blanket and sat with his back to a large tulip poplar. He could see the entire area on the top of his hill. Although he was worn out from the day's ordeal, he found it difficult to sleep, as his mind continued to churn with thoughts of self-incrimination.

I've lost my own true love—my dear Julia. Was I the one who could have avoided her death? And now she's gone and I dream of another—one who can't understand me, neither can I her. What sort of heathen man have I become—and with a young boy to bring up now by myself—by myself if ever I get back alive to Gunter's Harbour.

With each new thought that would crash into his restless mind he found himself arguing over what he had done in the past to produce his present life. And terrible was the shame he felt over that extreme notion that he had been responsible for his wife Julia's death.

He slept fitfully that night and slept very little the following nights as well.

CHAPTER FOUR

Apprentice Seaman

Morning had broken and the sun shone brightly through the kitchen windows of the house of Captain Laird Murphy and his wife Cynthia.

"Good morning, my little man," said Captain Murphy. "And how's Nathan, me seaman, this fine morning? Shall we go to the *Southern Swallow* and see what that lazy crew of mine is up to doing today?"

Nathan O'Connell sat on the kitchen floor, paying little attention to what went on about him. He was playing with a small boat that Fian had carved for him. He was growing quickly, a pleasant boy with his mother's green eyes. He bore the handsome look and the curly, tousled hair of his father. The captain often asked his wife to keep the boy's hair cut short, but she enjoyed seeing every feature of her grandson that reminded her of Julia and Sean.

"Now Laird," Cynthia warned, "Don't be getting him all excited about going unless you plan on taking him with you. And mind you, it'll be for the entire day if he goes. You needn't be sending him back home with Fian as you did last week when you thought he had become a nuisance."

"Now love," began the captain, "Don't you be so harsh when speaking about this old sea dog. Fian O'Niall has never in his life had a sprig of a lad

29

around him, and I can tell you he enjoys having Nathan about—although I'll say that he pays more mind to the lad than to his own tasks."

"Humph—an he don' be cleanin' that boy when he messes hisself," Missy the servant offered.

"Never you mind, Missy, this is not something that should be a matter to you," scolded Cynthia. "This is a matter between the Captain and me and you simply do as you're told and stay out of this affair."

Under her breath Missy muttered, "Humph—don' matter none lessen I has to be the one gonna clean him up."

"Well, dear," Captain Murphy continued, "I surely do understand your concerns. But I insist that Nathan go with me. I intend to make a seaman of him. That's my plan, so that when his father returns he'll not be as apt to run off into the wilderness to the west with the boy. Hopefully Nathan and Sean will stay here and ply the bay with me."

"That brings to mind his ship, Laird. Has the Swedish man made a decision about buying Sean's sloop?"

"No!" answered the captain emphatically. "But I've made the decision for him. The Swede intends to steal the sloop, and I mean for that to never happen. That Anders Larson thinks he can pay for Sean's Bermuda sloop, the *Julia's Fairwinds* as a landowner would pay a common laborer for a day in the field. And I'll have none of that."

"I'm sure of that dear. But then, what will you tell him," Cynthia asked.

"I'll tell him what I'm telling you, woman—the *Julia's Fairwinds* is to be neither sold nor traded."

"But when Sean left you told him that you'd sell it and put the profit aside for his future."

"Well, I'm telling you now and I'll tell Sean when he returns what I'm telling you—the *Julia's Fairwinds* already has a profit—and that profit's a heart, and the heart of that sloop belongs to Sean and no one else. He'll come back to join us here in Gunter's Harbour to become the captain of his own vessel, the *Julia's Fairwinds*. And that'll be his profit, and Nathan's, for the future. Wouldn't that please you to have your grandson close by instead of fearing for him in the wilderness?"

"Of course it would please me to have him near. But Laird, you know better than I that there's danger in the sea as much as there is in the wilderness—and you assured him that you'd sell the sloop."

The room became silent, except for the sounds Nathan made as he played with his boat.

"I've changed my mind with good reason, and you'll have to accept that—and so will Sean," the captain insisted. "It seems the Crown has no immediate plan for Dawn Light, seeing as how they've left it abandoned. And, who knows, when he returns perhaps Hough will be able to make another appeal in Annapolis and Sean may have the land restored to his ownership."

"Oh Laird, I know you can't really believe that. They'll refuse every plea that he . . . ."

"I'll not hear another word for now," snapped the captain. "You're probably right about not recovering Dawn Light—but when Sean returns, he'll be returning to find that he has a seafaring son, not a wandering fool somewhere out in the wilds with neither home nor heart. I tell you that I'll not have him taking young Nathan off to God knows where."

With that the captain slammed out of the door and in a moment came charging back in.

"And Nathan's going with me," he shouted firmly. "Come along, Nathan. You and the Captain are going to the harbor. You're going to become the finest seaman that I can make of you so that you can teach your own father a nautical thing or two. Come along boy."

With that command, Nathan jumped up from the floor and marched out with the captain—once again the kitchen door slammed as he left, without so much as a fair-thee-well.

"Boy gonna come home hisself all dirty as ever, and I can tell you so," said Missy.

"Now, you just never mind, Missy. I've told you it's not your matter. You have enough work of your own to do without concerning yourself over others."

"Humph—that's the same thing I says," Missy muttered in her lowest voice, "I gots enough work to my own self, 'cept it gonna be my matter when the boy has be cleaned up all over again."

Cynthia knew that Missy was probably right. But a young boy being dirty didn't bother her as much as the idea that the captain had decided that he would not sell the sloop. After all, he had assured Sean that he would do so.

Cynthia's hands were neither wet nor dirty yet she wiped them absent-mindedly on her apron then looked up with a prayer in her heart.

Lord, I told Sean that I'd care for Nathan just as Julia would have done. And, haven't I done that Lord? I've told Nathan of Sean and his mother every day since Sean left and—just as I promised—I'll continue to tell him every day of his life until Sean returns for him. Lord, please show us the right way. And Lord, please bring Sean safely home—soon"

"Look to now lads—would you look at this," shouted Fian O'Niall. Fian had been assigned a new and important role aboard Captain Murphy's ship. The former first mate, Brenan Connor, had met some old friends on a vessel in Annapolis and decided to return to Ireland with that ship. So Captain Murphy chose Fian as his second in command—a role for which Fian O'Niall thought himself well suited.

He was announcing to all who might hear that he saw the captain riding up to the quay[4] where the *Southern Swallow* was berthed—and Nathan was holding on tightly to the captain behind the saddle.

"Here's Fian's lad coming to help ol' Fian and this motley crew of the *Southern Swallow* on such a fine morning as this."

—— CHAPTER FIVE ——

Native Skills

Fall seemed to arrive early and winter was turning very cold in the wilderness. Fortunately, as Sean lived without the benefit of the shelter and warmth of a sturdy house, his body adjusted to the cold in ways he did not fully understand.

Sean had endured well as he learned to live off the land. He had acquired some tools from an Irish trader named Pádraig ÒNualláin—"But call me Paddy," the man had said.

Sean came across him at the mouth of the Conestoga Creek as it emptied into the Susquehanna. The man was badly wounded and Sean tried his best to tend to the man's infected cuts.

"Aye, Sean O'Connell," ÒNualláin had told him before he died, "A sad day it was when I left the blessed land of our fathers. Not that it was me idea to come here, you know. It was them beggarly English that sent me here a prisoner. A prisoner Sean—and me, Paddy, a native son of me own dear father and of our own Ireland."

"I know—I do Pádraig. But you need some rest now, the fever's getting worse. Try to sleep now."

"And I'll do just that. Could I expect that you might have a bit of the rum, Sean? What's an Irishman without his cup?"

"I have none, now you must sleep—please."

"And it's right you are, Sean. How can I thank you for your kindness, for lookin' out for me?"

"You'll thank me by getting some rest now, Paddy."

"No doubt you're right, Sean. Never should I have taken up with the Spanish man and his wife tradin' with Indians along them rivers," he said closing his eyes as if to sleep.

Then his eyes opened wide and he continued. "Never should I have done as much. Then, when them thievin' Shawnee came to trade, before long they was arguin' with the trader's wife concernin' the values of goods. Then, all sudden like, here comes more of them. They fell upon us did they Sean. They killed the Spaniard and carried the woman away with them. They thought they'd done them in an Irishman too, but we folk from the Isle don't die easy, do we Sean?"

"No, we don't and we don't quit, but you must rest now," pled Sean

With a smile on his face he said, "Aye, Sean, we don't quit. Then, without another word Pádraig ÒNualláin the Irishman closed his eyes and slept the endless sleep.

Sean wondered if the Indians that had attacked the Spaniard and Paddy might have been the same band that killed Benoit, but decided it was probably a different group, because unlike those that killed Benoit, these Indians had scalped neither of the men.

The few tools Sean scavenged from the Irishman would prove to be of great value to him, because as that first winter approached he abandoned the hill near the Pequea River and headed north, where he had come across the Irishman.

He buried the Irishman then built a small raft and crossed the Susquehanna using a series of small islands, taking advantage of the current and finding water shallow enough for him to use a pole to guide the raft. He tied his unwilling horse to the raft and the animal was able to swim and at times found a foothold for walking through shallower water.

For some reason Sean felt somewhat safer on the western bank of the Susquehanna, especially when he located a place that he considered would be ideal to spend the winter.

It was a hill that Sean calculated to be more than 500 feet high and it provided a position from which he could see anyone approaching. In fact, once the leaves had fallen from the trees he could see all the way back to the river in the distance.

An axe the Indians had left behind when they attacked the Spaniards and Paddy Sean made use of to cut trees as support beams for the interior and as an entrance to the small hut he dug into the hill with a shovel—it was a man-made cave.

As winter days came and the air became colder and snow fell, he was glad to have the earthen living area, because it held the heat of even the smallest of fires so well. This was important, because he knew that the sight of the smoke of a large fire might bring intruders his way to do him harm.

Sean had given up hope that Nokona and Lomasi might somehow surprise him and show up again as they had done in the past. Then, one day Sean caught a glimpse of two lone Indians traveling near him and he watched, hoping it might be his friends. But as they drew near he could see it was two men and they were setting snares to catch rabbits.

They noticed him watching and cautiously approached to offer a rabbit to Sean. He wasn't sure what might be the wise thing to do, but chose to accept their offer. This seemed to please them and Sean gave them some salt that he had found among the Irishman's belongings.

However, he had no idea from which tribe they had come, so for several days after they left he was very vigilant, suspecting that they might have gone off after a larger band of Indians before returning to kill him.

He doubted that he would ever be able to discern the difference between those who really sought to befriend him and those who wanted to set him off guard so they could slit his throat and take his hair. As far as he knew, he never saw those two Indians again.

The temperatures were bitterly cold that first winter in the wilderness and he was glad he had thought enough to purchase those three extra blankets from Benoit. He had cut a slit in one of the blankets and it doubled as a cape for warmth during the day and for sleeping at night.

Fortunately the snowfall was moderate and he was able to get about rather easily. From time to time he was able to kill a slow moving porcupine. The meat was greasy and had a pleasant taste, but the process of skinning and dressing the animal was a difficult one and he had many puncture wounds that gave evidence of his lack of proficiency.

So, he decided to apply what he had seen the Indians doing as they set snares and after several days without success he finally became somewhat adept at trapping rabbits.

However, one day he was surprised to find what at first he had thought was a grey chicken in his snare—it was a ruffed grouse and Sean enjoyed the variety the bird gave to his diet of rabbits. From that time on he determined to set his snares in areas where he felt he could catch both rabbits and grouse.

Occasionally he saw deer foraging further down the hill and had considered stalking one and risking a shot with the pistol to add yet another variety of meat to his uninteresting food source. However, he thought better of it, for even if he were able to kill a deer with a single shot the risk that some hostile Indian might hear the loud report was too great.

As the days began to warm and spring was teasing with promises to return, he thought: *This would be the time to abandon this winter home. I'm thinking that I might venture out a bit and if things don't turn to my liking I can always return here in the fall. But then, that would depend on what I might encounter as I travel.*

He did not return to his earthen home that following winter, nor the winter that followed. As he traveled west he came upon hills that he knew must tower well above 1,000 feet and were making it increasingly more difficult for him to traverse terrain that was becoming true mountains. He had never been at such elevations in his life.

He was also encountering more Indians as they passed through mostly in groups of two or three. Occasionally a band of 10 or more passed his way and it became evident that he was being observed long before he became aware of their presence.

At first these meetings alarmed Sean, because he could never lose the vision of Benoit being killed and scalped. However, more often than not he would be invited to eat with the Indians—often venison, and he had seen many deer brought down through their accuracy with bow and arrow.

Most meetings were friendly and Sean believed that these chance encounters with Indians were becoming increasingly more amiable. It never occurred to Sean that their kindness might have been based on the fact that he was alone and so he posed no threat to the Indians.

One morning four Indians came into Sean's camp. They gave him what he had learned was a greeting then went to examine his crudely built shelter. He had built a lean-to and had added pine boughs as needed. They stood talking, looking first at the shelter, then at Sean. Without any warning, two of the Indians began to tear the shelter apart. The other two picked up Sean's axe and walked off, seeming to be uninterested in what was going on behind them.

Sean tried to hide his anger as he approached the two who remained. One Indian held his hand up as if to stop Sean, then said something to his companion and they both laughed. One man motioned in a way that Sean clearly understood—so he followed his crude instructions and sat down. Then, the other man went off in the same direction that the first two had taken and Sean began to wonder if this would be his last day alive.

The Indian sat opposite Sean. From time to time he would say something that Sean didn't understand. The Indian would repeat the same utterances two or three times, then would fall silent again. After what seemed a very long time he heard noises coming from the direction in which the other three Indians had disappeared.

The three men were dragging branches and birch bark on a sled of pine boughs. They greeted the man who had waited with Sean and the four men began to create something that seemed marvelous to Sean. They were constructing a new shelter for him—Indian style. He tried to offer his help, but the Indians laughed and motioned for him to sit again. In less than two hours a sturdy shelter had been built, a small version of an Indian long house.

The Indians signaled for Sean to look inside. He had to bend over to enter but what he saw amazed him. This shelter looked as though it would withstand even strong wind and hard rain. He noted with admiration how they had woven branches they had chosen that had just the right flexibility and then covered critical areas with birch bark.

He turned to exit the shelter and thank the Indians—but they were walking away.

"Hello," Sean shouted. "Thank you. Will you have food?"

The Indians stopped, turned about and one of the men shouted something. They all laughed then disappeared into the forest.

Sean enjoyed the comfort and protection from the elements of the shelter the Indians had built. And he believed that he was becoming quite skilled at communicating with the savages. He had learned a few words—however, because different dialects were spoken, most of his communication was accomplished through gesturing. Slowly, Sean began to understand the truth that when the Indians found a friendly lone white man as they traveled through the wilderness, that he posed no threat to them and the meetings were mostly amicable, and he was very glad for that.

He found that they were very sociable and always eager to give him something. Nevertheless, it took him a time or two to learn that they expected a gift in return—and Sean quickly ran out of gift-trading materials.

On one occasion three Indians had passed through his camp in the morning and returned later in the day with two small turkeys. They plucked, cooked and ate the turkeys, sharing the meal with Sean. After they had eaten their fill, they sat around the fire talking to one another, occasionally trying unsuccessfully to include Sean in the banter. They seemed impressed with Sean's shelter, gesturing toward it and sometimes laughing. Sean wondered if they actually believed he had built it.

One man had taken long feathers from one of the turkeys and was twining two of the feathers into blades of grass, fitting them in with a leather thong that formed a long braid.

When it appeared that he had completed his task he got up and walked to Sean and handed him the feathers. He pointed, indicating that Sean should place the decoration on his head just as was the custom of some Indians Sean had seen.

Sean obliged him and when he did the Indians laughed in a good-natured manner at the amusing sight of a white man with feathers in his hair.

Sean could tell that the man expected something in return. He pointed to Sean's hatchet—the one with the carved handle. The others seemed to agree that this would be a good exchange and Sean could easily see that his hesitation troubled the Indians.

Fearing that the situation could get out of hand and might turn to something very bad, Sean reluctantly reached for his hatchet and handed it to the Indian. Approving headshakes followed as each Indian in turn wanted to look at the hatchet. Satisfied with the trade of gifts they soon left.

The next morning Sean arose to discover that his horse was gone. He couldn't be certain, but strongly suspected that his three recent guests came during the night and took the animal. Thoughts of following after them to recover his horse were soon replaced with the more sane decision that the horse was not worth his life.

Determined to forget the loss of the horse, Sean decided to go out and set fresh snares in his favorite location for catching grouse, that deep ravine where he had seen so much of the bird's activity. As he walked along enjoying the crisp cool air of spring on this sunny morning, he suddenly froze in his tracks when he heard voices coming from above.

He quickly stepped behind a cluster of birch trees and looked up. There, walking along a rocky ledge about 150 feet above him were perhaps a dozen people. From their dress, he could tell that two white women were tied to an Indian and he in turn was tied to a young white boy. Several Indians led the group and others followed behind the prisoners.

As Sean watched, suddenly the boy slipped and fell just over the ledge of the ravine, trying desperately to hang on to the rocky shelf and screaming. The Indian to whom he was tied lost his balance when the boy fell and also began to slide over the side.

One of the Indians who followed the captives came quickly to them. However, instead of helping them get back up, Sean watched in horror as the Indian cut the leather thongs that connected the man and the boy to the women.

They came plunging headlong down the rock face of the ravine, bouncing from ledge to ledge until they struck the ground no more than 30 feet from Sean. He heard a small whimper, probably the boy, and a man's groan—then the bodies lay silent.

The other Indians pushed the women to the ground and looked over the ledge. They watched for several minutes and he could hear loud talking as they apparently waited for movement from either of the bodies. When they were satisfied that those who had fallen were dead, they engaged in a brief, but even louder, conversation then yanked the women to their feet and were on their way.

Sean suspected they might come down to verify that the two were dead, and a cold chill of fear shook his body as he wondered if these were the Indians that killed the Frenchman. He was afraid to move, because he couldn't be sure if they would see him if he were to break away from the cover of his hiding place.

So he waited for a long time, until his legs began to cramp from his squatting position. Then very cautiously he arose, stretched his legs and leaned against the tree listening for any sound that might indicate that they were returning. When he was satisfied that they had continued on, he went to the bodies.

He kneeled to touch the boy's cheek. It was already cold and he could tell there was no breath coming from his lungs. As he stared at the lifeless face, Sean's first thought was that the boy was probably about the age of his Nathan.

Getting up he went to the man's body. The Indian's legs were bent awkwardly under him in a way that Sean knew that both must have been broken by the fall. The Indian had a scalp lock, but unlike Nokona's hair lock, this man's ran from his forehead to his neck, shaved bald on either side. Sean could see that Indian was a young man and wondered if he might be from the Minqua tribe. But, seeing no badge on his chest, Sean decided that he was not of the Black Minqua—unless of course his captors had taken that identifying badge the Minqua wore.

With some difficulty he removed the cloak the man wore. It was black probably made from the pelt of a large black bear Sean guessed, and the sleeves were made of many small pelts that had been sewn together. He slipped into the garment and found that it fit reasonably well. And, although it had a terrible smell Sean decided that if needed, and he chose to wear it, the smell would be overridden by the value of the good warmth it might provide next winter.

He searched both bodies and found nothing that would be of value to him. Nevertheless, thinking that he might find some use for it later, he did remove the boy's wool coat and then pulled the bodies close to the bottom of the rocky precipice, turning them back-to-back against one another. Then he covered the bodies with some of the same fallen rocks that had caused their death. By then the sun was high and he decided to return to his small shelter.

He was exhausted, more from the mental anxiety of the presence of those Indians than the physical exertion with burying the bodies. He decided against a fire, climbed into his shelter and, as was his custom, he placed the loaded and cocked pistol next to him and covered himself with his blankets. He lay there for a long time, listening to the noises of the forest and at last he fell asleep.

Sean bolted upward, groggy and confused, not knowing whether he had been awakened by the loud clap of the pistol going off, or the screaming Indian with the blackened face who had dropped the smoking pistol and was falling backwards from the shelter.

Wasting no time and fearful for his life, Sean grabbed the sword Fian had given him and pounced on the Indian. He was about to drive the sword into the Indian's neck when he looked up and saw Lomasi on one side of the shelter and turned in time to see Nokona jumping on him, knocking him to the ground and wrestling the sword from his hand.

Sean's first notion was, *haven't I thought just this—none of them can be trusted.*

"No kill—friend. No kill," Nokona was shouting.

Sean wasn't sure if he should be happy to see Nokona and Lomasi or frightened because of what was happening.

Lomasi, in her usual and unassuming manner, quickly began the process of building a fire. She held up the carcasses of several small animals for Sean to admire and continued in her pursuit of meal preparation.

Nokona helped Sean to his feet and for almost an hour tried to explain what had happened. The man who had come with them sat staring at Sean in an unfriendly manner. He had a scalp lock that was greased so the hair stood erect. The face that had frightened Sean was the result of black tattooing across the man's forehead and under his eyes, and was embellished with a black turtle tattooed on each cheek.

"See three men with horse of Sean," Nokona said holding up three fingers. "See hatchet of Sean with carved handle. See men with Sean hatchet and horse—think they kill Sean."

Sean thought he was beginning to understand. Nokona had run into three Indians, undoubtedly those who had taken his horse.

Nokona reached behind him and pulled a familiar looking axe from his belt then handed it to Sean.

"This is it. Yes, this is the axe I traded to them. But, then later they came back to steal my horse. Where is the horse, did you capture the horse too?"

"No horse," Nokona said. "Kill men, one man take horse run away. No catch man—no catch horse."

As they talked on, Sean realized what had happened and thought: *Nokona believed the men had killed me and had taken my axe and horse, so in a rage Nokona retaliated. I feel some regret over their deaths, because aside from stealing my horse they were good visitors and meant me no harm. After all, that night when they took the horse they could have killed me and taken everything, but they hadn't. Will the ways of these savages ever become something I'll be able to understand and live with?*

Nokona then pointed to the man with the blackened face and said, "Bone Man!"

"I—what did you say—bone man?" Sean asked. "What's a bone man?"

"Him Bone Man—no say true name. Him Lenni Lenape[5]. Lenape no give true name so other man can steal away."

So, thought Sean, *This black-faced buggar thinks I'd steal his real name if I knew it. Not on my life, he hasn't anything I'd want to steal—especially*

41

that evil looking sharpened bone he carries. Looks like the upper leg bone of a very large animal and—so, that's probably where he gets this name, that's why he's called Bone Man. No, I don't want that bone weapon and I especially don't want to steal his name.

Then reaching out to touch the tattoo of a turtle on the man's cheek, Nokona said: "Lenni Lenape—Bone Man, turtle clan."

Just then the sound of Lomasi's voice caught Sean's attention as she took one of the small animals from the fire and handed it to Bone Man. She smiled as she gave him the meat, then turned and smiled at Sean. Nevertheless, the next piece of meat went to Nokona and Sean received his last—a rather small piece at that.

The rest of the day was spent trying to get more information from Nokona, and Sean felt that his linguistic abilities were improving. As the shadows lengthened and the forest began to darken, Sean wondered what the sleeping arrangements might be on this night.

The thought had no sooner passed through his mind when Bone Man got up and walked into the forest. Lomasi picked up the shawl she had been holding around her as the day grew cooler and followed closely behind him.

Puzzled, Sean looked at Nokona. All the Indian did was to shake his head affirmatively and say, "Bone Man wife."

Wife? thought Sean. *Lomasi is that savage's wife? Perhaps this ugly savage does have something I might want to steal. Lomasi—pretty flower—she is a pretty flower but how could I ever have had such lustful thoughts—and over a savage—O Lord, what sort of man have I become?*

CHAPTER SIX

Annapolis Journey

Once again morning was breaking as the sun shone brightly through the kitchen windows of the home of Captain and Mrs. Laird Murphy.

"Good morning, my dear wife Cynthia," the captain said.

"And a gracious good morning it is to you, my dear husband," she responded reaching up to grasp his collar and pull him down toward her so she could kiss his cheek.

"And where's me best seaman today?" the captain asked no one in particular.

"Be yonder getting' more work I should be doin'," Missy complained in her best loud mumble.

"No such thing," Cynthia said. "He's gone out to feed and curry the horses, and, Missy, I'd say that's more than you've done recently."

"Now, Cynthia, Missy has her work and we mustn't chastise her for not doing something that Nathan can do—and he does enjoy doing it so."

"Humph," Missy agreed, with the safest comment she could make.

Just then Nathan came bursting into the room.

"You be wiping those barn dirty shoes off 'fore you be comin' in my kitchen," Missy ordered.

"Here's where I stop the conversation Missy—do you hear?"

"Yessir Mas' Cap'n. I hears."

"So, tell me my fine young seaman, what did I say we'd be doing this day?" the captain asked.

Nathan responded with a huge grin, "We're going to Annapolis to meet the lady and bring her to our house, Grandfather."

"Aye, Nathan, and just who is this lady we'll be bringing to visit?"

"She's—why she's—I think she's—who is the lady Grandmother?"

They laughed and then Cynthia responded. "Well, the lady's name is Sarah—Sarah Fitzpatrick, and she's Grandfather's niece. She's the daughter of Grandfather's brother, Liam Murphy."

"Grandfather's brother's—then why isn't her name Murphy, the same as yours and Grandfather's—is she a nice lady, Grandmother?"

"Well, I've never met her, but I'm sure that she is—isn't that what you'd say Captain?"

"Eh? Well, of course I—that is, the last time I saw her she was a fine one, a pretty little girl, even younger than Nathan here I think—a sprig of a girl she was. But, aye—that's what I'd say. I'd say she's a nice lady; she's bound to be a nice lady. Well, what am I talking about here—she's me own brother Liam's daughter—of course she's a fine lady!"

"And I'm thinking the same thing, Nathan," said Cynthia. "And when you find her at the Reverend John Hubbard Sikes home, you must be sure to tell the Reverend's wife that you're my grandson."

"But doesn't she already know who I am, Grandmother?"

"Well, of course. But it's the polite way to behave. You'll tell her who you are and then you'll get to know Miss Sarah really well as you sail back from Annapolis to Gunter's Harbour. You be sure that you're very polite and address her as Miss Sarah. And, you can show her how much you know about being a young seaman and of all those things you've learned from Grandfather, Fian and the others. And do you know what?"

"No, Grandmother—what?"

"I'm thinking that you'll like her very well and she surely will love. . .—she'll surely like you. And when you come back home Missy will have corn biscuits for you."

Missy offered an unrequested. "Humph."

"That will be nice," Nathan said unconvincingly. "But when will father be coming home, Grandmother—will it be soon?"

That afternoon, as they returned from the harbor, Missy kept glancing at her mistress waiting for her to say something. When she didn't, Missy could contain herself no longer.

"You and Captain, I knows what you does. You be conjurin' up somethin' with Miss Sarah, that's what you be doin."

There was no response from Cynthia.

Chapter Seven

Going Home

Sean didn't know what month it was, but he knew that he had been roaming around these forests for a long time—probably three years or more—and something inside him was pleading for him to return soon to see his son.

How old would he be now—eight—nine? Would he be nine years old—is that possible? Surely the lad will have forgotten who I am by now. Even if Cynthia truly kept reminding Nathan of his mother and me, I couldn't expect the lad to remember well a father who had as much as abandoned him. And for what—to find a new life—what life is there here for me or for my own son? The life of a trapper or of a trader is a life that I've seen lasts not long at all. I may not be God's best man, but I wouldn't care to make a life by cheating Indians in matters of trade. What is there for me besides my son? The sloop is sold, but I'd be able to sign on as a seaman with the captain. God, what is there for me—for us—if you really have a plan for my life, then why did you let me come to this wilderness? I could have stayed in Gunter's Harbour to see people dying and being killed, I didn't have to come out here in this desolate land for that. And if you have a plan why didn't you show me that plan God?

It had been months since he had last seen Nokona and Lomasi. And the thoughts and dreams of Lomasi that had at one time so beleaguered him no longer troubled him.

Sean had taken up the habit of reading poems from Julia's book of verse and as time passed he discovered that he was able to regain a sense of her presence as he read the poetry she loved so well.

He had remained in the same area where the four Indians had built his sturdy lodge, but he had moved higher up the side of the mountain and there he built another dwelling, patterned after the one they had erected.

This newer lodge was built so he didn't have to bend over inside, and it was even more water tight than the other. Sean took some pride in the things he had learned on his own and from those Indians who had befriended him.

But, what is it that I have really learned? he wondered. *I could take my new-found skills to Gunter's Harbour and build Indian lodges for others to live in—or perhaps I could travel about, showing others how to snare rabbits and birds for their supper. I wonder—have I become too much a savage to ever return home?*

Sean had come upon a young deer with a broken leg and the animal's disadvantage became Sean's opportunity. He killed the deer, skinned it and decided to smoke most of the meat and dry some to make jerky. The activity with the deer was a welcome change to what had become a very routine life. He had also been cooking some of the wild vegetables he had learned to gather and was enjoying eating some tubers and a variety of berries—although he had discovered that many berries not only tasted bad but were very destructive to his digestive system.

He was alternating his time, drying the deer meat for a few days then going out to collect tubers. He considered that he might try to cure the deer hide, but thought better of it when he recalled his unsuccessful attempt with a rabbit skin.

One day as he was keeping a smoky fire going as he made jerky, a voice called.

"Hello, the camp. Can I come in, I mean no harm, but I've seen your smoke and could use something to eat."

Sean stood and turned to see a burly man coming his way. He had a strange looking pack on his back and when he came closer the man reached back, pulled a strap and threw the pack on the ground. It was a collection of furs.

"I be John Peters," the man said with an outstretched hand. "Some calls me John, but I can't say I won't come when you call me Jonny." With that he laughed and grasped Sean's hand with a grip that Sean thought might turn his fingers numb.

"Sean—I'm Sean O'Connell. At least I think that's who I am. It's been so long since I've talked with someone I could understand, that I'm not sure if I'm dreaming."

"Dreaming? No, Sean O'Connell, you're not dreaming. That's unless you're having a nightmare because old Jonny's here." Again he laughed and Sean enjoyed the sound of this man's energetic laughter.

"You say you're hungry? Well, I've plenty to eat, but I won't lie and tell you that my way of cooking appeals to all—but you're welcome to it. I see you have furs, what are they?"

"Beaver—it's what they're wanting in England these days makin' theirselves hats and such. At first I trapped them meself, but I make a better life just trading with the Indians for the pelts they gather. They're far better at trapping and dressing the hides too. And I see you're hiding a deer skin yourself. Would you sell it?"

"Sell? No, I think not—I've had no success curing hides, but then, I never thought of selling hides either. Come, let's eat and we'll talk more of these things. You must tell me if you've been east of the Susquehanna and if you have news from there."

"Susquehanna? I'd say so," Jonny said as he reached for a large chunk of jerky. I used to have a horse to carry me furs, but the Indians are beginning to like horses. They're not easy to come by and they'll bring a pretty price. But some Indians will take your scalp and your horse. So, I sold me horse to keep me hair and I carry me own furs now—as I'm doing now as you see."

Then they ate some of the smoked venison and some berries that were sour but tasty. And they enjoyed the fire and companionship as the day turned to night.

"How did you come to this wilderness—by way of Maryland?" Sean asked.

"Maryland, oh no, it was Philadelphia where I started, or at least south of there on the Delaware River. What about you?"

"I've never been to Philadelphia, but at one time I thought of living near there. No, I've come up from Maryland—Gunter's Harbour on the Chesapeake Bay."

"I see, on the bay it was. And what would bring a sane man from the bay out here, Sean O'Connell? I can see by your beard that you've lived here for some time now."

"You're right, Jonny. And I'll say this without meaning no offense to you personally; for I can see by the way you talk that you're from England. But, I had to run from your English countrymen when they took away my land in Maryland—land that had been given to my family more than fifty years ago."

"Hush now, Sean. It's them same countrymen of mine that brings me out here to gather pelts. As you've found for yourself, the Crown's soldiers don't like to dirty their pretty red coats out here in the wilderness, do they?"

Sean laughed and said, "At last, I've found a true Englishman." Then suddenly his face became sad and he said, "And I married a beautiful true English woman, Jonny—but she has gone to be with her Lord God."

"Oh, I'll not like to hear that sort of thing, Sean O'Connell—Sean— Sean O'Connell! Well, where's my empty head today—your name should have struck the sound of the bell. Didn't I meet a man—oh it was last year as I recall—and when he discovered that I was crossing the river he said to me, 'Should you ever come across Sean O'Connell, you tell him that'—now what was his name? He was a short stout man and belonged to that religion that Penn was part of. Now what was his name?"

"Was it Hough—Francis Hough?"

"That's the very one—Francis Hough. Then you do know him. Well he says to me, 'Should you ever come across Sean O'Connell, you tell him that Samson,' and some others, but I can't recall their names. 'You tell Sean O'Connell that Samson and them others they're fine as can be and safe,' yes, that's what he says, they're safe too."

"That is very good news, Jonny, thank you for recalling the message."

"As you can see," Jonny said with a smile, "I'd have told you sooner, but I don't recollect as good as once I did."

"Nor do I," Sean said and then they both laughed until tears were falling from Sean's eyes.

Then Sean said, "Did you say the same 'religion that Penn *was* part of'? Then is Penn no longer a Quaker?"

"It's not that he's not so much a Quaker, Sean. No, but Penn's not much of anything. He died more than three years ago."

The following morning Jonny was gathering his belongings to continue his trek eastward.

"I'd say you'll probably come across many a different person in your travels Jonny—am I right?"

"Oh, right you are and I'd say most are of a good sort, Sean. After a time you come to be aware you do. Something inside tells you who to trust and who to take your leave from as quick as jumping over a candlestick."

"Here's what I'd ask of you, Jonny. Would you be willing to take a letter with you and give it to someone you feel you can trust who might be passing near the home of Francis Hough?"

"Why would you even ask? Now, I couldn't give me pledge that I'll find such a man, but for any man to show Jonny your sort of hospitality—why I'd consider it a true honor to do it for you."

Sean went to a nearby growth of young birch trees. He gathered what he wanted and returned, sharpened a stick to use for writing, pulled a well charred small log from his fire, and began to rub the stick on the charcoal and painstakingly wrote:

To Francis Hough tell Captain Sean will return soon

"Do you know the month and the year, Jonny?"

"Well now, Sean. It's the year of our Lord 1721, of that I feel quite certain. I'd have to tell you that the month must be April or maybe it's May. From the looks of the forest I'll say May if that pleases you."

"That pleases me fine, Jonny."

Then Sean added *May 1721* to the birch bark. He purposely kept the message brief so that the bark could be easily rolled and protected, keeping the words readable—brief, but enough information so that Hough would understand the message and communicate the news to Captain Murphy that Sean O'Connell was well and would soon return home.

Sean handed the small scroll to Jonny who lifted the pack of beaver skins to his shoulder then vowed, "Sean, if ever we meet again—the next time it'll be over a cup of something more flavorful than spring water."

Then John Peters turned and headed east, laughing and waving his huge ham of a hand in farewell to Sean as he went.

———— CHAPTER EIGHT ————

Captain's Niece

"Well now, Nathan," Captain Murphy said, "What did your grandmother tell you about meeting the Reverend Sikes and Mrs. Sikes?"

"I'm to say that she's my grandmother," Nathan said to Mrs. Sikes. "Is that right, Grandfather? No—I remember! I'm to tell you that I'm very pleased to meet you Mrs. Sikes and that I'm my grandmother's grandson."

"And I'm sure you are," responded Mary Sikes with a pleasant smile.

Nathan liked the way that Mrs. Sikes smiled.

"You're a handsome grandson too, and I expect that you look very much like your father Sean. Does he Captain?"

"Do I Grandfather? Do I look like father?" Nathan chimed in.

"Well, I'll have to say that I see some of Sean in this seafaring grandson of mine—yes indeed."

"I haven't seen my father for a long time," Nathan said rather sadly. Then, breaking into a grin he said, "But grandfather says he'll come home soon and he'll be a seafaring man just like us—won't he Grandfather?"

"Soon, yes, we'd like to see him very soon. Aye, Nathan, very soon it'll be and I'm sure he'll make a fine seafaring man." With that he glanced at his niece Sarah.

Sarah had married Michael Fitzpatrick, a man schooled in navigation who came from an affluent Dublin seafaring family. He was serving a marine apprenticeship to an English sea captain aboard the frigate *Snow Lamb* authorized by the Crown as a privateer and he had participated in several expeditions against the Spanish.

However, three years earlier Fitzpatrick had been killed, along with the entire crew, when the *Snow Lamb* was sunk in a furious battle with the Spanish ship *San Juan del Cielo* as it returned from the Caribbean.

Sarah had been pregnant with their first child and when she was given the news of her husband's death at sea, the child was born prematurely and died within three months. Since then she seemed unable to lift herself from the cloudy veil of despair—most thought it was because of the loss of her husband and child.

After her husband's death she had gone to live with her father, Liam Murphy, Captain Murphy's brother. Sarah's mother had died from a fever when Sarah was very young and her father never remarried.

Some time had passed and Sarah's father thought that perhaps the change that might come from a visit to the colonies could lift her spirits and perhaps help her begin anew. He contacted his brother and Captain Murphy and Cynthia agreed that Sarah should visit with them in the colonies—perhaps even for an extended stay.

"Well now, Sarah," the captain began, "What do you think of life here in Maryland?"

Sarah's pleasant face was framed by coal black hair and that made her appear paler than she actually was. She was seated with her hands folded in her lap and as she looked up her grey eyes were pooled with tears when she answered the captain.

"Maryland? Oh, yes, Maryland. Well, of course I am pleased to have the very generous hospitality of the Sikes family here in Annapolis, and I . . . . That's a very difficult question Uncle, and I'm afraid that I have no true response. I've been here less than a week and . . . ."

"Now Laird," said Reverend Sikes, "I think you'll have time for answers when Sarah knows more—much more—about your question. After all, as she says, she's only now arrived these past few days and she hasn't much to consider about Maryland, has she?"

"Of course, Sarah," replied the captain. "You must forgive your barnacled uncle. I'm much too accustomed to talking with coarse seamen— rough seamen much like our young Nathan here."

There was some nervous laughter by everyone except Nathan and Sarah. No one really knew the things that Sarah Fitzpatrick had experienced and how those events continued to impact her spirit.

Later that day Nathan was playing in the garden, rolling a large wooden ball that the Reverend Sikes had given him. He had devised a game with two stones that he placed a foot apart and then would try to roll the ball between the stones. Frustrated after several misses, he rolled the ball much too hard and the foot of Sarah stopped it.

"My, but aren't you a very strong boy," Sarah said as she picked up the ball and handed it to Nathan.

"Thank you, Miss Sarah."

"You are very welcome. So do you enjoy your game Nathan?"

"Yes I do. It's a game I decided on all by myself," he replied. Then with frankness he asked, "Why are you sad, Miss Sarah? Do you never smile? Do you miss your father too?"

She was somewhat shocked by the guileless innocence of the boy.

"Why yes, Nathan. Yes, I do miss my father, and it does make me a bit sad."

Then with an effort she had not even considered in a long time, she smiled and said, "And I know you must miss your father as well."

"I have no mother Miss Sarah. Did you know that I have no mother?"

"Why, yes I did."

"Sometimes I try to think of her but I can't remember what she looked like." He paused and with a contemplative expression said, "I'm not sure I remember what father looks like either. I hope he'll be home soon."

Sarah's mind reached back searching for images of her mother too, but she was unsuccessful.

"Yes, Nathan. Yes, I'm sure you miss him and you do want him to return soon."

Then smiling again, this time more naturally, she added, "And do you know what? I'm sure of something else too—I'm sure that when you see him you'll know him and recognize him as the father that you do remember."

"I think so too, Miss Sarah," he quickly responded; then paused and asked, "Why is your name different than your father's name? Why isn't your name Sarah Murphy?"

She said, "Well, you're right Nathan, my name should be the same as my father's. And I was Sarah Murphy—for a very long time—but then I married and took my husband's name, and that's when I became Sarah Fitzpatrick."

"Oh, so that's why—you're married and you have a husband."

Then with a puzzled look Nathan asked, "Well then, if you're married, where is your husband and where are your children?"

"What are you two doing out here in the garden," called Mrs. Sikes from the house. "It's getting cool, so you must come inside for tea and biscuits. I've many things to talk about with you, Sarah, and we have only one more day until you sail to North East with the captain."

"Come Nathan," Sarah said, "Doesn't hot tea sound good? Let's go inside for tea and biscuits. We'll talk about these things when we sail to North East, Nathan—then we'll learn more about each other."

Two days later they sailed for Gunter's Harbour on the evening high tide.

CHAPTER NINE

Back Together

Sean was noticing larger groups of Indians and seeing them more regularly. Often it appeared to be entire families or perhaps small clans and almost always they were traveling westward.

In the past, most of the Indians had made some kind of effort to meet with Sean and deal with him in a friendly manner. Now, although they did not try to avoid Sean, it appeared that the Indians had no desire to engage in social encounters with him.

He never saw anyone from the Black Minqua, but there were many Lenni Lenape, from Bone Man's tribe, who passed through the area. He knew this when he recognized symbols of the turtle on men and women and often on the warriors' shields.

On a few occasions some of the younger men would run angrily toward Sean shaking weapons in their hands and shouting at him until an older man would call them back. None of the groups, whether large or small, seemed interested in slowing down long enough for Sean to enjoy their company.

It seemed almost as if they were fixed on arriving somewhere—and that was exactly what was happening.

Since the death of William Penn, many of the promises made to the Indians were continually in the process of being broken or ignored. Whites were moving onto lands that Penn had assured would always belong to the tribes, and these moves were supported and enforced by small units of British soldiers who drove the Indians farther west.

Of course, Sean was unaware of these political policy changes until one day when two of the men who had shown him how to build a sturdy shelter passed by with their families. They were Shawnee and they told him they were being driven from their ancestral land. He didn't understand everything they said, but he could see that the more they spoke of it the more agitated they became.

Sean offered them food and they refused it, which was not a good indication. Fortunately the men then left with their families, and from that moment on Sean determined that whenever possible he would stay clear of the Indians.

Leaving behind most of what he had accumulated since his journey to the wilderness, he armed himself, gathered what food he could easily carry, abandoned his sturdy lodge and started his trek toward the Susquehanna.

Fortunately, the vast majority of Indians who were migrating westward were in groups that he could hear and then easily avoid. However, one time as he was coming down a steep hill he lost his footing then slid and rolled until he ended up at the bottom—at the feet of two Indians. They were almost as surprised as he was. And even though they looked fierce enough, fortunately for Sean they did not seem to be in a belligerent mood, but laughed and walked off into the forest—another reminder to Sean of the need for extreme care in the future.

Often Sean found that he had to backtrack or take a different direction entirely simply to keep away from the Indians that he sensed were becoming more and more roused in their behavior. One day as he hid himself, waiting near a creek for a small group made up of mostly women to cross over, a larger group came upon them, killed two of the men from the smaller group and ran the rest off.

It appeared to Sean that they had done this for no more reason than to be able to cross over the water before the others.

Unfortunately, John Peters had discovered even worse behavior as he traveled back toward Philadelphia. After leaving Sean, he had come upon a group of Shawnee. Of course he had bargained with Shawnee before and as he approached them to see if they might have beaver skins to trade, they attacked and beat him, took his pelts, scalped him alive and left him to die.

The Indian who had taken Jonny's scalp, Kaweequa, called Six Toes by the other Shawnee, wiped the blood from his knife with a piece of rolled up birch bark that had fallen from John's tunic.

As the Indians became more emboldened and aggressive, the British responded by sending more troops into the areas where whites were moving and they also began an effort to conscript able-bodied colonial men to help them.

All during this time many of the Indians were submitting to the demands of the white men and were moving further west, However, Six Toes continued to wreak havoc by pillaging and killing other Indians as well as the small groups of whites who were moving onto the land.

Six Toes had sent two men ahead to determine if the farmers in one small community could be easily overcome. From the forest, just outside the edge of a field, the Indians watched for more than an hour as six white men and three blacks worked hard trying to pull a large stump from the ground.

However, Six Toes' renegades were unaware that they also were being watched—by two other Indians, Nokona and Bone Man.

Kezie, Sean's former slave, and two white women were carrying food and a small pail of water out to the men working in the field. Included in this group were Samson, Obadiah and Ezekiel.

One of the white farmers saw them and said, "This is a grand sight; the women are coming with bread and water."

Samson, Ezekiel, Obadiah and the other farmers laid their tools down. The men still hadn't pulled the stump entirely out of the ground and they welcomed this opportunity to rest and to be refreshed with food and water.

They were sitting on the ground discussing ways that they might try to burn part of the stump to more easily break it up when—just as the sun began to set over the trees—Six Toes and his band came screaming from the western edge of the field toward them.

One of the farmers grabbed the rifle he had laid against a large rock and the other men took up available tools to defend themselves.

Samson shouted, "Obadiah, Kezie get to the house and warn them others."

But, those in the buildings had already heard the screaming Indians. A shot rang out from the direction of the buildings and one of the running

Indians dropped in his tracks. The others stopped, looked at the leader and then continued to charge toward Samson, Ezekiel and the others.

The man who retrieved his weapon knelt down and steadied the rifle on the rock and fired. Another Indian went down.

Suddenly two more Indians came screaming from the forest, but these were running toward the attackers. The man at the rock finished reloading his rifle and was about to shoot at the large Indian who had just broken from the cover of the trees.

"No! Don' be shoot him," shouted Ezekiel. "Don' be shoot him." Although he didn't know his name, Ezekiel recognized Nokona as the man who had saved his life several years earlier.

So the man took aim at the closest man in the larger group and fired. This time two Indians fell as the shot tore through the first man's neck and into the side of the other. Four others turned to attack Nokona and Bone Man, who were approaching rapidly, Nokona with his war club and Bone Man with his leg bone knife-club, both weapons raised to strike.

Another shot rang out and the Indian who was leading those who were attacking Nokona fell. The other three stopped in their tracks when a call from Six Toes sent them all scurrying back toward the forest.

Bone Man wanted a taste of blood and threw his weapon. It struck one of the retreating men just behind the knee and he went tumbling to the ground. Before he could recover and get to his feet, Nokona was upon him and ended the man's raiding days. Bone Man recovered his weapon and threw it at another man but he was already out of the range of his throw.

Nokona and Bone Man then ran to the wounded Indians and without hesitation or any suggestion of mercy, dispatched them to their eternity.

Samson and Ezekiel started toward the two Indians to greet them. Nokona made eye contact with Ezekiel, then he and Bone Man turned and trotted off to the forest—for even though Nokona knew he would have been welcomed and comfortable with the blacks, he could not be sure of finding a welcome haven with these unknown whites.

It was more than two months later when Sean walked into a clearing and saw Francis Hough's house. It was just before dusk and Sean called, "Hello the house. Sean O'Connell comes to call—is he welcomed?"

The door flew open and Hough came hurrying outside to greet Sean.

"Welcome—yes—welcome you are. Oh, my how good to see you. We wondered if you were alive."

Sean suspected that he bore an unpleasant odor and asked if he might spend the night in one of their sheds. He knew from the relieved look on Mrs. Hough's face that that she was pleased with his request. Sean and Hough set up a board over two barrels and the meal was provided outside the entrance to the house. Sean had forgotten just how good food tasted when prepared by someone other than himself—or and Indian.

They talked well into the night and when Hough told Sean that he had never received his message saying that he was coming back home, Sean thought the worst of what might have happened to John Peters.

Hough told him of the attack that the Indians made on the farmers to the north where Samson, Kezie, Obadiah and Ezekiel had been safely located.

"Indeed, safe I thought they would be from those who might be after escaped slaves, but never thinking how much danger there would be from Indians. My friends said two Indians who were not with the marauding Indian band actually drove the others away. They said that Ezekiel knew one of the Indians and . . . ."

"And I know him as well," Sean interrupted. If Ezekiel recognized him then he was the one known as Nokona and I'll need a week's long time if I were to tell of those times I spent with him in the wilderness. But, would you excuse me Francis, for I must get some sleep. I'll leave before daybreak, so I'll thank you now for the kindness that you and your dear wife have shown me. I'd not like to think what life might have been if God hadn't brought you into my life. You're a good man, Francis Hough."

Somewhat embarrassed, Hough replied, "Well—certainly—that is, thank you."

Sean went to the horse shed and lay down on a small packet of straw. He was asleep before his head touched the ground.

He could not tell how long he had slept or how soon dawn would come, but when he awoke he was anxious to continue the rest of his journey toward Gunter's Harbour. He walked for almost three hours and just before the sun began to rise he came to a creek that seemed familiar.

Finding a bend in the creek that was hidden from the view of any who might come along to cross over, he removed all of his clothing and carried them into the creek. He sat down and soaked the clothing, then twisted it as streams of dirt muddied the clear water. Shocked that he had been wearing these items on his body, he continued soaking and wringing them until at last he achieved a reasonable resemblance of clean water.

Then he hung the clothing on some bushes in the sun and went back into the water to get some of the grime from himself. He laid his head on the branch of a tree that had the appearance of bending down to take a drink, then relaxing he looked up at the clear blue sky, rested and enjoyed the refreshing cool water washing over him.

He awoke with a start when his head slipped from the branch and he went underwater then came up choking with the water he had inhaled. Looking around to be sure no one was there he climbed from the creek and tested his clothing. It was still damp, but he could wait no longer. He could not be this close to his son without seeing him as soon as possible, so he dressed hurriedly and was on his way.

"A man's coming, Grandfather," Nathan said to the Captain who sat rocking on the front porch.

"He is, is he now? Is it Ben?"

"No Grandfather, it's not Ben. He's walking and he looks like he's not a very clean man."

With that, Captain Murphy got up to look down the lane.

"Is that you? Sean—is that you Sean?" the captain shouted.

When Sean heard the captain call he started to trot toward the house.

Nathan went inside to tell his grandmother that some man named Sean was coming down the lane.

"Sean is coming down the lane?" Cynthia cried out incredulously. "Sean's here, Missy, Sean's here—Nathan, it's Sean. He's your father."

Captain Murphy was laughing uproariously at the sight of Sean.

"Sean, me boy, it'll take us a week to scrape those whiskers off and we'll have to burn them clothes you're wearing as we did when we got you out of the prison in Annapolis. Oh, Sean, how good it is to lay these old eyes on you."

They all ran down to the front garden as Sean came through the gate—all but Nathan and Sarah. They waited on the porch.

"Oh Sean, just look at you, such a fine sight you are," Cynthia said as tears rolled down her cheeks. "We are so happy that you've come back."

"I'll not say as much about being a fine sight, Sean," the captain said and once again began to laugh. "But, it is good to have you here where you belong, lad."

"I can't explain how wonderful it is to be here with you," Sean said and then looking at the porch and lowering his voice asked: "And Nathan? Is that Nathan on the porch—and who is the woman he stands by?"

"Come down here now, Nathan, won't you?" Cynthia called. "And Sarah, please come dear to meet Sean."

Sarah came down the porch steps with Nathan behind her. As they approached the captain said, "Sean, this is my niece, Sarah Fitzpatrick. And, well, maybe you know who this young seaman is."

Sean didn't even acknowledge the introduction of Sarah.

"He's grown so," Sean marveled. "Is this the small child I was first afraid to hold when his mother gave birth? Is this the little man who cried so hard because I left him here that day three years ago? And those eyes—those green eyes—no one would dare say this was not Julia's child."

Sean squatted down with outstretched arms. "Come here, my boy. I'm your father. And son I've come back for you."

Nathan ran to his father's outstretched arms and never noticed the odor of the man the others seemed hesitant to embrace.

—————— CHAPTER TEN ——————

Troubled Relationships

"In Julia's room—but why must she be in Julia's room?" Sean was asking Cynthia.

"Well, Sean," Cynthia replied, "we felt it was appropriate because it is a lovely room, a room that would be pleasant for any woman, And I simply think that Julia would be pleased that Sarah would be able to sleep there and use the room just now—don't you Sean?"

Sean thought, *No, I don't think it would have pleased Julia, not at all, and it certainly doesn't please me. I've thought of her room as mine—as our—room.*

"That's right, Father, Miss Sarah likes the room very much," Nathan agreed. "And sometimes I take an afternoon nap with her. Maybe you could sleep with me in my room sometime too Daddy. We could do that couldn't we Grandmother?"

"Well, of course you may—would that be suitable for now, Sean?"

"No, I think it would not. Look here, dear lady, the idea of a strange woman being in Julia's bed is not an easy thought for me to deal with just yet. And, well I've been in the wilderness much too long to behave in a decent manner and to stay in such a pleasant home as this."

"Oh now, Sean, how can you say that. Sarah is not a stranger in this house. She's the captain's niece. And, Sean, this is as much your home as ours, and I thought it would please you if we were to open our home to help this woman," Cynthia insisted.

"I'm sorry Cynthia, but it doesn't please me at all. But perhaps you're right, and I apologize for behaving so toward you—you of all people."

"No need to apologize, Sean. I do understand. Your love for my daughter is very clear and I would not wish to disparage that love in any way. So Sean, may Sarah remain in Julia's room?"

"Yes—yes, of course dear lady. And it works well, because the captain told me that the soldiers haven't come back to Dawn Light for more that three years as far as he could tell. I'm thinking that I'll ride over there to see for myself and Nathan can come with me. If it seems safe, we could spend a few days there. Would you like that Nathan? It would be a bit like living in the wilderness with your father, just as I've been living."

"Would that be fine with you Grandmother? May I go with Daddy?"

"Of course you may, Nathan. He's your father, why shouldn't you go? And I'll have Missy make some of your favorite things to eat and Grandfather will bring them to you tomorrow. How would you two like that?"

They settled on that plan after Sean had assured Nathan that he need not fear any Indians while he was with his father. And it also seemed to Cynthia that the situation of having a stranger in Julia's room was also settled—at least for now.

Sean took Nathan to the second floor of Dawn Light and showed Nathan the room he had once slept in when he was very young.

"Did I sleep in this very room Father? Where is my bed?"

"Yes, son, this very room, and then the soldiers took your bed away along with our other beds, chairs, lamps and everything else that belonged to us, But, let's clean these pesky little visitors out of the room now so we'll have a decent place to sleep."

Sean found a broom and cleaned out some of the cobwebs and swept the floor as clean as he could. He found that many things such as candles had been left behind, so he chose two large candles and lit them, then Nathan and his father talked into the night. Once Nathan fell asleep, Sean could not take his eyes from his boy's face for the longest time.

Sean snuffed both candles and as he laid on the floor his mind went around and around, trying to capture and align the thoughts that were spinning through his head and finally sleep came.

"Hello, the house. Food for your majesty and the prince," called the captain's unmistakable voice.

At first when Sean sat upright he was unaware of his location. Then, remembering he looked about for Nathan, but he had run outside as soon as he heard his grandfather call.

"There you are, you rascal," the captain shouted. "Now where's that father of yours. Must I eat all of this food myself?"

"No, Grandfather, don't eat all of the food. Daddy will want some too, and I'm very hungry."

"I'll say you'd better not eat all of the food," said Sean stepping through the door. "Good to see you Captain. Oh my, you have no idea how good it is to see you and my son."

They ate and Nathan wanted to explore the buildings around Dawn Light.

Sean cautioned him, "Nathan, be aware of snakes, because they've had the place as their own for a few years."

Then Sean and the captain sat on the porch steps as they began the attempt for each to understand what the past few years had been like in their lives while he was away.

Occasionally, Nathan would return, listen for awhile and then go off on a new adventure. When it seemed they had both explained what had been going on in their lives during the separation they sat quietly for awhile.

"You haven't asked much about my niece, Sean."

"And why should I? Is there something you'd want to be telling me that you think I should be asking?"

"It's not that you should be asking, Sean. But, here's the way the sails are filling. My brother, Liam—you've heard me speak of him—we've not seen the other for years, but I received a letter about a year ago asking me if we might take Sarah as a guest for awhile."

The captain went on to explain Sarah's background, the death of her husband and loss of their child. Then he said, "So, you see, Liam had the idea that spending time here with us might mend her heart, because it had been broken over the loss of her husband and child."

"And why does Nathan seem so drawn to her? I'll tell you Captain this to me seems as though I'm being placed in a compromising position. I'd not like to say as much to you, because to me you're an old and trusted friend—like the father I was never able to really know. But, Captain, it seems to me that some sort of trickery or deceit is going on with this matter of your niece."

"Now, I'll say be careful with the jib of that sail, Sean. My Cynthia and I would do nothing to deceive you. We saw this plan as something that might be good for my niece. And tell me if you can, Sean O'Connell, would there be something wrong if it were to be of benefit to you and Nathan too?"

Sean had no response that seemed suitable.

"And while we're out on the yardarm[6] in this here storm Sean, I'll tell you this as well—I never sold your sloop *Julia's Fairwinds*, and I'll tell you why. The only purchaser I had was that Swede and I never cared much for the man. Then, when he wanted to steal the sloop I set my mind, and here's what I set it to. I says—and I told Cynthia as much, and like her you might not respect what I've done—I says, I'm thinking that Sean will be back soon from his wilderness wandering and then what?"

"Then what?—then what?" Sean interrupted. "How is it that you might be the one who would decide 'then what' for me?"

"I knew as how you'd see it as Cynthia did. But look Sean, you've a fine vessel in the likes of that sloop and what would keep you from joining me in shipping goods up and down the Chesapeake? I'll tell you this," the captain said as he saw Nathan coming around the corner of the house. "And haven't I prepared a fine first mate for you in young Nathan here?"

"Will I be the first mate, Grandfather? I thought Fian was your first mate?"

"We'll talk more of this later," Sean said. He went to the shed where the horse had been bedded, saddled the horse and walked him back to the front of the house.

"You'd best be going back to the house with your grandfather Nathan I have things to tend to." He mounted and rode off without another word.

"What does he mean, Grandfather? What does he need to tend to?"

"That's something your father will do by himself, Nathan. Come now let's get up on this tired old horse and go back home. I think I smell some of Missy's biscuits."

Sean was gone for several days and no one had an idea of where he might be.

"What do you think Laird," Cynthia asked with deep concern in her voice, "Might this wilderness life have done something to him? Why has he gone off again?"

"You're asking the wrong man, my wife. Sean's the only one with that answer. He's a man that can care for himself. My concern is with you, Nathan and Sarah—and of course Missy as well. This talk about the Indian they call Six Toes gives me disquiet for you."

"But, you're here with us, Laird, and I don't see why such a man would come near us here. There are far too many people who would see him and warn others—don't you think as much?"

"It's as I've said about Sean, the same goes for this savage. I've no idea how or what he's thinking. What I'm saying to you is that I'll not have you alone outside the house. And when I'm not here I'll have you bolt the doors. Can you do that for me?"

"Of course Laird, I'll do as you ask, but I don't see that we'll be bothered by such a man—and for what purpose?"

The following day Fian sent word to the captain about a problem with two new members of the crew.

"I'll be going to Gunter's Harbour today, Cynthia, and Nathan will be with me," the captain announced. "I fear that Fian may be ready to put a lash to two of the crew—either lash them or hang them, you can never tell about Fian." He laughed, kissed his wife on the cheek and he was out the door with Nathan just a step behind.

They had been gone only fifteen minutes before Cynthia remembered that she had promised Elizabeth that she would ride over to the Dixon's to introduce Sarah, and the captain was supposed to have gone with them.

If he had any concerns about me taking the short trip to Dixon's, thought Cynthia, *he certainly would have said something before he left for the ship. I'm sure he would have told me to wait until another day when he could go with us if he'd had unease about us traveling there alone. Yes, I'm certain that he would have said something.*

An hour later Missy had the horse hitched to the large cart and the three women started out on the path toward the Dixon home. Just before they came to the first turn at the large tulip poplar tree, three Indians blocked the path and as Missy reined the horse in two others jumped on the cart.

In minutes the women were bound and had disappeared with Six Toes and his men.

Sean was about to leave Ben and Elizabeth Dixon's farm with the promise to return and share a meal with them later that week. He had come to his senses and determined that he would not allow the situation with Sarah to allow his relationship with Cynthia and the captain—and especially Nathan—to be affected.

When Sean came to the turn at the tulip poplar he was surprised to see a horse and cart in the path. He dismounted and recognizing it as the captain's cart he thought the women might have gone into the lightly wooded area to look for berries.

He tied his horse loosely to the same shrub that held the cart-horse and then as he turned around he glanced back toward the path and saw a bonnet lying on the ground, the same bonnet that Cynthia had worn when last he saw her.

CHAPTER ELEVEN

Friends Part

"Here comes Sean," Elizabeth Dixon called to her husband Ben. "He's racing down the path."

Ben looked up from the log he was trying to split. He laughed and said, "Didn't think he'd be coming back so soon—and in such a hurry—to eat with us."

Sean was dismounting before the horse had fully stopped and Ben knew that something was wrong.

"They've taken the women—I fear that Indians have taken Cynthia, Missy and the captain's niece."

"Saddle my horse Elizabeth and then get to Gunter's Harbour as fast as possible and tell the captain, I know he must be at the ship."

"What of the Tubbs cousins," Sean asked, "Where do they stay now?"

"Didn't the captain tell you? No help there, Sean. They've gone off to Philadelphia—left a few years back. I'll get my rifle and sword. I see you're unarmed except for that stout short sword, so I'll get powder and shot for the pistol too. Help Elizabeth saddle my horse."

In less than ten minutes they were mounted and headed back toward the place along the path where Sean had found the horse and cart.

Elizabeth Dixon came careening much too fast toward the ship, and it was obvious to Fian that something was not right.

"Captain—Captain! Ben Dixon's wife's comin' just thrashin' away at her beast."

Captain Murphy quickly went down the plank from the ship to the quay and grabbed the horse's bridle.

"Here now Elizabeth, what's amiss?" the captain shouted.

"It's your wife. It's Cynthia and the other women. They've been taken by Indians and . . . ."

Before she could finish, Fian had called up two crewmen and then he went to the captain's quarters and came back with pistols for himself and the captain and swords for the men. The captain had left the horse hitched to his cart so he turned his cart about and the men jumped in.

"How does Sean know all this?" he asked Elizabeth. "Where were they last seen?"

"He found the cart and horse on the path to our house—and I'm sure that the cart will still be there, because Ben and Sean have gone to that very place to see if they can follow after the Indians and recover your wife."

"Then we're off," the captain said and then he shouted to two crewmen who leaned over the port side of the ship, "You two there—take Nathan with you and accompany Mrs. Dixon to her home and stay there until her husband returns. Be quick now."

"Grandfather I want to go with you and Fian . . ." Captain Murphy didn't hear his grandson's plea, but whipped the horse into a gallop and they were off in a cloud of dust. As they approached the large tulip poplar there was the horse, still hitched to the cart and tied to the shrub—just as Elizabeth had suggested.

"I'm thinking that here's where they must've gone in," the captain said. "Fian, have the men take the harnesses from the horse. I'll ride on ahead and you should be able to follow in the wide wake that so many of us traveling through these woods leave behind. Now, be at it."

"Aye, Captain, and we'll be followin' just after you, you can be sure."

Sean and Ben walked their horses through the wooded area at a pace faster than a man could walk, being careful to make as little noise as possible. They would stop as one or the other men gave a signal if he thought he had heard something.

Sean had the feeling—a sense that brought the hackles up on his neck—that they were being watched. He was about to say something to Ben when an arrow glanced harmlessly off of the brass buckle on his horse's bridle and another arrow thumped into a tree about two feet from Sean's head.

He turned in the direction the arrows had come from and saw two Shawnee about fifty feet from him and they were about to release a second wave of arrows. One did let loose his arrow, but it flew to the ground as he fell forward. Sean recognized a familiar object in the man's back.

The other Shawnee turned quickly, just in time to see Bone Man bringing his war club down on the arm in which the man held his bow. Nokona was right behind him and they quickly dispatched both Shawnee and turned toward Sean and Ben—Ben looked at Sean in panic.

"They're friends," Sean hastily assured Ben. "You remember the big man, don't you? He's the one who . . . "

"Yes," Ben shouted with a look of some relief. "I do know who he is—but the other?"

Before Sean could say more, Nokona motioned for them to dismount and follow. This they did, leaving the horses then trailing them with haste. Ben thought the noise they were making as they followed Nokona and Bone Man might warn those they were following of their presence. But before he could complete that thought, Nokona and Bone Man dropped to a knee and Sean and Ben did the same.

They heard loud voices ahead of them and what sounded like the sobbing of a woman. Just then a man shouted, then others made strange calls and then Sean saw Missy running towards them, with two Indians pursuing.

Nokona held his hand as a sign for stillness and within a few moments Missy saw Nokona and screamed, because she thought she had run off only to be quickly recaptured. Those who chased were focused on Missy, so when she stumbled and fell they caught up with her and began to beat her. The beating was brief as Nokona and Bone Man rose to protect her. Bone Man was struck with a knife but rather than slow him down it enraged him and in seconds another two Shawnee lay dead.

Shouts came from ahead because the rest of the band of Shawnee had heard the ruckus. They were calling to the men who had pursued Missy and when they did, Nokona dared to respond in the Shawnee dialect.

Nokona called to the Shawnee for help. Sean told Missy to stand against the tree with him and Ben and they pretended to be trussed up.

Nokona and Bone Man hid in a shallow depression in the ground and before long Six Toes and another Indian came upon the scene.

Six Toes was perplexed when he saw Missy, Sean and Ben apparently tied up, but before he could decide what was happening, Nokona and Bone Man stood and the battle was on. Sean ran toward the direction from which Six Toes had come stopping briefly to be sure his pistol was charged.

A shot rang out behind him and the forest fell silent. Then, he heard a blood-curdling scream—it was Bone Man claiming victory.

Sean forged ahead and soon came upon Cynthia and the captain's niece. They were still bound, but they were alone and Sarah sobbed uncontrollably

"There was only one Indian who remained here, Sean," Cynthia advised. "When he heard the shot and the scream he ran off—I think we'll not see him again."

Sarah was on the ground and Cynthia sat beside her and put her arm around her shoulder and said, "It's all right, dear. It's all over now. Don't be afraid; please don't cry dear. We're safe now. Sean and the others are here." Then, turning to Sean she said, "Is the captain with you?"

"No, Ben's with me but you can be certain that the captain will be here before long. Elizabeth went to Gunter's Harbour to get him and—well, here he comes with the others now."

As Sean expected, the captain, his men and Ben, with Nokona and Bone Man following, approached them with smiles on their faces.

Sarah screamed and fainted when she saw Nokona and Bone Man.

Cynthia and Missy spent a good amount of time cleaning the wounds Nokona and Bone Man had sustained in Six Toes' final battle.

Sarah recovered from her the initial fright of seeing the Indians with Ben and Sean—especially the frightening face of Bone Man.

"Let me tear some cloth from your petticoat, Sarah, it will make fine dressings for their wounds."

"No—no, I cannot do it," she responded between sobs. "Not for these or any other savages. I only want to be alone and safe. Is there nowhere to be safe here—nowhere?"

The captain was satisfied that there was no more to fear for the moment and he tried to comfort his niece as the group walked back to the cart path. He sent Fian and the others back to the ship with his cart.

Sean was agitated over Sarah's comments about his Indian friends and he wanted to explain to Sarah how important this "savage"—as she had said—was in his life and the lives of his friends.

However, because Sean had asked to speak to Sarah, without informing Captain Murphy, the captain, Cynthia and Missy rode on in their other cart back to their home, leaving Sarah behind. That was not exactly what Sean had wanted—to be alone with Sarah.

After Ben went his way, Sean decided to face Sarah. He tried to explain to Sarah the important part that Nokona had played in the lives of those of her own family—meaning saving the life of her uncle, the captain. He wanted her to meet Nokona and Bone Man, but she refused. Sean could not determine if her refusal was based upon fear, unconcern, or stubbornness, but her rejection of his friends did nothing to change his feelings toward this immovable woman.

She had quieted down somewhat, but would unexpectedly begin to sob again. Sean didn't know just what to do with Sarah and so he decided that she should return to Murphy's house, yet somehow he had missed the fact that the others had already left in the cart.

Now what am I to do? I could put her on my horse and walk the animal back to Murphy's, but I'll not march back there just because of this willful woman.

Sean walked away from where she sat sobbing on the side of the path and spoke to Nokona.

"Again, old friend, I am in your debt. You have saved my life and the lives of these others once again."

Nokona grasped the forearm of Sean as his sign of deep friendship. Then, Bone Man surprised Sean when he did the same and said something Sean didn't understand.

"Long time friend, Sean," Nokona said. "*Sean anákawa sheénay kawa[7]*—Nokona always be Sean's friend. Nokona go—more to wander."

Once again the two Indians slipped away into the forest. Sean had no way of knowing that it would be a very long time before he would see Bone Man, the *wanderer* Nokona or his sister Lomasi—*pretty flower.*

When the Indians left, Sean said to Sarah, "I'm riding back to Murphy's. You have a choice. You can ride with me, or you can walk back to your uncle's house."

She made her decision quickly. She wasn't about to chance seeing more Indians today. So Sean mounted then helped her get up on the horse, where she sat very uncomfortably, straddling the horse's rump behind Sean.

They galloped along at a breakneck pace and all the while Sean was thinking, *I'll not mollycoddle this woman for anyone's cause—not even because she's the captain's niece.*

Rather swiftly Sarah brought her sobbing under control as they rode back to Murphy's, because now she was occupied with the activity of holding on for her life—to Sean—and rather taking pleasure in the sensation of the contact..

CHAPTER TWELVE

Renewed Appeals

The sun had run its course for the day and shadows were turning to the dark of night as Captain Murphy and Sean sat on the porch steps of the captain's home.

Sarah, the captain's niece was upset, because after the Indians had been driven off they had left her behind with Sean. Leaving her behind and alone with Sean had been a very awkward experience for both of them. And then, to add to discomfort to her embarrassment, she had to ride back with him on the horse's rump.

The captain wanted to talk to Sean about Sarah and tell him something of her life before she came to the colonies. However, he was somewhat puzzled because of the changes that seemed to have come over Sean.

On the one hand, since his return, Sean seemed much more self-confident, a characteristic the captain attributed to having been alone and independent in the wilderness for quite some time. On the other hand, the captain sensed what he considered a distant attitude, which was not at all like the Sean of the past.

The captain and Ben Dixon had managed to recover some of Sean's clothing from Dawn Light after the English soldiers had ransacked and then abandoned the house, and Cynthia had stored some of the clothing for his return.

The tunic that Cynthia had given him that morning hung a bit loosely on his body. Life in the wilderness had brought a more muscular and lean Sean back to Gunter's Harbour.

The captain heaved a sigh and leaned back on the railing of the porch steps.

"Sean," the captain began, "Do you remember much about the *English Pale*[8]?"

"The English Pale? Do you mean the pale around Dublin, Captain?"

"The same," the captain replied. "They tell me that bloody pale has been there 100 years and probably longer, a series of damnable barriers of posts, ditches and fences—and what for?"

"What for Captain? Well, I'd say to keep the Irish from having their rightful land."

"Aye, Sean, and you'd be right. But they weren't satisfied with just Dublin. Oh no, they gradually fortified County Meath, County Louth, and County Kildare as well. Irish land—land the English fortified just to prevent the Irish from attacking and regaining their own homes—our own land, Sean."

The two men sat silently for several minutes as both considered the injustice of that situation.

Then Sean said, "Much like it is here in the colonies, isn't it Captain?"

"What's that Sean? Much like what?"

"Well, think of it," Sean began. "Now, I've never traveled outside the pale in Ireland myself. But here's how the English understand it I'm thinking. To go outside the pale is to be *beyond the pale*. And to an Englishman that means to be outside of civilization with no expectation of civilized treatment."

"Aye, that's what I'd agree to as a right way to explain it, Sean. The English have a way of thinking that allows them to say that it's themselves what's the only civilized men there are."

With that, both men laughed and then Sean continued.

"Modest these Englishmen, would you agree Captain?"

"Modest—agree?" the captain responded. "No, Sean I can't agree with that—I'd say that I'd have to *insist* that the English think they have a way of life above all others—I'm thinking they'd call it an 'English society.' And that English way of life—in all the English humility they can muster don't you know—is a society they consider the same thing as civilization itself."

The captain laughed at the clever remark he thought he had made, but Sean was silent.

"What is it Sean?"

"Oh, you'd have to excuse me, Captain. I've just thought about the English Pale in Ireland and how it disgusts and angers those of us who are Irishmen."

"Aye, Sean, I'd say it does make me blood boil at times."

"But, Captain—I've been *beyond the pale* right here in the colonies too. Only this time, the English aren't taking Irish land and driving out the Irish—it's the white men who are taking land from the Indians and driving them out. English, Spanish, Dutch, Swiss, German and I'd have to include the Irish. Captain, do you understand? I've seen it myself. I've been beyond the pale."

"You have, Sean. That you have. I do see your meaning about the pale and I'd agree that you've been beyond the pale. You've been to the wilderness, Sean, but now you're back. Do you see Sean? We need to have our Sean truly back here with us, back from the wilderness. Away from the wild ways you've had to live. You've returned, Sean. Will you give us back the Sean we knew here in civilization?"

The clouds were slipping silently across the moon and Sean stared at the captain for a few seconds and then, as if expecting to see someone coming, he looked off down the path toward Gunter's Harbour before continuing.

"You see, Captain . . ." he began, but then he fell silent for several minutes.

"What, Sean? What is it you want me to see?" the captain asked.

"I've been to what we've called the wilderness, but there I found a civilization too. Men who are surely as civilized as any Englishman I've ever met. And although with different ways and their own speech, men I'd trust with my life—and have trusted with my life—just as you and I have trusted each other."

"Aye, but it's a different matter when we come to the savages, Sean."

"No, Captain. That's what you don't understand. You see here's what I'm saying to you. I've been to the wilderness, and that's beyond the *pale* where white men consider that they're outside of civilization with no expectation of civilized treatment. But, I tell you, Captain, I've found that men are men, whether in England, Ireland, or the colonies. They can dress in fine linens, white wigs and red coats and all the while they'll lie, cheat and steal from you—as they've done from me. Or, with tattooed faces and hair greased to make it stand upright, they'll share with you whatever they have—be it much or little. Yes, Captain, I've been beyond the pale and now I'm back—and Captain, the Sean I'm bringing back to you is the only Sean I know."

Just then the front door opened and Cynthia said, "Would you two prefer to sit out here in darkness or come in for a tasty warm meal?"

"We'll choose the meal, my dear," the captain said.

The men arose to go inside and the captain said, "We must talk more about these matters, Sean."

The next day, just before dawn, Sean decided to put a new plan into action. He had continued to sleep in Julia's bedroom at Dawn Light since his return from the wilderness, even though Cynthia begged him to stay with them. Of course there was no bed and he slept on a pallet made of blankets on the floor, but this wasn't much different than what he had become accustomed to these past years.

Dawn Light—The Manor House

After watering and feeding his horse, he saddled the animal. Sean was hoping that the day might become a pleasant blend of conversation and good food with old friends—so he rode to Ben Dixon's place.

"Well," said Elizabeth as Sean rode up to the front of the house where she sat on the porch, "You're too late for breakfast and too early for a noon meal, so what business do you have with us on this day, Sean O'Connell?"

"Don't try to deceive me, Elizabeth. I know you always make more corn cakes than Ben can eat. But, I'll tell you this—I have a hunger enough for three men today and I'll eat whatever crumbs you have left on the table."

Elizabeth got up from the chair and laid the small pan of beans that she had been shelling on the floor.

"You must have been looking in the window, because I think I can find a fried corn cake or two that Ben hasn't carried off to the field with him. Now, you sit out here in my chair."

Ben had seen Sean riding in, and no sooner was Sean seated in Elizabeth's chair than Ben was at the house.

"Sean, you're too late for . . ."

"He knows, Ben," Elizabeth said. "I've already told him he was too late. But he insisted and you can see that he hasn't had decent food for awhile."

"You're right you are," Sean said patting his stomach and smiling. "And I appreciate your kind and generous hospitality to a wanderer like me."

The moment Sean called himself a wanderer a mental picture of Nokona, his wandering Indian friend, filled his mind.

"We're glad to have you back here where you belong, Sean," Ben said, and Elizabeth nodded in agreement.

"And it pleases me to be back," Sean responded, "but I don't yet have the sense that I belong here."

"Well, of course you belong here Sean," Elizabeth admonished. "This is home for you—of course you belong here. Where else would you belong?"

"I think I know what you're saying Elizabeth and I can't explain just how I'm feeling. But, enough of that—I have a plan Ben and I want you to tell me if I'm mad."

"No need for telling me the plan, Sean," Ben said laughing, "I can say plain as day that you're mad—as mad today as the day you left."

"And maybe you're right, friend. But here's my plan. I've been thinking about Dawn Light—and I can tell you that I thought much of it as I was coming back to Gunter's Harbour. Here's my thinking—even though the thieves in Annapolis have taken away my family's heritage from me and they've taken it all, buildings and land and whatever was left there—still, I'm thinking that because they've left it abandoned, maybe they've given me an opportunity. I'm thinking there's a possibility that Hough could make another appeal for me. In my way of thinking, I'd say that the band of thieves in Annapolis owe me that much. I'll ask Hough if he'd be willing to present another appeal from me for our land—for Dawn Light."

"Oh Sean, that would be wonderful," Elizabeth said.

"Wonderful?" asked Ben. "Oh yes, it would be wonderful all right, if it was possible. Have you forgotten what you went through in Annapolis when you lost Dawn Light, Sean? Are you wanting to spend another enjoyable respite there in the military dungeon—have you really gone mad?"

"I can't say I have, Ben, but I won't say I'm not mad either. Here's what I'd ask of you. If you can give me paper, pen and ink, I'll write to Hough and let him give me the response that's right. If he says 'No,' then I'll take it as a true sign that it's not possible. But, if Hough were to give me the smallest chance to succeed and says 'Yes,' then I'll give it my best at regaining Dawn Light with every bit of strength and ability I have."

Just as Sean finished, Elizabeth came back to the porch with paper and pen. "This small piece is the only paper we have. Give me a moment Sean, and I'll find some ink, I know we have some."

"Now Ben—Elizabeth—I must ask that you say nothing to the captain or Cynthia about this affair," Sean insisted. "I'll not want to have them bothered with the matter. I know they'd be willing to help, but they have enough to trouble them with the captain's niece being here. Can I count on you for that?"

"I can't say it'll please Cynthia and the captain," Elizabeth said. "But, no need to ask such a thing, Sean—you have but to tell Ben and me something and we'll keep it to ourselves. I've already told you that it would be wonderful if you could return to Dawn Light."

"You get that letter written Sean," Ben said. "I know a man named James Smith who has only recently come to the colony from England and looks to establish himself as a shaper of metal objects—something of a tinkerer, a metal smith. I told him that my wife had some utensils she wants repaired and he promised to stop by here before moving on to Nottingham Lots. I'd say you could pay him to deliver your letter to Hough."

Francis Hough was mildly irritated when someone was pounding on his door. Looking through the window he saw a small handcart filled with different types of metal objects. His irritation then turned to curiosity as the beating on the door once again began.

Throwing the door open Hough saw a small man with a large grin.

"Yes? Well, don't stand there—what is it?" Hough asked.

"Me name's James Smith and a smith I truly am. And I've come with a message for Master Francis Hough I have."

"Well, so you've come to the proper dwelling, now what's the message?"

"That I can't say as it's writ down on paper and I'll tell you that I'd oblige the words, but me eyes don't allow me to read words."

"Don't be bothering me," Hough said, "unless you truly have a paper for me—now, where is this paper? And what's that littering your cart?"

"Oh, I've a paper all right, and me cart bears treasure not litter. I'll mend pots and pans and metals of all sorts. I'm a tinkerer by trade and an honest man by practice. I'd expect you're the same—an honest man. Oh, and generous as anyone can see, one who would be grateful for the letter I bear. Am I right Master Hough?"

Hough reached into his tunic and pulled out a coin that he held out in his hand for Smith to see.

"I don't read words, but I read a man's nature when I sees him. Thank you, Master Hough," he said as he took the coin and pulled the letter from his shirt and gave it to Hough.

Hough said, "Thank you my good man and now I have things that press for my attention."

He closed the door, went to the window and watched as the tinkerer walked away pulling his small cart of treasure. Then he sat down at the table, took his quizzing glass from his pocket and began to read.

> *Friend Hough, I've thought to make another appeal in Annapolis to recover* Dawn Light. *If you think this is at all possible, will you help? I'll accept your decision as being providentially given. Please respond when you can. In your debt, Sean O'Connell*

He smiled as he read the brief letter and then chuckled, which was certainly a rare occasion for Francis Hough.

CHAPTER THIRTEEN

Shocking Revelation

Almost two months had passed since his return and Sean continued to spend most of his nights at Dawn Light. Nathan wanted to spend time with his father, but he liked sleeping in his own bed at the Murphy's, so most of their time together was on the *Julia's Fairwinds*. Some days they would take brief excursions on the bay and Nathan always liked that, because he could demonstrate to his father all the things that Fian and Captain Murphy had taught him about sailing. At other times they would simply work together on small tasks aboard the sloop.

There had been little change in Sean's relationship with the captain's niece Sarah and although he never brought it up again, he remained somewhat annoyed with the captain and Cynthia because they had allowed her to stay in Julia's room.

Sean began to wonder if James Smith the tinkerer had actually delivered the letter to Hough.

Perhaps I should have paid him more he thought. *But then, he did insist that the coin I gave him was ample. But then, I have no way of knowing the mind of Francis—Hough may have thought another appeal would be useless.*

However, if he would have thought so, I'm certain that he would have told me that too. Maybe I'll hear from him soon.

Three days later a man from Kennett village rode into Gunter's Harbour with a letter for Sean. When he saw men loafing about the *Southern Swallow* he asked one of the seamen, "Can you tell me where Sean O'Connell might be found?"

Fian O'Niall heard the man, and before the seaman could respond, Fian said: "And who is it that's asking after Sean O'Connell?"

"I'm Elias Woolman from Kennett village and I've come with a message for Sean O'Connell. It's from Francis Hough of Nottingham Lots. Do you know where O'Connell can be found?"

"Are you one of them sheriffs?" Fian asked.

"Sherriff? Not at all, my trade is that of a surveyor and I've only come this way to deliver a letter, find stabling for my horse until I return, do paid work of surveying and then take the next ship bound for Annapolis."

"Then fortune's smiled on you," Fian said with a grin. "If you'll turn your animal about you'll see the mast of a small sloop there portside about 100 yards I'd say."

"Portside?" Woolman asked.

"Aye, portside—once you have your animal turned about it'll be down to your left," Fian said. "You'll see the mast as I've said and there you'll find Sean O'Connell and his son Nathan."

Woolman rode to the edge of the quay where *Julia's Fairwinds* was berthed.

"Hello aboard the ship," Woolman called.

Nathan heard the unknown voice and stood up from his task of scraping tar from the deck.

"Hello sir," Nathan responded. "Have you come to see my father?"

"That could well be, young man. Is his name Sean O'Connell?"

"It is," Sean responded as he came topside. "And for what reason do you seek me?"

"I'm Elias Woolman of Kennett village and I think I may have seen you before."

"It's possible," Sean responded still not sure of the man's purpose. "I've been there. Now what brings you to Gunter's Harbour?"

"I've come from Nottingham Lots with a letter for you from a mutual friend, Francis Hough."

"Then it's welcome you are, friend. Will you come aboard? My son will tether your horse."

Turning to Nathan he said, "Do it the Indian way as I showed you, and mind you, give him room to move about so he can find grass."

Woolman came up the short narrow plank and shook hands with Sean. Then, pulling the letter from his blouse he sat on a small barrel.

"Mr. Woolman, I've nothing to offer you for refreshment. But I thank you for this letter. Now please excuse my lack of manners, but I must read this letter."

"Please do," Wolman responded, "and I'll rest here while you read."

Sean sat on the deck, carefully broke the wax seal on Hough's letter and began to read.

Friend Sean,

How unexpected your letter. You must know that I have had similar thoughts as you in this matter and I agree that we should appeal once again. My reasoning is this. Since Queen Anne's demise, her cousin Georg Ludwig of Lower Saxony has ascended to the throne as King George I. I have been informed that his reign has provided many changes in the colonies, not the least of which in Maryland I think these changes must have fallen well for your purposes.

Barristers from Philadelphia have informed me that the entire Assembly of the Maryland Upper House has been changed completely by the king and that the speaker and all assemblymen that were engaged with our first appeal have been removed and, I suspect, have returned to England.

While I know nothing of those now filling those positions, I have also been informed that George I is a monarch that willfully has lessened his control considerably as compared to former rulers.

It is my considered opinion that the diminishing of these monarchial powers may provide us with opportunity to engage in what could be a successful appeal for the return of your ancestral home, Dawn Light. Yes, Sean. Indeed I agree that we must appeal again. You must come soon and we will confer regarding the plan I have in mind. In friendship, Francis Hough

Sean's heart began to pound in anticipation while at the same instant he felt a cold chill, remembering the terrible days he spent as a military prisoner in the filthy stone jail shed.

Recovering, he thanked Mr. Woolman and offered to pay him for his trouble.

"Not at all, sir, I could do no such thing. This I've done as a favor for our mutual friend Francis Hough. And I can now tell you where last we met. It was at the home where you sold Francis Hough that printery machine. Do you recall?"

"I do recall, and again I thank you, but I must be off to deliver this news to others."

"Very well, and because it seems the news must be of a good sort then I feel well in that I've accomplished my business."

After Woolman left, Sean rode to the Murphy's and that night after the evening meal, the captain and Sean took a short walk down the path toward Gunter's Harbour.

"Captain, there's something I'll tell you that I want you to keep to yourself for now."

"Of course, Sean," the captain replied confidently. "You know that what you want me to hear between us can stay that way. Now, what is it Sean?"

"I've had thoughts of regaining Dawn Light, and I . . . "

"Dawn Light!" the captain stopped and turned toward Sean. "Haven't you had your fill of those English thieves? What makes you think they'd have a change of their well-blackened hearts?"

"I've thought the same, and that's what's been troubling me so." Sean paused for several seconds then continued. "I want what's mine by right and yet I've thought it impossible to regain Dawn Light. I didn't reveal this to you before—and for the very reason of what you're telling me now. I thought you'd convince me that the idea of regaining Dawn Light was impossible."

"You're right as a pleasant wind in the sail, Sean," replied Captain Murphy. "It's impossible—they'll never give their prize back to you."

"Well that's why I didn't tell you before I wrote to Francis Hough asking him if he thought they might respond favorably to another appeal—I feared you would try to convince me otherwise."

"No, Sean, no—not the English," the captain said as he turned to walk back toward his house.

"Wait, Captain—then let me tell you what Hough said," Sean insisted.

Then Sean began to lay out for the captain all the changes that Hough explained—changes that he thought might tip the balances in Sean's favor.

"Understand, Captain," Sean insisted, "Whether the new Maryland assemblymen would look with favor on me because of the way those other thieves dealt with me I can't say. But, I'll tell you this Captain, if I wouldn't be willing to appeal to them anew for what's rightfully mine—well, I'd say that I wouldn't deserve Dawn Light in any case."

"You're right about that, Sean. And I do understand—Dawn Light is rightly yours. So, what do you propose to do next?"

"I'll be leaving for Nottingham Lots in the morning. I'd be pleased if you'd join me, Captain, but I don't know how long I'll be gone."

"No, Sean. I'll be staying here. But, you tell Francis Hough that we'd be pleased to have him in our home as you pass through on the way to Annapolis."

The following week Sean returned from Nottingham Lots. Two days after his return, Hough followed. After a night of rest the next day was spent in pleasant discourse at the Murphy home. Then, after a fine meal, Hough, Sean and Fian O'Niall and another crewman from the *Southern Swallow* left on the evening high tide aboard the *Julia's Fairwinds* and they were under sail for Annapolis.

Captain Murphy had driven the men to Gunter's Harbour in the carriage, and while he was gone, Sarah was emboldened to ask Cynthia some very personal questions.

"Uncle seems to be very kind to most people, and in that respect he is very much like his brother, my father," Sarah said.

"Why, yes, he certainly is a kind man. And it pleases me Sarah that you recognize that very excellent quality in him. Yes, he is a very fine man. As you say a kind man much as his brother—whom I have never met of course."

"I was very young when mother died," Sarah continued, "and I feel certain that father was as kind to mother as he has always been to me."

"What a wonderful memory to have of your father. But, Sarah, I feel that you have something more that you want to say to me. Please speak on, say whatever you will, dear. What is it you want to know?"

Sarah sat staring for what seemed to Cynthia to be a very long time.

Then suddenly the question came bursting from her, "Is the captain kind to you when you're alone?"

"Why, of course he is dear. He doesn't change just because no one else is about."

"But some men do change when no one else is about, don't they?" Sarah said in a pleading tone.

"Well I—there are probably—Sarah, what are you saying?"

"I'm so ashamed to say it, Aunt Cynthia—may I call you aunt?"

"Of course you may, Sarah. But what is it that you think shames you?"

"He beat me when we were alone," she said as she began to sob.

"Your father beat you—Laird's brother beat you?" Cynthia was shocked.

"No!" Sarah managed between sobs then she cried out, "Not father—my husband beat me!"

"Oh, Sarah," Cynthia said as she knelt on the floor next to Sarah's chair. "I had no idea, I had no idea."

Cynthia pulled Sarah to her and embraced her as she would have her own daughter Julia, and for several minutes she held Sarah until the sobbing settled down.

"There now," Cynthia said as she took a kerchief from her apron and dabbed Sarah's cheeks. Then rising she said, "Come sit over here with me and we'll talk more of this matter."

Once Sarah became calm Cynthia said, "That must have been very terrible for you. But your husband is dead and you must try your best to put this in your past."

With that, Sarah began to cry. "But you don't understand. I prayed for God to take his life, and God did as I asked."

"Now, you must explain what you mean by this—praying for God to take his life. When your husband died at sea did you think it was because God had done your bidding?"

Immediately Sarah stopped crying, and with a stunned look said, "Of course that's what I thought. I prayed for him to die and he died."

"Oh my dear," Cynthia said with an understanding smile. "You think that your husband died because of your request to God? Sarah, dear, if that were so easily done, then when I prayed that my daughter wouldn't die from the fever I would think that she'd still be alive. From what your Uncle Laird has told me, your husband—what was his name—Michael?"

"Yes, Michael—Michael Fitzpatrick," Sarah responded.

"And as I say, from what the captain told me, Michael died from greed as a privateer—killed by the Spaniards—not because of your prayers. I know they call themselves privateers when the Crown pays them to kill and steal—but they're no more than pirates from what I know. Because the same Crown that pays privateers to steal for the Crown, will then hang pirates who steal on their own. Being a privateer is stealing and thievery and just that, no matter the fancy name it might be given. No my dear, prayers weren't responsible for Michael's death—it was his greediness. You're no more responsible for Michael's death than I am for my daughter's demise."

"But you don't understand; there's more—I was with child when Michael was killed and when I received news of his death the child birthed early. He was a sickly child and I was slow in giving him much milk. Even after I was able to satisfy his need he remained weak . . ." then Sarah began to sob.

When she recovered she said, "And then he died before his third month. Don't you see Aunt Cynthia, it all points to my wicked heart and God punishing me for . . ."

"Hush now, Sarah. No more of this talk. It's past the time for you to rise up from this hopeless place of despair. God does not want you to go on punishing yourself for something that was none of your fault. Yours is a new life to be lived, not destroyed—and I'm certain that's exactly why God has you here with us now. We must not continue to reprove ourselves because of our past. What really matters is the everlasting present that God may choose to grant us."

"Do you, Aunt Cynthia—do you think God would be gracious enough to grant me this—as you say—this new life to be lived?"

Smiling as she recalled the blessing of how the Lord had given her the captain as her companion in her new life that she now lived, she said, "Oh yes, my dear Sarah. You see, I believe that if we are right before God, whatever our mistakes may be, they are never blunders of the heart—and I believe God may have already set His plan in motion for you."

The next morning Sarah was in the kitchen with Missy before sunrise.

"Good morning to you Missy," Sarah said with a smile.

"Be as good as mos'," Missy replied as she fanned the flame in the fire pot. "What brings you here so early Miss Sarah?"

"I couldn't sleep well after I had a long discussion with Aunt Cynthia."

Surprised, Missy stood up and said, "Who? Didn' never hear say 'Aunt Cynthia' before." She smiled then said, "I likes the sound—Aunt Cynthia."

"Well, I like the sound of it too, Missy. Tell me, Missy, is this a good home for you?"

"Good home?" Missy said somewhat surprise. "Be only home I has. Be a fine home."

"Does Captain Murphy treat you well?" Sarah asked.

"Don' think Miss Cynthia be havin' me talkin' this way."

"Oh? And what way is that, Missy?" Cynthia said as she walked into the kitchen.

"Good morning, Aunt Cynthia," Sarah answered, and then to salvage the situation said,. "I've been asking Missy about her life here and how she liked it."

Missy looked at Cynthia hoping that she wouldn't be rebuked, but Cynthia simply said, "I think that I might like having her here with me more than she likes being here. Sarah, I can tell you that Missy has been a great help to me after losing my first husband and then losing my daughter Julia. And I can tell you this—many people didn't like the idea that Julia and Missy were much more like sisters or good friend than they were like mistress and slave. But, what are you doing up so early—and why so many questions?"

"I wasn't able to sleep well after our conversation last night," Sarah responded.

"And why should that be dear, I would have thought that what we talked of might have been to your benefit."

"Oh, it was. Oh yes Aunt, it was. And there's the difficulty. I had so much to think about—so many things to consider, that my mind was swirling with thoughts of the future—delightful and wonderful thoughts. But no, not even so much the future—it's more like thoughts for today— this very day."

"And there you have it," Cynthia replied. "It took me many years to recognize that all we really have is our loved ones—one another—and that life is really only for today dear. We must not become anxious or worry about tomorrow. I should have learned that with the death of my first husband—but it took the death of Julia to make me aware of the importance of the present—today. In many ways, my dear, today could be all that any of us might have, and we must take hold of what we have and live it to the fullest. And, dear Sarah, remember that last evening when we spoke, you agreed with me that you have a new life to be lived—so let's live our lives today!"

Sarah and Cynthia embraced and Missy smiled her approval.

--- CHAPTER FOURTEEN ---

Morgan Glasfryn

When they arrived in Annapolis the following day, Francis Hough insisted that they should lodge at the Eagle and Lamb Ordinary, owned by his friend Stanley Shaw. It was the inn where Hough had stayed during the first appeal. Shaw's friendship had proven to be very beneficial and he had helped Hough by laying some groundwork as he made some important contacts in Annapolis.

Shaw, also a member of the Religious Society of Friends, arranged comfortable rooms for Hough and Sean. Fian O'Niall refused to go ashore for quarters and preferred that he and the other crewman should sleep on the sloop.

Stanley Shaw suggested that Hough should confer with a local barrister named Morgan Glasfryn, an elderly man from the Isle of Anglesy in Wales. He had lost his wife and children years earlier in a house fire and then, alone and unhappy, he had gone to Bermuda looking for relief from his sorrow. Later, on a whim, he decided to leave Bermuda and come to Maryland. And now, because of his age he had no desire to leave.

Morgan Glasfryn lived in a cramped room that was filled with stacks of books and smelled of tobacco. Glasfryn actually had served in the Royal

Court as a legal counselor to Queen Anne herself, and that fact alone was going to make him an invaluable ally to Hough in the matter at hand.

It was mid-morning when Francis Hough found the building where Glasfryn lived. He opened the door at street level, walked up four narrow stairs to another door and heard it unlatch before he could knock. Morgan Glasfryn opened the door to his small room.

"Come in, come in. I knew it would be you—Francis Hough, am I correct?"

Not waiting for an answer he cleared several books from a chair. "Here you are. This is the only place for you to be seated, Francis Hough. Is this suitable?"

"Oh yes," answered Hough, "I assure you that it is quite fitting, fitting indeed."

Hough found Glasfryn's Welsh accent a wonderful recipe of vowel sounds that were combined with the unique tapped 'r'—the sound of the tip of the tongue as it made brief contact with the roof of the mouth. The sing-song lilt of the Welshman's voice caused Hough—not overly accustomed to smiling—occasionally to beam.

However, Hough soon was to discover why it was that when Glasfryn spoke, men would listen. It was more than the lilting Welsh speech and the booming of his strong voice that captured one's attention. Hough learned that Morgan Glasfryn was more proficient with English law than anyone else in Maryland.

Hough thought, *Perhaps one could say that this Morgan Glasfryn seems to know English law better than anyone I've known in the American colonies.*

"Here now, we'll need more light than this small transom affords" Glasfryn said. "I must light another candle. One moment Hough—now where are those candles."

After finding the candles behind one of the many book stacks he tamped tobacco into his pipe, lit two candles and his pipe and then sat down across the small room from Hough.

After Hough explained what had happened more than three years earlier when Sean lost Dawn Light, he waited for Glasfryn to ask questions. Instead, Hough listened.

"Very well," Glasfryn began. "There have been many errors made by the former speaker of the Maryland Upper Assembly. As you have already suggested, he went far beyond his authority and his odd actions made that quite clear. Oh yes, matters such as these often result when small men pretend to be what they are not, nor may they ever become."

He paused for several minutes with his eyes closed and occasionally small puffs of smoke came from the pipe. Hough wondered if perhaps the elderly gentleman had simply fallen asleep.

Then just as unexpectedly he opened his eyes, removed the pipe from his mouth and his booming voice pronounced, "I strongly believe that we shall find that Sean O'Connell is still the master of Dawn Light—but we shall have to see, haven't we?"

Hough removed the documents he still had from the first appeal, several years earlier. Glasfryn quickly read the documents and then for several hours the men laid out their plans as they discussed strategy. Hough left late in the afternoon and hadn't noticed his hunger until he had almost arrived back at the Eagle and Lamb Ordinary.

Sean sat at a table near the fireplace and was happy to see Hough as he walked into the inn.

"Francis," Sean began as he stood, "I wondered if you had decided that an appeal was useless. What have you determined?"

"I've made good discoveries, Sean, good discoveries. Allow me to go to my room for a brief rest and then I'll return to take a meal—and will you join me?"

"I will dine with you indeed," Sean said. "But would you not care to tell me of your discoveries now?"

"Shortly, Sean, shortly—you've waited this long." Appearing somewhat annoyed Hough started up the stairs and said, "Now be patient and give me opportunity for a brief rest."

Hough didn't return from his room 'after a brief rest.' In fact it wasn't until the next morning that he came to the dining area for breakfast. Sean was waiting patiently at the same table.

"Ah, yes. Good morning, Sean. I was more exhausted than I suspected. I slept through the night after inviting you to dine with me."

"I waited for some time," Sean replied. "But considered that you must have been more fatigued than you were hungry and I had my supper without you."

Hough sat on the bench opposite Sean just as innkeeper Shaw's wife brought warm bowls of corn mush to the table.

"I'd prefer fried corn cakes if you have them," Sean said to Shaw's wife.

"This is what we have," she replied unsympathetically then turned and walked away to the back of the room.

Sean smiled and said, "Then this is what I'll have."

Shaw's wife turned and glared at Sean.

"Now, tell me Francis, what have you and this Welshman decided?"

Hough laid the plan out before Sean.

"Glasfryn is an excellent barrister," Hough began. "And he's extremely confident that either he will be able to have a private audience with the speaker of the Maryland Upper Assembly and resolve the situation without further deliberation, or else we should be able to present the appeal before the entire Upper Assembly. Of course, my hope is that his private conversations will resolve the situation."

"This seems difficult to believe," Sean said. "When do you think he'll be able to see this speaker of the assembly?"

"Why, today of course," Hough replied as if this should have been obvious.

"Today—he will see him today?" Sean seemed stunned. "I thought we would have to wait as we had before."

"No, Sean. As Glasfryn has assured me, unlike those who were in power when we first appealed, this speaker is well founded and, in fact, knows well the fine repute of Barrister Morgan Glasfryn."

Greatly relieved and yet anxious for word from Glasfryn, Sean decided to take some air.

"I'll be going to the dock, Francis. Would you care to join me?"

"No, Sean. I've a mind to wait about. I'll go to my room and perhaps do some reading. If I'm right, I expect that we'll hear from Morgan Glasfryn before this day is out."

Sean spent the day going over the sloop with Fian.

"Beggin' your pardon," Fian began. "As a seaman I sees things in a sloop such as this one here that most don't see so good. This I'll be tellin' you, she's many a small crack what could use some tar. Now, I ain't about to say we'll be sinkin' soon, but I ain't sayin' that it won't be a problem neither if we don't caulk her up a bit."

"I count on you to tell me such things, Fian. You're a man to depend on and I'll tell you that as true as can be. I'd be obliged if you'd show me what you see and let's be about making it right. I've no notion to be sinking on the sail back to Gunter's Harbour."

They busied themselves with making small repairs for most of the day until Sean said, "I'd best get back to the inn, Fian. I'm needing to see if there's been word from the barristers."

He entered the inn and there at the same table where Sean had left him sat Hough with the Welshman.

"Well, now we were beginning to believe you might have gone back to Gunter's Harbour without me," Hough said in an unusually lighthearted manner.

"Gunter's Harbour is it?" Glasfryn asked. "You'll do well to call it North East, as do the English now. You'll do well, I'd say, to do things as much their way as your own conscience will allow, at least for the very present time."

"Well, now," Hough began. "Allow me to introduce you to Sean O'Connell. Sean, this is Morgan Glasfryn—I make no exaggeration when I say that barrister Morgan Glasfryn is your beneficent benefactor."

Sean extended his arm across the table and offered his hand to the Welshman. Sean long had considered that barristers and others who made their living by their wits were somewhat over refined and lacking strength—he was surprised by the sturdy grip of the man.

"I am honored to meet you sir and am in your great debt simply because you have seen fit to consider helping us in this matter."

Then sitting down Sean turned to Hough who was sipping a small mug of rum. "Tell me, have you had any success with gaining a meeting with those in authority?"

"Success?" Hough asked taking another sip. "Of course, that would depend on what you might consider being successful, eh Morgan?"

Glasfryn responded, "Very much so. It would depend very much on what one might consider success. Of course, I must say that in the past I have had what might be considered greater successes . . ."

"Then you've been unable to make the appeal?" Sean asked.

"Respect, young sir," Hough offered. "Allow our friend Glasfryn respect and give way for him to complete his statement."

"My apologies sir," Sean said. "Please do continue."

"As I've said," Glasfryn began. "Other efforts of mine have brought more notoriety and were considered greater successes. But, I'll say this to you Sean O'Connell; I've not found greater pleasure in many other opportunities than I have in this."

Sean was bursting to know the man's response.

"Sean," Hough said reaching into his leather pouch and removing a rolled document, "This is what I believe you've been wanting for and what our good friend here has been able to deliver."

Taking the document in hand, Sean walked to the window for light, unrolled it and read:

The following has been examined & shall now be deemed a certifyed copy of the original document having ben appropriatly recorded & was received by the O'Connell family to wit

The Honourable Lord Baltimore grants unto Alan O'Connell, Nathan O'Connell, Thomas O'Connell, Edward O'Connell, & Elayne O'Connell, their unmarried sister, all that tract of land to be called O'Connell Manor, lying on the north side of the Chesapeake Bay, & on the west side of a river in the said bay, called Gunter's Harbour, on the westernmost side of a creek in the said river, called Beacon Creek, and running northwesterly up the said creek of the length of two thousand perches[9] to the southernmost bound marked by an oak tree of the land of Philip Calvert, Esq., & from said oak running southwest for the length of three hundred and twenty perches until it intersects the easternmost side of a creek called Principio Creek, and running southerly down the said creek until said line reaches the bay. Containing & now laid out for four thousand acres. These lands & manor to be held by them and their heirs, in free and common socage[10], by fealty[11] only for all manner of services, by even & equal portions, the rent of four pounds sterling, in silver or gold, or the full value thereof, in such commodities as we or our heirs shall accept in perpetuitous discharge thereof.

Cecilius, Lord Baron of Baltimore (signature)

The authenticity of the above stated document being recognized in its authenticity, & Sean O'Connell, having been granted possession of O'Connell Manor, known as Dawn Light, is to be known as tenant in possession & the lawful & undoubted heir having been wrongly & falsely relieved of his tenancy in 1718 has now been legally represented & has lawfully appealed & shall now have these rights of tenancy restored from this day forward, July 4th in the year of our Lord 1721.

In presence of   William J. Baker, Honourable Speaker of the Maryland Upper Assembly

Sean was stunned as he read the paper and stood at the window briefly before returning to the table. Vigorously shaking the hands of Glasfryn and Hough, Sean remained speechless.

"Well Sean" Hough asked, "Have you any words for your benefactor, Morgan Glasfryn?"

"Words?" Sean repeated. "I have no words to tell you sir what this means. You have recovered in a matter of hours that which I thought never to receive again. Master Glasfryn, this man stands before you with a grateful heart but lacking the needed speech to express to you what I am feeling."

"Of course," Glasfryn responded. "I sense your sincere gratitude and further speech concerning the matter only would prove to be superfluous."

Changing the subject Hough asked, "Then what shall we say about fees, Morgan? We've not come to any agreement, because in fact we've had no discussion of the matter. I, of course, have known Sean O'Connell for some time and am accustomed to negotiating fees using a somewhat different set of scales. However, sir, we can only ask that you inform us of your requirement for these unproven and distinctive services and we shall gladly respond to your claim upon us in any amount you may declare."

"Then I'll give you my claim. But first—innkeeper," Glasfryn called, "three fresh mugs of your finest."

Innkeeper Shaw presented the men with rum and Morgan Glasfryn lifted his pewter mug to the others

"Not many a man can be a king," he began. "And not many a king is a kindly man. But this I'll say to all who hear, I'd rather be a king maker than a king, and on this I stand. And, to you, Sean O'Connell, I have the sense that today I may have made a king—and it's you. Now drink your mug dry and I'll tell you my fee."

They raised their mugs and drank.

"Your fee then, Glasfryn," Hough said. "Tell us your fee."

"Oh yes, my fee," Glasfryn responded. "I only hope you'll be able to afford it, for it's an immeasurable amount."

Sean's heart almost stopped beating when he heard those words, but the Welshman continued.

"Here's my fee then and I won't bargain. I believe that my efforts have worked a fine thing in the life of you, Sean O'Connell. I have good sense enough to know how important this has been to you and how much you appreciate it. Now, instead of blathering on as you Irish do, I'll get to the point of it as a good Welshman. My payment would be this—that you be aware of the needs of another as I have been of your need. But not only must you know of the need and understand it, you must willingly do that which will correct the need."

"I'll not say I understand, sir" Sean said, puzzled.

"Here's the best of what I'll say is the heart of the matter," the Welshman began. "I dare to say that without me you would not have become owner of Dawn Light again. Can you agree to that?"

"Yes, of course," Sean said. "I agree."

"Then I further say," continued Glasfryn, "that there is someone in your life right now, or there will come someone at some future day who will be in need, perhaps also unable to recover what he needs, unless you yourself provide for that person. Do you understand my terms and will you pledge to do so?"

"I believe that I understand well what you've said, but I see no one in my life I'd be able to help in the way you've done for me."

"Then you'd better think more carefully and perhaps look deeper," Glasfryn said.

Sean responded, "I'm not certain that I could make such a vow because . . ."

"Then if that's as you say, we've had enough talk about kings and such—I've already told you I don't bargain, so now we'll talk of coins," Glasfryn said. "Just as others, I've need of sustenance and my purse is not always as full as I would like it to be. So, Master Hough—would you care to offer a suggestion to the young sir regarding a fee?"

"Well, I'd feel—I think I'd be somewhat out of sorts discussing it in this manner," Hough stammered. "Perhaps you and I should sit down and come to an agreeable amount."

"An agreeable amount? I've given my best offer," the Welshman said. "An agreeable amount? Are you both unwilling or simply lacking understanding? All I've asked is that Sean O'Connell provide for another person in the same manner as I've provided for him. I've done for him that which he could not do for himself. Do you understand? My fee is that Sean O'Connell does for another that which that person cannot do for himself—or herself."

The three men sat silently for a long time. Finally the Welshman called for another drink, but only for himself.

He drank it down and said, "I'll be off to my lodgings, Sean O'Connell. What will your answer be? I believe I've made you a king. What sort of king shall you be? Will you do as much for another?" Then he stood to leave.

Sean rose and grasped the Welshman's hand. "You have my word. I'll do as you have said and try to accomplish this work—as you call it—of a king maker. Yet the fee you have asked will never repay the gain you have given me."

Morgan Glasfryn smiled and said, "Oh, you're wrong, Sean O'Connell. You'll learn that king making is as fine a labor as can be found and it pays one's soul very well. I'll leave you both now. Remember that you'll need to begin to call your Gunter's Harbour, North East instead—it will please the English and they do so like to be pleased."

Sean walked ahead to open the door for Morgan Glasfryn.

As he walked out he said, "To you both I'll say this—no matter whether we see one another on this side again, we'll always have the memory of who we are. I'll tell you Sean—and you too Hough—the world is always in need of king makers."

As the Welshman left Hough said, "I believe we've accomplished what we came to do, Sean. Let's have a good night's sleep and in the morning we'll head back to Gunter's . . . back to North East."

As Sean prepared for his last night in the comfortable bed at the Eagle and Lamb Ordinary, his favorite Scripture, from the Apostle Paul's second letter to Timothy, in the first chapter, verse 12, kept repeating in his mind: *I know whom I have believed, and am persuaded that he is able to keep that which I have committed unto him against that day.*

Sean's last thoughts as he prayed before falling asleep were, *Thank you Lord, thank you. Thank you for the kindhearted Welsh gentleman, Morgan Glasfryn. And thank you Lord for using him to teach me that, in a sense, he has made me a king so that now I'll know how to be a king maker. Thank you Lord. And show me that person—that man—that you would have me to encourage, just as I've been encouraged by the grace and kindness of Morgan Glasfryn. May I ever remember the Welshman's words: 'Not many a man can be a king' he began. 'And not many a king is a kindly man. But this I'll say to all who hear, I'd rather be a king maker than a king, and on this I stand.' And, Lord, show me how I am to do that.*

CHAPTER FIFTEEN ———

Difficult Request

Upon their return to North East, Sean insisted that he accompany Hough back to his home in Nottingham Lots.

"Completely unnecessary, Sean," Hough had argued. "I rode here myself and I can return alone—you now have much to consider here for yourself."

"Francis Hough—what sort of friend would I be if I were not to accompany you as you return to your home? It's and honor and privilege for me to do so. I've waited this long for the O'Connell manor to be restored and now, thanks to you, I need wait no longer. I agree that I will have much to do in order to bring Dawn Light back to its comfortable condition. But I assure you that my work can wait until after I've delivered you safely to your kind wife."

When Sean returned from Nottingham Lots, the captain was eager to know the details of what had transpired in Annapolis and, of course, Sean was happy to report what had happened.

"This Welsh friend that Hough came across was surely a God-send," the captain said to Sean. "I've known many a Welshman in my day and have had a few as crew on the *Southern Swallow*. They're a quick-tempered lot, but I've found them warm-hearted, talkative and concerned with their families—not at all unlike many an Irishman, eh Sean? And one of my Welsh crew as I recall was given to reciting poetry. Not a bad sort, but, Sean, I've never come across the bow of a Welshman like your Morgan Glasfryn seems to be. God bless him is what I'll say. And God bless all Welshmen like him."

"Right you are, Captain," Sean responded. "I've not met a man as quick to give of himself as was Morgan Glasfryn. To think that he served as counsel to royalty and yet he was willing to give me—to give Hough and me—his hand of friendship along with his great and respected knowledge, his time and more. Never have I met a man like Glasfryn."

"Well, now you must know that if you're to be staying at Dawn Light as a legal tenant and not as some sort of intruder, you'll have need of some furnishing. I'll not have my grandson Nathan sleeping on the floor or the ground like that wild man of a father he has."

They laughed at what had really been true and then the captain continued.

"You know, Cynthia and Elizabeth Dixon have plans for Dawn Light I can tell you that. Why, even Missy wants to give you some of her furnishings. And, if I know Elizabeth, she will already have given notice to every female—married or not—within a half day's walk of here, that there's a need for furnishing the recovered home of Sean O'Connell."

"I'm not at all surprised. I thought that's what she meant the other day, Captain. She mentioned something about how I needed to clean the place, scrub and freshen it up so some furnishing could be provided. I told her there was still a bed and a small table and some stools in Samson's old cabin I could use. But she'd have none of that—said she'd not have her grandson sleeping on the bed of a slave."

"Now," Sean," the captain began, "I'll not say it's to your liking, but you must allow the women to do this. And even if you don't think so, I suspect it's as much for you as it is for Nathan, although the women do still see you as something of a savage." With that the captain released his most boisterous laugh.

The captain was right about what the women had already done. They responded generously to the exciting news as it swept through the community of North East—Sean O'Connell had regained his ancestral home.

Of course, it was tempered somewhat by the reality that people had no surplus of furnishings to speak of. And Dawn Light had been ransacked by the English soldiers of anything of significant use. In fact, aside from the buildings themselves, there was little of value left on the land.

However, rather than being an obstacle, the reality of such a great need of furnishings and so many other things stirred excitement among the women, and by the end of the week Dawn Light was well equipped with furnishings and a variety of house wares.

Sean and Nathan were on the porch busily sorting through some of the cooking objects. Sean didn't recognize most of them but was pleased that Nathan knew the purpose of many.

"How is it that you know so much about that—what did you say it was—a toe toaster[12]?"

"Yes, Father. Grandmother brought it from England when she was very young. Sometimes when it was very cold and Missy had made bread, she would bring it inside to the fireplace and Grandmother would toast bread with it."

"But," Sean said with a grin, "I thought you said it was for toasting toes?"

"No, Daddy! It's used to toast bread in the fireplace. And you can turn the bread using your foot to keep your hand from getting burned."

"I can see that you've learned many things since I've been gone and I'm very proud of you son."

The sound of a horse's hooves caused them both to turn and they saw Cynthia and Missy coming down the lane toward the house with their large cart loaded with wares of every kind.

Stepping off the porch to greet them, Sean said, "Cynthia, I already have more furnishings than I could think to ever use. And, although I'm not certain, would some of these items in the cart once have been owned by my family—perhaps those that your brother, the Reverend Topping purchased from my family?"

"Yes, they are among those my brother had purchased. But, as I told you when you and Julia first married, it was my pleasure to restore some of your family's possessions to you."

Stolen property Sean was thinking. *Stolen from my family by your rogue brother and yet, how can this be held against you, dear and gracious lady?*

"I thank you for your kind generosity," Sean replied. "I'm learning that my son has discovered many things since living with you. Not only has the captain made him quite a seaman, but he knows his way about these household tools as well." He held up the "toe toaster," as he spoke.

"Oh my," Cynthia said. "I am embarrassed. Laird should not have brought that here. It was broken when my first husband was alive, even before Julia was born. I only kept it about because of its sentimental importance—it was my mother's and given to me as a gift. Besides, who would know how to bake bread at Dawn Light—you Nathan? It would have to be you, because it's certainly not your father."

"It's true enough," replied Sean. "I'm quite able to eat the bread but preparing it is rather another matter."

"A woman's touch, Sean—you need a woman's touch here."

"I've managed for more than three years without such a touch, Cynthia."

"Well and good. But now, once again, you're responsible for more than yourself, Sean."

"Even so," replied Sean, "Please take this 'toe toaster' with you. It has much value to you I know. Besides, we seldom toast toes here—isn't that right Nathan?"

Nathan didn't respond. He had climbed onto the cart and was busy trying to discover what else Missy and his grandmother had brought with them.

"Laird's niece sends her greetings, Sean," Cynthia announced. "I'm sure you'll be pleased to know that her spirits are somewhat lifted. In fact, Sarah would have come with us, but the cart was too full. We do want to give your home a feminine touch, Sean. Perhaps she'll come another day to help us do that."

"Perhaps," Sean snapped. "But I hardly think that would be necessary. Nathan and I can do fine by ourselves, can't we son?"

"But Daddy, I'd like Sarah to come and see our house, wouldn't you?"

Before Sean could respond, Cynthia said, "You see, Sean? You'll want to allow Sarah to visit for the sake of my grandson if for no other reason—won't you?"

Then, before Sean was able to reply she added, "Well, let's be about unloading these things—Missy, Sean, Nathan let's be busy now."

That afternoon Ben and Elizabeth Dixon stopped by Dawn Light with their daughter Annie.

Nathan was happy to see Annie. They were about the same age and through the years they had many opportunities to play together.

"Come on, Annie. See the room where I sleep—it's the very next room to father's. Then we'll go outside and sit next to the porch—we'll recite rhymes or whatever else you want to do."

After the children went back outside, Sean brought some fresh water to the porch and Elizabeth unfolded the cloth she had brought with her. Elizabeth was the sort of considerate person who was hospitable whether she had visitors or she was the visitor. Sean was pleased that his suspicions were correct when she revealed fried corn cakes—Sean's favorites because Elizabeth almost always included fat cracklings in her corn cakes.

Elizabeth smiled at Sean and said, "Come children, have a corn cake before they're all gone."

"Aye, and you'd better hurry," Ben added. "I've a hunger myself."

"I could only find two cups and I hope you won't mind sharing your water," Sean said.

"Of course not—in fact," Elizabeth added, "I'm not at all thirsty."

After eating the cakes, Elizabeth said, "Are there any utensils that you need that we may help you with, such as cups or other articles?"

"For now," Sean began, "we have more than I can deal with. Nathan and I have been sorting through the many items that so many generous people have provided. I'm very grateful, of course, but I'm somewhat overwhelmed by it all."

"I can tell you that it's because we're all so glad to have you back here, Sean," Ben said. "Seems you're part of our own family just as I'm thinking you feel the same toward us."

"That's as true as the sun rising, Ben. You are family to me."

"While we're speaking of family, Sean," Elizabeth began. "When do you think you'll want the women from your family coming over to set your house in proper order? I was speaking with Cynthia and Sarah just the other day and we all agreed that it would be a fine thing for us to come by, to give this place a woman's cleaning and something of a feminine touch."

"Yes, yes, I know," Sean said. "I've already been given that same sort of instruction by Cynthia. You'll excuse me for being so forthright Elizabeth, but it seems this 'feminine touch' nonsense is getting out of hand."

"It's not nonsense—it's more important than that, Sean," Elizabeth continued. "Captain Murphy's niece seems to be regaining her serenity some, and Cynthia and I—well, we're thinking that it would be a good thing for Sarah to be able to do something for someone else. Not that Cynthia is unhappy having to do for her, mind you—but eventually Sarah must stand alone. Isn't that what we think, Ben?"

Before Ben could answer, Sean shot back a response.

"Elizabeth, while I'm sure you charming ladies have nothing but good intentions, I'll thank you to leave the captain's niece out of my life. I have enough to do trying to raise my own son in a proper way. I have no need to take on another assignment for which I have no concern whatever. Now—fine ladies that you are—I can't say for certain what any of you might have in mind, but I've some suspicions that I think you'd have difficulty denying."

"Elizabeth, I think we'll be riding back home now," Ben said as he stood and called. "Annie, come now girl, we're leaving. Hear me, Sean. When you have a plan for something you'll want me to help with, I'll expect that you'll let me know—am I right?"

"That I'll do, Ben, and there will be many things that I'll need to have the help of a man. I'll count on you and the captain for that. Thank you. And Elizabeth, you're always welcome at my home. Please forgive me for my bad-tempered responses. They were not because of your suggestions. In fact I'm not sure what my bad temper's all about."

"I'm confident you don't know Sean," replied Elizabeth with a smile. "But Sean, you can be quite certain that I do understand the reason for your annoyance. Come now Ben, Annie, let's be off."

Women! Sean complained to himself as the Dixons rode off. *They seem to have the idea that what we think and the way we appear can be read as easily as a book. Well, here's one book no woman will ever be able to read.*

Mid-morning two days later Sean heard a familiar voice.

"Avast the house, wishin' to come aboard we are," Fian called.

Walking out of the small shed, Sean responded, "Out here behind the house."

"Captain Murphy and his first mate comin' aboard we are," Fian responded just as he was almost knocked to the ground when Nathan came around the corner of the house and jumped up on him.

"Fian, Fian," Nathan squealed, "I knew you were coming soon to see me."

Fian lifted Nathan as high as he could and said, "Where have you been, lad? If you're to be crew of the *Southern Swallow*, the first mate always has to know where his crew's off to."

Then they both laughed as Fian roughly threw him to the ground and began to tickle him.

"Here now, Fian," Captain Murphy cautioned. "That's no way to be treating a first-class member of our crew, is it?"

"Beggin' your pardon Captain, it won't happen again," Fian replied as he rolled Nathan over and began the tickling process again.

"Fian, see if you and my grandson can stay out of mischief long enough for me to have a talk with Sean."

Sean was still walking toward them, wiping his hands on a small rag, then extending his hand to the captain.

"Always good to see you, Captain. And what brings you about on this day?"

Looking over his shoulder to be certain that Fian and Nathan were out of earshot, he began: "Sean, you know I'm no one to drag me anchor when I've sailing to do. So, let me say what brings me about on this day."

"Elizabeth's been talking to Cynthia, hasn't she?" Sean asked, more as a statement of fact than a question.

"Of course she has—they talk often. But let me have my say before you tack off in another direction."

"All right," Sean unwillingly agreed. "Let's go back to the open shed—we can sit in the shade and I'll hear you."

Sean sat on the ground and the captain seated himself on a small log and began talking again.

"It's about my niece, Sarah . . . ."

"That's not a matter I'd be speaking of, Captain. Is that what's brought you here?"

"Hold right there Sean, belay—you've said that you'll hear me, and hear me you will," the captain said forcefully.

Sean began to respond, thought better of it and pulled his legs up and wrapped his arms around them. "All right then Captain. I'll hear you."

"Every person I know is pleased that you've returned, Sean. None more than meself, and I'd say you know that. Folk from far and near have been part of helping you found your home here at Dawn Light once again. And the very idea that Hough and that Welshman from Annapolis were the ones who've had your home returned to you—well Sean—that's a fine thing, a fine thing indeed."

"It is, Captain. And I'm not about to forget that. And as you say . . ."

"As I say," the captain continued, "I'll be the one talking I will. Understand, Sean, all of these good people have helped you in your time of need. And it wasn't as though you've had to go about begging for it, have you? No, you haven't. People saw you had a need and they took action. Now, let me tell you this . . . ."

The captain paused for several moments, wiping his nose with the back of his hand before starting anew.

"Let me tell you this, Sean, my brother's girl, Sarah—well, Sean, she's a woman with need too. We haven't known just what we could do to help her. Even Cynthia's been baffled by some of Sarah's ways—until recently. Sean, my niece told Cynthia that she'd had a terrible marriage to a wicked man. This Fitzpatrick coward would beat her whenever he wasn't out to sea, and the woman feared for her life at times."

"I'm sorry to hear such as this, Captain. But this sort of thing does happen and, Captain, it can have nothing to do with me."

"But it can, Sean—and it does. You see, Sarah's very nervous around men, and having a husband who beat her—well, that's enough to make anyone uneasy. But, Sean, she's noticed how caring you are about Nathan and how he acts in response to you. She has seen your manner around Cynthia and Elizabeth and even Missy. But Sean, she has even wondered if you had beaten Julia—and asked Cynthia as much."

"What?" Sean shouted as he stood. "I've heard more than what I need, Captain."

"No you haven't, Sean. Now, sit down and let me finish. You must hear me out."

Sean was glaring at the captain, but his respect for the man would only allow him to do as the captain asked, so he sat once again.

"She was even unsure about Liam my brother, and wondered if he had beaten his wife, her mother, but was never bold enough to ask her father—her own father. Of course Cynthia assured her that you had never behaved in such a way with her daughter Julia."

There was another pause and Sean thought he saw a tear form in the captain's eye.

"And, Sean," the Captain continued with a broken voice, "She asked my dear wife if I had ever beaten her! It made my blood boil to first hear that she'd asked. But when Cynthia explained the reason for her question—well, Sean, I tell you that I wept with the sadness it brought to me. My own brother's flesh and blood was beaten by a cowardly pirate of a man."

The captain paused again and looked off toward the field where Fian and Nathan seemed to be looking for something on the ground. He sat watching them for several minutes with a smile that reflected his thoughts.

"Even hard talking ferocious fighters like Fian—Sean, just look at them two would you? Like two boys in a field rather than a boy and a bad-mannered sailor. But, I'll tell you this, Sean, Fitzpatrick wouldn't have lasted a day at sea if he had sailed with the likes of me Fian."

"I thank you for telling me these things, Captain. It does help explain your niece's conduct. But, Nathan and I have things to do now."

"Do you Sean? You've not heard me out—not yet. What you have to do has waited for more than three years, a few minutes more will be no grand loss for you."

Captain Murphy waited as Sean leaned against the post of the shed and settled down again.

"I have no idea why you seem to be so unkind to Sarah," the captain said as he paused to see if the expression of Sean's face would change. He continued when it did not.

"You know, Sean, if you purposely ignore someone else—or perhaps physically or emotionally injure someone just because you dislike the person—soon you'll find yourself liking that person less and less. I'll tell you that I know this because of my own past actions. And Sean, here's another thing. You know that I believe in God. And even though I've not the same sort of friendship with Him that you tell me of, nevertheless I've learned some of the sayings of Jesus through my years."

"I'm certain you have, Captain. And I've found that even if you didn't know what God has to say in His Bible, very often somehow you knew in your heart what God wanted and have done as God directed."

"I'd be watchful about saying such as that, Sean, I would. But, here's what I do know. I know that Jesus said something like, 'You ought to love your own neighbor as yourself,' or some such thing. And here's my way of thinking, Sean. If we begin to behave as if we like someone, or as Jesus said, 'Love your neighbor,' I'm thinking that we'll presently come to like that person. That's what I'm thinking, and now, that's what I'm asking of you. I'm asking that you begin to see Sarah as a person. You may not love her or—you might not even like her—I know that'll be up to you. But I am asking you to do as God says and begin to behave as if you do like her."

"Oh, Captain, that's . . . . "

"No, Sean. Please say no more. I beg only that you consider this. Think about beginning to behave toward Sarah as if she were a person you like. You see, Sean, she loves your son Nathan dearly. And although she may not even know this, Cynthia tells me that Sarah requires that you treat her in a friendly manner. Now I don't know how women know such things—but it's so, that's what Cynthia tells me."

They remained silent until Nathan came running up to the open shed.

"Look what Fian found Father—he says it's the head of an Indian's arrow. Is it Daddy?" Nathan said holding the arrowhead in his open hand for Sean to see.

"It looks to me that you and Fian have found exactly that, Nathan. You'll need to thank Fian and then put it some place safe in the house and then later you can take it out and look at it whenever you please."

"That's just what I'll do, Daddy. And I already thanked Fian, and he said that this won't be the last thing we'll find together."

"We're off to the quay, Sean," the captain announced. "Can Nathan join us? He can dine aboard with the crew and I'll have him back home before dark."

"As long as the dining doesn't mean that he'll have to eat the crew's green salt pork. I think he'd like that—wouldn't you Nathan?"

"Oh yes, I would Father."

"Then let's be off men," the captain said. "I've had enough of this lazy crew of mine—there's toil enough to do aboard the *Southern Swallow* without idling the time away. Am I right Fian?"

"Aye, Captain. Right like always I says, is what I says. Let's jump to then, seaman Nathan."

They headed down the path toward North East and Sean was alone again. Captain Murphy had left him with many matters on which to reflect and he thought long and hard about those things.

Later that day, just before dark as Sean sat on the front steps enjoying the lengthening shadows, he saw Nathan coming down the pathway with the captain in his cart.

"We've a favor to ask of you Sean. My grandson would like to stay with us tonight. He says he wants to see his grandmother and Sarah. I told him you wouldn't mind and I know I was right. And Sean, don't be taking love from the boy because of your stubbornness—he'll soon be seeing right through your actions and outlook. Or, better yet, Sean, he'll be seeing the best part that we talked about."

Before Sean could object, the captain called, "Come get Nathan in the morning, Sean." Then he turned the cart around and was headed toward his own home

"Good-bye Father," Nathan shouted above the noise of the pounding hooves and the creaking cart.

CHAPTER SIXTEEN

Disastrous Decision

That night Sean had already decided that very likely he would have difficulty sleeping—and he was right. He went to bed fully intending to gain a good night's sleep, but was unable to think of anything except the requests the captain had made of him.

The moon threw shadows across Sean's bed that caused his imagination to envision every sort of distraction that could possibly keep him from sleep. So he decided to go outside to sit on the porch.

Everything appeared almost as clearly as if it were day in the glow of the bright moon. Sean looked up to the heavens and reflected on some of the thoughts that had been racing through his mind.

Lord, I've trusted you since that day I gave myself to you. I sat right here in this very place, on this porch when I was with the Tubbs cousins, Ethan and Edward. Lord, I'm in need of men like them once again in my life. I know I've not been the kind of man I should have been at times, but I try Lord.

Sean looked down at his clasped hands and wondered: *Why would a loving God allow my wife to die? Lord, if anyone's life needed to be taken it should have been mine, not Julia's. It's so difficult to make sense of this world—it seems that circumstances are more in control than You are. Why is this so, Lord?*

He raised his head and cried out, "Why?"

The sound of his voice stirred the night and he heard the muffled noises of small animals scurrying about. The sudden soft thumping of a night hawk's wings startled Sean as the bird glided past him within arm's reach.

He sat very still almost expecting to hear or see other birds or animals, but when he heard none he began to think again.

The Welshman is a man that I wish I could be close by. He seemed to be a man blessed of great wisdom. And the captain—what the captain was saying about liking someone even if I thought them unlikeable—was that an echo of Glasfryn Lord? Just another way the Welshman had of demanding me to be aware of the needs of others? After all, Morgan Glasfryn said that he had helped fulfill my need—and he did. And I pledged to him that I would help to fulfill the needs of others.

Looking up he spoke aloud. "Ah moon—you have worked your strange magic on me. You have me talking to you and babbling to myself and I cannot discover the proper sense in myself to have the right answers. Yes, the spell of moon magic is what I think it is. I've fallen under the spell of the moon."

For the longest time he sat there in the cool of the night waiting for answers that he believed God owed him.

Then he thought, *I remember the Welshman's very words, because he spoke them as one would sing a song:*

"Not many a man can be a king, and not many a king is a kindly man. But this I'll say to all who hear, I'd rather be a king maker than a king, and on this I stand." And on this I must stand as well. I pledged my word to the good Welshman. It's the payment I owe him for his kindness. I could do nothing for him, yet he did much for me. And isn't that just as God has done for man through our Lord Jesus Christ—has done for me? Sean O'Connell, you're a thickheaded Irishman, and I've become a cold-hearted man as well. The captain has shown me the first opportunity to pay my fee to Morgan Glasfryn the Welshman, my benefactor. Thank you, Lord. I understand. Captain Murphy's niece Sarah Fitzpatrick is one who is in need. She's my neighbor just as Christ said, although I've shut her out as an enemy—and all the while seeing how she behaved so lovingly toward Nathan. She's a woman so I'm unable to make her a king. But with your help Lord—a queen she'll be.

Sean went back up to his bed and slept well through the night.

The first rays of morning sun wakened Sean and he decided that he would try to get to the Murphy house in time for a warm breakfast. Even though Missy had never learned to make the good bark tea that Sean enjoyed when Kezie was with him, he knew he would have a better meal with the captain and Cynthia than he would have alone—a much better meal.

He saddled the horse and was off at a trot. As he rode along he enjoyed the beauty of the early morning sky as the sun reflected its rosy hues on the gathering clouds, and soon he arrived at the side gate of the Murphy home.

"Hello the house!" Sean shouted. "A passing vagabond is in need of a meal."

"Be havin' cook for everybody come 'roun this house, and how am I suppose to know who be here an' who don' be here?" Missy grumbled, not caring if anyone heard or not.

"Missy," continued Sean, "I've come because they tell me that the best breakfast in Maryland can be found at Captain Murphy's house. And, today I've come to see for myself if this is true."

"Don' make me no care what they say. All the same means more work for Missy, that's all I knows."

"Oh, hush, Missy," Cynthia scolded. She had heard Sean's voice and Missy's mumblings and came out to greet him.

"I'm glad you came," Cynthia announced. "We're having a special treat today. Nathan was playing in the forest last week and came across some beautiful purple Fox grapes. Then yesterday, Missy and Sarah went out to harvest some for our pleasure. They are plump and sweet and will be a very juicy treat to begin one's day."

"Then I'd say that I've made a fine choice of inns for this vagabond's travels." Sean said, laughing.

Everyone seemed cheerful this early morning and all were enjoying the special delight of fresh grapes. Nathan was the object of many favorable comments for the part he had in finding the abundance of grapes.

"But Missy and Miss Sarah gathered them. I couldn't reach most of the grapes, because they were too high. But, next year I'll be taller and then I'll help too, won't I Miss Sarah?"

"You certainly shall, Nathan," she responded with a smile.

With that, Sean thought, *it appears that God is presenting just the opportunity I need to practice what I have promised the Welshman and captain.*

"Nathan certainly seems to have found you to be a special friend, Miss Sarah," Sean offered.

"I'm certain that he find me as friendly as I find him," Sarah responded without looking at Sean. "I believe that is quite scriptural, for the Bible tells us that if one wants a friend, one must be a friend to others—or some such thing. And Nathan certainly has been my good friend."

Before Sean could respond, Sarah pushed her chair away from the table.

"If you would, excuse me please," she said as she left the room.

Sean was perplexed and thought, *How am I to be expected to deal with such an uncooperative person? Why did I agree to go through with this matter with captain's niece? It all seems so contrived and very unnatural—for her and certainly for me as well.*

117

Sean hurriedly finished the meal and said, "Nathan, we must be going now."

"But, Father, can't we stay the whole day here with Grandmother and Grandfather?"

"I'd say that's a suggestion I'd agree with," the captain added. "Sean why don't you . . ."

"Yes," Sean snapped. "Why don't I—why don't I do this and why don't I do that. Well, what I say is that Nathan and I are leaving. We'll do what I say, not what someone else might say. And we're leaving right now. Thank you, Cynthia, for the breakfast. Now, Nathan, we're leaving—now Nathan!"

Nathan began to cry and Sean grabbed him by the arm and yanked him out the door as the captain looked at his wife and shook his head so as to warn her not to say more.

Nathan had to hold on to his father for fear of falling as Sean whipped the horse faster and faster toward North East.

Fian saw them coming and came down to the quay, because he thought something might have happened to the captain.

"What's the hurry this morning Sean. Is everyone well?" Fian asked.

Without dismounting, Sean replied, "If you mean the captain and his family, yes, they're well. But, don't be asking about me—not today, Fian."

Not to be bullied by anyone, Fian responded. "Well now, I wouldn't be after making words just as those Sean. Is there something you need to say—something you're thinking I've done to displease you?"

Sean glared at Fian for a moment then said, "No, it has nothing to do with you, Fian. Here's what I'm asking—would you join Nathan and me today? I'd like to sail *Julia's Fairwinds* across the bay today, because I need the air to clear my head."

"Aye, Sean, the sea will clear your head—it'll do that for you. But not today, because I couldn't sail with you unless the captain agreed, and I can tell you this as a seaman, Sean—today's not the best day for sailing your sloop. I'm sure you and Nathan will make fine seamen one day, but no, today's not the day. I know you've heard us say at one time or another, 'Red sky in the morning, sailors take warning.' Well, Sean the sky told us this morning that a storm's on the way. And you don't have to be much of a seaman—just look and you can see for . . . "

"Very well, Fian. If you can't or won't go—then Nathan and I'll sail the sloop alone."

"I tell you, Sean," Fian warned, "you'd do well to stay ashore on this day. The wind's blowing evil already."

Bermuda Sloop—*Julia's Fairwinds*

As Sean and Nathan rode off toward the quay where *Julia's Fairwinds* was berthed, Fian stood wondering what had upset Sean in such a manner.

Sean struggled to free the sloop from its berth. He needed the strength of another man but finally he was able to catch enough air with the small forward sail and managed to get them to open water.

The wind began to blow fiercely and Sean wondered if perhaps this plan of his to sail across the bay should be withdrawn. But, when Nathan called out to him, he decided that he would continue on.

"Father," Nathan shouted above the wind. "Look how the wind is blowing water from the waves. It's almost like rain that's blowing sideways. Look—look at the big waves, Father!"

And that's when the trouble began. With the large waves Nathan had seen came an enormous gust of wind. Unfortunately, Sean's inexperience in such dangerous waters had allowed him to loose the sheets[13] that released the second sail. As it filled with the gale force wind that blew up from the southeast, driving rain began to pelt them like shot from a gun.

"Stay down low there, Nathan," Sean shouted above the howling wind and crashing thunder. "Don't get up unless I call to you. Do you understand?"

By now Nathan was not as eager as he had been just minutes earlier to watch the roaring waves that seemed to come crashing upward from the depths, and he shook his head in agreement.

No sooner had Sean ordered Nathan to safety in the lower part of the deck than he realized that the excessive load on both sails was driving the sloop dangerously fast. If Sean were to allow the sloop to continue at such an uncontrolled speed he knew the result would be disastrous.

And disaster is exactly what happened. Sean pulled hard as he could on the whipstaff[14] trying to bring the helm about. But when a flashing crash of lightning startled him, he made the unskilled mistake of forcing the rudder too far in his attempt to slow the sloop. The blustering wind caught the mainsail and swung the boom across the deck with great force. The unrestrained boom began to slam back and forth to the limit of its range, placing excessive stress on the rigging.

Fear gripped Sean as he saw the boom crashing wildly from side to side until he finally heard an explosive sound as the mast snapped and came down. This sudden change in control resulted in the sloop almost steadying itself, but then it continued on, heeling precariously for a few minutes still driven by the gale even though the mast and sails were down.

Then, in those chaotic moments, with waves washing the deck and lightning seeming to illuminate the entire world, for some strange reason Sean thought: *Why didn't I do what the captain told me to do—why didn't I add more ballast?*

Before this thought had the opportunity to pass through his mind, the sloop took a sudden change of direction and an unwary Sean lost his balance and he slipped backward and fell overboard. All he could think about as he went underwater was Nathan.

He surfaced, disoriented and coughing water from his lungs he shouted, "Nathan! Nathan! Where are you Nathan?"

Unknown to Sean, Nathan had gone overboard at almost the same instance that Sean had lost his balance, and he was tangled in the sheets of the forward sail. That could have choked him or held him underwater, but instead Nathan was able to grasp one of the mainsail sheets as the wind and water angrily twisted the mast from its mooring on the sloop.

Sean didn't see Nathan in the choppy waves, but he saw the mast as it broke loose from the sloop and in desperation he swam toward it. Exhausted, in the growing darkness, at last he was able to reach out and his hand established a good grip. As he pulled himself closer to the mast, he looked in horror as *Julia's Fairwinds* capsized, rolled back almost upright and then sank from sight.

"Julia!" Sean screamed as the sloop went under.

Through the clamorous howling wind, Sean heard a weak voice calling, "Father—father!" And there, not ten feet away from him, he saw Nathan hugging the mast too.

Sean pulled himself toward Nathan and thrashed about trying to tie himself to the mast while he held on to Nathan. Even though Sean ardently prayed that the tempest would subside, the rage of the storm didn't waver. Although they were in water it seemed that the whole earth was shaking. Finally, Sean managed to use a part of the torn sail to wrap around Nathan and he secured Nathan to himself as he struggled to keep both their heads above water. All the while the clouds continued relentlessly to pour water down upon them.

Captain Murphy had no idea that Sean had taken the *Julia's Fairings* out into the bay and he was shocked when Fian came in the driving rain and pounded on the door.

"What in the world has happened? Get in here Fian," the captain said as the driving rain came washing through the open doorway. "Why did you walk all the way out here? Is something wrong with the ship?"

"Not the ship, Captain. It's Sean and Nathan, they've taken the sloop out to sea and they haven't returned—it's been hours it has, Captain."

"They have done what? What has this foolish man done? Why didn't you stop him, Fian—couldn't you see the storm brewing?"

"Aye, Captain. I knew it would be blowing and I told him as much, but he wouldn't hear me. He was behavin' his self like a man of no sense, Captain. And now I fear that . . ."

"What's this about, Laird?" Cynthia said as she came down the stairs. "Fian, why have you come during such a storm?"

"It's Sean and Nathan," the captain answered. "They took the sloop from berth and haven't returned."

Then, turning back to Fian he said, "You're already wet, get the cart horse hitched, and get back to the ship. Have the crew ready and we'll be taking her out. I'll follow on horseback."

"No, Laird," Cynthia pled. "You can't go out now, there's no use in it. There's nothing that can be done in the storm."

Captain Murphy took his wife by the arms and said, "Cynthia, I'm captain of a ship and I've seen storms raging at sea that make this one look like a spilled bucket of spring water. I'll be safe—besides how could I not go out after Nathan and Sean?"

Cynthia stood at the door as the rain blew in and she watched the captain ride off toward North East.

By the time he reached the *Southern Swallow* darkness had fallen as the storm continued to rage. The captain knew that putting himself and his crew in peril in the darkness would do nothing to help Sean and Nathan.

"Fian," the captain ordered, "Have the men put in for a night's sleep and we'll set sail at daybreak. Let's hope this wolf loses some its teeth by then."

"Aye, Captain. We'll be ready to sail at your word."

Through the night the captain was unable to sleep as the rain beat down on the deck and the wind continued to howl, and he only hoped that his crew would be rested and ready for what might prove to be a difficult ordeal on the next day.

However, sometime after midnight, the wind quieted, even though the rain continued, and just before daybreak Fian pounded on the door of the captain's quarters.

"Crew's up and we're waiting for your order to sail, Captain," Fian reported.

"Then sail we will," the captain said as he stepped out of his quarters and up to the quarterdeck. "Away all lines, Fian."

Anticipating the order, the crew quickly responded to Fian's loud call and the *Southern Swallow* pulled from the quay. All hands that were not working the sails were assigned to stand watch.

As they raised the mainsail the *Southern Swallow* moved gracefully toward open water, all eyes cast toward the four points of the compass looking for any clue that might lead them to Sean and his son.

The captain set a course that took them back and forth, crisscrossing as they moved from as close to the shoreline as he dared sail and then back to deeper water. A tattered piece of sail was pulled from the water. Fian recognized the stitching on the sail's edge and identified it as being from Sean's sloop.

The rain stopped and the day wore on. The sun came out and a gentle breeze drifted clouds quietly along, revealing no hint of the chaos of yesterday's weather. Captain Murphy allowed no one to rest, including himself, and he paced the deck looking outward and hoping to see something—anything—that would give him hope. He saw nothing but water.

Then suddenly, just as the sun was dipping to the western horizon, a cry rang out.

"Off the bow, Captain— off the port bow," called a seaman. "Wreckage off the port bow, it's a man, Captain—off the port bow."

Running forward, the captain strained to see where the crewman was pointing. Fian brought the helm about and they were swiftly drawing near the wreckage. The crewman was right and as they closed the distance a man could be clearly seen and he appeared to be tied to some debris—possibly a mast.

Fian gave the helm to another crewmember and ran forward. Immediately, upon assuring himself that it was Sean, he jumped overboard with a line from the boat. When Fian reached him Sean was semi-conscious and his face was battered and swollen as he bobbed up and down in the water.

Fian struggled to loosen the unconscious Nathan from where his father had bound him to himself. Holding Nathan's head above water with one arm he struggled trying to tie the line securely under Sean's arms. Another crewman had jumped in to help and when they had Sean secure, Fian signaled for the crew to pull him toward the ship and then they raised him aboard.

Fian stayed with Nathan and although he had difficulty swimming back, he soon was able to make it to the side of the ship. When the crew pulled them up to the deck and all were safely aboard the *Southern Swallow*, they headed back toward North East.

CHAPTER SEVENTEEN

Reclaimed Ruin

It had been ten days since Sean and Nathan had been rescued. The captain insisted that they stay with Cynthia and Sean was so weak and despondent that he had agreed.

"I know that I thought I saw her go under, but maybe it was just large waves that kept her from my view. Are you certain there's no possibility that she's still afloat, Captain?" Sean asked.

"No, Sean. Fian and the men have gone out several times. And they've alerted other seamen and watermen too and have asked them to report any wreckage they might see afloat—but there's been none reported, not even torn rigging."

"What has become of me, Captain?" Sean pled. "Am I mad? I've lost my wife, and then I take my son out in the sloop facing winds that howled like banshees. It was as if I wanted to die myself—and my own son—my own son with me. Captain, am I mad?"

"Mad? No, I think not. Although I'd have to tell you that I've not had many acquaintances who were mad men—so I can't be certain," the captain replied with a laugh. "But, I can tell you this, Sean O'Connell, you're an angry man. And I know this—that you should do well rather to be grateful than to be angry."

"Grateful? I should be grateful? My wife is dead, Captain. I sank the very sloop that I built and then named for her. And I almost killed my own son and myself. Grateful—and I suppose you can tell me why I should be grateful?"

"Now," replied the captain smiling, "Isn't that just what I'd like to be doing? Oh yes, Sean, I can tell you why you should be grateful. I can tell you as straight as a compass pointing north why you should be grateful."

"Will you tell me as well, husband?" Cynthia asked as she came into the room.

"We're having a talk, my dear wife. But, I'm afraid it's not the sort of talk from which women could benefit or enjoy. Oh, no—you see, we're talking about things that are a concern only to men—eh Sean?"

Sean didn't answer, but Cynthia could see from the dark expression on his face that something was terribly wrong.

"Well then, if that's the way it must be, I'm off to the kitchen shed to see how Missy is coming with our supper. And Laird, don't spend too much time talking about these things that only concern men—we'll have supper very soon—and I know that concerns men as well."

Sean walked to the window and looked out, then the captain came alongside and put his arm around Sean's shoulder.

"Here's the cut of the jib, Sean. I wouldn't be telling anyone such as I'll tell you if we weren't the very best of friends."

Sean pulled away and turned to face the captain.

"Friends, Captain?" Sean said irately. "Why would a man like you be calling someone like me your friend? I almost killed your grandson—my son!"

"And isn't that where being grateful shows itself, Sean? The captain inquired. "Our Nathan is alive! If you can't see cause to be grateful for that, then maybe you are mad Sean O'Connell."

Disgusted, the captain turned and walked from the room, leaving Sean staring from the window again.

Sean's mind began to churn and the thoughts that had brought him to this state of despondence began to boil over again in his mind.

Why do I have this persuasive sense of guilt? Is it because of my angry departure from Murphy's? They seemed to accept my appeal for pardon and said they did forgive me. Then why must this shame stick to me like spilled molasses? The Captain says I'm not mad—but no good man of reason would spitefully

*and knowingly risk the life of his own son by foolishly setting sail into the teeth
of an impending tempest, and then lose the* Julia Fairwinds *in a raging storm.
Oh, Lord, take my hand—lift me God from this dark bog of despair.*

A light knock on the door broke his contemplation and then he heard
Missy's voice.

"Miss Cynthia says bes' be comin' to eat some."

By the end of the second week since being saved from the shipwreck,
Sean's cuts and bruises had healed. Even though Nathan had not been
physically tossed about as much as Sean had, nevertheless he suffered from
coughing spasms, which Cynthia attributed to getting so much water in
his lungs.

Missy knew of a cure for lung congestion and she had prepared a
poultice from herbs that she was using to nurse Nathan back to health. In
fact the poultice seemed to be working and he was improving. However,
Sean decided to leave him in the care of Cynthia and he went back to
Dawn Light to continue settling in to his reestablished home.

At first Nathan was disappointed that he couldn't go straightaway to
Dawn Light with his father. But before long he changed his mind, because
Sarah was pampering him with kindness. And especially because she had
said, "I know a game that I enjoy and maybe you'd like to learn how to
play it."

"Oh yes, Miss Sarah. I want to learn how to play your game. What
is it?"

"Well, it's called Nine Men's Morrice[15]—and I've already asked Fian to
make a board upon which we will play the game. I'll go to my room and
fetch the board. I'll be right back."

"Don't you mean my mother's room, Miss Sarah?"

"Of course I do, Nathan. I'll fetch the board from your mother's
room."

She returned and they both sat on the floor as Sarah placed the board
between them.

"Now, each of us is to have nine markers. I've chosen to use these
dried beans and, Nathan, why don't you chose nine of your best small
stones—those you keep in your old stocking?"

"Yes, that's what I'll use," Nathan said as he reached under his bed—
the place he kept all of his treasures—to retrieve his stones.

"Now," continued Sarah, "the object of the game is that we should
make rows of three markers on these lines that Fian has scratched into the

board. Now then, I'll try to prevent you from doing this, and you'll try to prevent me. Do you understand?"

Puzzled, Nathan said, "I don't understand. Will you show me?"

"Of course, here's how we'll play," she said and they began the game.

At first, Nathan enjoyed himself. But he became frustrated and wanted to stop playing before the game was over. Sarah suggested that he carefully observed her as she played and before long he began to use his markers to advantage.

However, after a brief time he tired of the game. As Sarah was picking up the beans, stones and board, Nathan surprised her when he said, "Miss Sarah, do you think my father is a good man?"

"Why Nathan, I—well yes, of course I do. Why would you ask such a question?"

"But, you don't talk to him very much—do you?"

"Well, Nathan—no—you're right, we don't speak often."

"But, Miss Sarah, I've never seen you and father speaking at all. Are you certain that you think he's a nice man?"

"I've already told you that I think he's a good man. But, Nathan, a woman is not to be so bold as to suddenly begin to converse with a man such as your father."

"Why, Miss Sarah? Do you want me to ask him to talk to you?"

"No, Nathan," she blurted. "You will do no such thing, and now that we have played enough Nine Men's Morrice for one day—Nathan. I have things to do. We'll play on another occasion—we'll put the game away for now. And tomorrow—well tomorrow or perhaps another day I'll teach you some riddles."

Meanwhile, back at Dawn Light, Sean looked up when he heard the familiar shout of his friend. "Hello there, in the house or barn—or wherever you might be trying to hide from us—we're the Crown's royal colonial red coats and we're looking for land to confiscate."

Without stepping from the barn Sean returned the call. "Although it sounds much like my neighbor Ben Dixon, I'm hoping that it isn't Ben, because I'm about to cock and fire this musket—for I'll not lose my land a second time."

"Oh now, looks like I'm mistaken," came Ben's voice followed by, "It must be the house down the lane we were looking for."

Sean came from the barn shaking his head. "Ben, if you think your jesting is witty then you have come to the wrong house—and you're not even close to the right lane. But I'll say welcome to you just the same."

"You're looking a bit more like yourself, Sean. And to get you as well as can be, Elizabeth sent along some corn cakes with cracklings to bring you back to good health."

"Ah, bless that dear wife of yours, Ben. There's no finer fried corn cake I've ever tasted. Take them to the shade of the porch and I'll get us some water."

The two friends settled down and began to eat the cakes.

"Sean, Elizabeth and I—well, we've had some concern as to why you don't have Nathan back here with you, now that you both seem well again."

"You're concerned are you? Well, I am too. I'll tell you Ben that I've struggled with this matter, but I can't say my head's clear enough to give me a sound answer."

"What matter would that be, Sean—the matter of Nathan being with you?"

"That and more, because you see Ben, Nathan is thriving there at Murphy's and although Cynthia and the captain have been part of his prospering, I've come to see that there's been a strong tie come to be between Nathan and the captain's niece."

"His niece—do you mean Sarah, Sean? Friend, you can hardly say her name and why would that be?"

Sean's appearance didn't change, but he simply sat staring toward the path leading to the lane.

"Sean," Ben repeated, "why is it that you can't say her name?"

Turning to his friend Sean answered, "Ben, I can't say. These past three years—and it's been more now—out there in the wilderness, and even back here, I've had a vision of Nathan growing up with me—and that we'd have adventures and perhaps even see marvelous things together." He abruptly stopped speaking and after a few moments continued.

"But Ben, now that I've returned—well, you see what's happened. Dawn Light is returned to me and then I sail off trying to drown Nathan and me and in it all I've destroyed the sloop. And Ben, it seems I'm determined to destroy my life. But not only mine, but Nathan's and those who would offer their hand of kindness."

"You've told me what you've done, Sean. And I've seen you do it. But what is it friend that has changed you so?"

"It's this woman—the captain's niece—all right, Sarah. When Glasfryn the Welshman and I settled on payment for what he had done for helping me retrieve Dawn Light—I promised to help fulfill the need of someone who could not do so for themselves—just as I was unable without Glasfryn's help. He has this strange king-making proposal, and I agreed to abide by it."

"I can't say I see it, Sean. What's this matter about and why are you unwilling to do what he has asked and you have promised to do?"

"Because I fear it's not something I thought I'd agreed to do."

"From what you've told me, Sean, there was no bargain struck—you had nothing to pay the Welshman—so what have you to do?"

"You still don't understand, do you? The captain has told me of the great need that his niece—that Sarah has. And even though I've told the captain much as I've told you about my pact with the Welshman, the captain had no idea whatever of how the promise I'd made would result—and I didn't either. The captain does not know of the turmoil it's causing me. But—God forgive me if I'm wrong Ben—but I know that she—Sarah—is the one I must help."

"Well then, help her you must, for it seems plain as day," Ben said.

"Aye Ben plain to see and plain to say, but there's where the storm arises and I've had me fill of storms, Ben. Even if I really understood the deep need this woman has, how can I ever hope to be able to help someone in the way she requires help without having good feelings toward her?"

"Now you're troubling my mind," Ben said. "You have no good feelings toward her? Sean, she's taken Nathan under wing just as a mother hen would a chick."

"There, you see? That's the very thing I'm talking about. I'm thankful for the way she and Nathan have become such close friends, but that's no reason to—to meet someone's need—even if I was to know what the need was. Is it?"

"Sean, much as I'd like to help you, this is something you'll be untangling by yourself. Even if I really understood what this is all about, I'd have not the good sense to be a guide through such as this—and believe me Sean, I don't understand."

Ben walked to where his horse had been grazing, He took the reins in hand, mounted and as he rode off for home he said in a voice loud enough for Sean to hear, "You've some way of making a difficulty of things Sean O'Connell."

Sean stood in front of the house watching Ben ride toward the gate and thought: *Ben's right—the difficulty is mine, but I can't see how I'm its author. Even if Ben and the others seem to realize what I've told them they still don't understand how my soul struggles. How could I possibly think I'd be able to meet the needs of a woman I don't really know—and I've made no attempt to become gracious to her—Lord, are you certain that this loving your neighbor approach to life really works?*

The following day Sean rode over to Murphy's before noon hoping to be offered a meal. As he approached the side gate of their house he heard, "Miss Sarah, Miss Sarah—here comes father."

Nathan came running up as Sean dismounted to lead his horse into the back garden.

"Hello Nathan," Sean said. "How's my fine son this day."

"I'm glad you're here, Father. Miss Sarah and I are going to ask some riddles and you can join us. Won't that be grand, Daddy?"

"Well, I've only come to have a meal with you. Maybe you and the captain's niece—Miss Sarah—should go ahead and ask the riddles without me."

"Oh, please come join us, Mr. O'Connell," Sarah said as she stepped around the corner of the house. "I agree with Nathan, it would be grand if you were to join us."

Sean didn't know just how he should respond. But, thinking that this might be another opportunity to fulfill his pledge to the Welshman, he said, "I've never been able to solve riddles well. But perhaps I could listen while you question each other."

"No, Daddy, You must play too."

"There you have it, Mr. O'Connell, 'you must play too.' Please come and join us on the front porch where we're out of the sun."

"Very well," Sean replied, surprised at his response.

"But, if I'm to play—and because you cannot call me 'father,' Miss Fitzpatrick—you'll have to call me by my given name, Sean."

"I'll agree, but only if I shall be Sarah to you."

Sean felt his face flush, so he quickly took his son's hand and said, "Then let's be off to the front porch and solve some riddles."

Sarah and Sean each took a rocker and Nathan sat between them on the floor.

"All right, now, Nathan, how shall we begin? Do you have a riddle for us?"

"I do, and grandmother gave me the riddle—shall I ask my riddle now?"

Sean was pleased to see how at ease his son as with Sarah and said, "I'd like to hear your riddle son, why don't you ask it?"

Of course Nathan had hoped he could be the first to test others with his riddle and he smiled and said, "Here's my riddle and it's a very difficult riddle. Are you ready Miss Sarah? Are you ready Father?"

"Yes," Sean replied, "I believe we're both ready now."

"Then this is my riddle—what flies up, but is always down?"

"Oh my," Sarah began, "this does seem a very difficult riddle. Do you know the answer Mr.—Sean?"

"I'm afraid I don't know. This is very puzzling. I'm wondering how it could be possible that something could fly up but always remain down."

"I'm baffled too, Nathan," Sarah said. "You must tell us the answer." "Goose feathers," Nathan said, delighted that he had mystified them with his riddle.

"Goose feathers?" Sean asked. "Oh, I see, the feather of a goose can fly up but it always remains down—the down of a goose."

"Now it's your turn Miss Sarah," Nathan insisted.

"All right then, here's my riddle. When is a boy most like a bear?"

"I know," shouted Nathan. "A boy is most like a bear because he's a cub, like a young bear. Is that right?"

"That is a very good guess," replied Sarah smiling. "But here's the answer—a boy is most like a bear when he is barefoot."

"Now you must give us your riddle Father," Nathan insisted.

"Everyone bes' be comin' eat now, so Miss Cynthia say," Missy announced from the open door.

"And the meal has come just in time, said Sean. Let's be going inside to eat."

"No Daddy, no. Not until we have your riddle."

"We must not keep your grandmother waiting," Sean replied as he stood.

"I'm afraid Nathan is right, Sean," Sarah said, smiling as she stood and blocked Sean's way. "You must give us a riddle before you can eat."

Sean began to back away as Sarah placed her hand lightly on Sean's forearm but then he sat again.

"Well then, if this is the way it must be if I'm to eat—here's a riddle from the wilderness."

"From the wilderness," Nathan said excitedly. "Do they tell riddles in the wilderness, Father? Is it an Indian riddle?"

"You'll have to decide for yourself. Here's my riddle," he said. "What is it that falls down but never gets hurt?"

Looking at Sarah, who was still smiling, Nathan asked, "Do you know Miss Sarah?"

"Oh no, I don't know. This is a very difficult riddle. What do you suppose it might be that 'falls down but never gets hurt'?"

"I'm willing to tell you the answer," Sean announced, "if you then allow me do go inside to eat."

"Shall we allow that, Nathan?" Sarah asked.

"Yes, Father, tell us the answer and we'll allow that—and we shall all go inside to eat. Tell us Father."

"How can I know that you'll let me come inside with you? Miss Sarah blocked my way just now and I fear that if I tell the answer to the riddle, that you'll not allow me to eat."

"Oh no, we will let you eat, Daddy. Won't we Miss Sarah?"

"Perhaps your father has discovered our ways, Nathan."

"I believe that I have," Sean answered before Nathan could speak. "Now, here's what I'll offer both of you. We'll go in to eat, then when I'm certain that I'll be fed, only then will I give the answer to my riddle."

"No, Daddy, no . . ." Nathan began to complain.

"That seems very fair to all," Sarah said. "Now let's go to find a fine meal inside and then we'll discover the answer to this riddle."

Sarah reached her hand down to Nathan and as he stood he grasped his father's hand and pulled both Sean and Sarah close to him and said, "Isn't this just fine, Daddy?"

Once again Sean felt his face flush. "Fine it is, Nathan. Yes, fine it is—now let's go eat."

The captain and Cynthia were already seated at opposite ends of the table.

"You sit here, Daddy, with Miss Sarah and me. Then tell us the answer to your riddle"

"I'll just sit across from you Nathan and then we'll all have more room."

"Riddles is it?" the captain asked. "I've a riddle for everyone if it's riddles you're after. Sean's said he'll have more room, well here's my riddle. What kind of room is not in a house?"

"That's enough riddles for now, Laird," Cynthia said. "We're all hungry, now let's eat."

"O please, grandfather, tell us what kind of room isn't in a house."

"Why that's plain as can be," the captain responded. The kind of room that's not in a house is a mushroom."

"Enough, Laird," Cynthia insisted.

During the meal Nathan continued to trouble Sean for the answer to his riddle, but he kept putting him off. After everyone had finished eating, Sean pushed his chair back.

"I must be going now, I have much work today," Sean said. "Thank you so much for the very delicious meal—it was exceptional. But, I've always enjoyed meals here. I hope you don't mind me coming by unannounced."

"And has that troubled us before, Sean O'Connell?" the captain said laughing.

"We need no pronouncement beforehand if you care to eat with us," Cynthia assured him. "You're always welcome here. This is, after all, your house too, Sean. And I'm so pleased you enjoyed the meal. We'll have to thank Sarah for that, because she has shown Missy how to prepare the pork as they did at her father's home. Isn't that so, Sarah?"

Blushing, Sarah replied quietly, "It is, but Missy has done the cooking."

A familiar "Humph," was heard. "Ain't that be the only way 'roun' here," Missy grumbled. I do all the cookin' an' cleanin' an' . . . "

"All right, Missy," the captain said in mock annoyance. "We all know how important you are to us."

"Seems I be the only one does know," she responded under her breath—but loud enough for all to hear.

Nathan got up from the table and went to stand in the doorway.

"You can't leave, Father. Not until we hear the answer to your riddle. Please Daddy, tell us again what it was."

"Another time, Nathan," Sean said jokingly.

"I think not, Mr. O'Connell," Sarah said boldly. "If you are a man of your word, as I'm assured that you are, then you'll be allowed to leave as soon as you reveal this riddle of yours."

Somewhat shocked, Sean looked at Sarah briefly then said, "Very well then Mrs. Fitzpatrick—Sarah—this is my riddle. What is it that falls down but never gets hurt? Here's the answer, and it's well known in the wilderness—and yes, Nathan, it's known by white men as well as Indians. You see, whether in the wilderness or here in the garden, when snow falls it never gets hurt."

"I think that your father must have had the very best riddle today Nathan," said Sarah. "Don't you think so? Of course, yours was a fine riddle too."

"And mine?" asked the captain as though his feelings had been hurt.

They all laughed and then Sean thanked everyone again and excused himself. Nathan went outside as his father mounted his horse, then reached down to pat his son on the head and rode off.

Sarah stood behind the curtain watching him through the window as he rode off—then she sighed, not understanding why.

CHAPTER EIGHTEEN

Unusual Visitor

Sean enjoyed himself riding slowly along the pathway back to Dawn Light. He was particularly aware of the brightness of the sunny afternoon and thought that the leaves on the trees appeared especially green. He looked about and took in the natural beauty, even though he had passed this way many times before, it almost seemed as though he was becoming aware of things for the first time. Also, he noticed that the birds seemed to be so purposeful in their singing that he wondered if this might be their mating season and it prompted Sean to join them and he began to whistle.

What an amazing day, he thought, *although I can't say just what makes it so remarkable. But it gives me good reason to understand that this is today— today—and there'll never be another day like it. There have been so many days in my past—days that were very much like this—days that I have squandered. There are too many to imagine or remember—even if I were able to remember. And how many of those yesterdays can I recover? None—not even one, whether it was the most pleasant and thankfully not the most unpleasant or disastrous. And even though the memories of those wonderful yesterdays with Julia are with me now, yet those days with her can never be recovered. What am I to do?*

As he rode through the gate to Dawn Light he saw someone run along the side of the house and then duck behind the back of the house. He set the horse to a gallop and rode to the opposite side of the house thinking he would find the person running away. He was right and almost ran into the man, but Sean's horse reared up and the man staggered backward and fell.

Sean jumped from his mount and shouted, "Here now, who are you. Why are you lurking around my house?"

The man tried to stand but lost his balance and fell down again. He had a wild look in his eyes, his hair was matted, his clothing was in tatters, he was without shoes and Sean could smell him even though he was several feet away.

"I said who are you?" Sean repeated sternly. "Just what are you up to?"

The man sat staring off toward the forest and would not look directly at Sean. Then he started making sounds and bubbles of spittle formed around his mouth and Sean soon realized that the man was unable to speak and could do nothing more than babble incoherently.

"You can't stay here, you know." Sean said and then felt foolish for declaring the obvious. "You can't stay here—you must leave—do you want something to eat?"

With that question the man swung his head about and looked at Sean's feet. He held his hand out as if he expected Sean to fill it with something.

"All right now, you follow me. Do you understand?" Sean said but the man made no reply.

Sean left the horse behind and began to walk toward the back door. The man stood and took the long way around the horse watching to be sure the animal wouldn't rear up again and then fell in behind Sean and followed him. Arriving at the door Sean directed the man to wait outside.

Sean left the door ajar and watched as the man sat on the ground and began to babble again, rolling his eyes back occasionally, but otherwise he seemed to be calm enough.

Sean looked through what little provisions he had trying to find something that he thought would be suitable to give the man. He found some jerky that someone had brought to the house when the women of the community helped to restock his pantry.

"Well, it's better than nothing," Sean said aloud and took several pieces back outside.

"Now I'll have to tell you to get along," Sean demanded. "I won't have you prowling around my home. Do you understand?"

He expected no response and received none, so Sean handed the food to him as he remained seated on the ground. However, the moment he had the jerky in his hand he leapt nimbly to his feet and ran off toward the wooded area out past the large beech trees.

"Look at that fool run," Sean blurted in amazement. "He's running like a rabbit."

Through the rest of the day Sean worked in and around the house and the small barns, but he couldn't keep himself from frequently looking off in every direction almost expecting to see the strange man return—but he did not.

Sean wondered, *where did he come from and how does he manage to stay alive?*

The next day Sean rode over to the Dixons to see if Ben would be able to help him put some timbers in place so he could repair a shed roof. Ben quickly agreed to help him and together they rode back to Dawn Light. Sean seemed to be in no hurry and told Ben of his unusual experience with the strange man from the previous day.

"And I tell you Ben, I was alarmed by the man. I've been in too many difficult situations and seen and done too much that I shouldn't have been frightened by such as him. Nevertheless, there was something about the man that terrified me."

"I can imagine," said Ben. "And like you, I'd wonder where he had come from too."

"You know," Sean continued, "when I was in the wilderness I once saw a man—not much different than the one I experienced yesterday—traveling with a small band of Shawnee warriors. He behaved very differently from the other Indians he was with. He wore unusual regalia unlike what the others wore and would unexpectedly cry out with strange sounds. Yet, unlike the man yesterday, the Indian seemed clean and well kept and it appeared that the Indians were treating him with respect—actually I'd say with uncommon respect."

"That does seem odd, doesn't it?" Ben asked.

"Yes, very odd," replied Sean. "And some time later I mentioned this to our friend Nokona. If I understood what Nokona told me, he pointed out that Indians consider a person like that—someone I suppose we might consider mad—to be a very special person indeed. A man like that would have many needs and the Indians honored such a person and treated him with esteem. He never had to fight as did the others and was always cared for by members of the clan. They considered him very special, almost as a holy man—a person with a sensitive spirit."

They continued riding slowly and Ben said, "Makes me grateful to be as well as I am."

"Right you are," Sean replied. "That poor soul yesterday seemed to have no ability to take care of himself. And another thing, unlike the Indians, I didn't see him as having a sensitive spirit—but more of a wicked spirit. And I'll tell you Ben, the smell of the man would make you rather choose to bed down with a skunk. How fortunate we are to be able to do things for ourselves and be as well as we are."

"Puts you to mind of what your Welsh friend told you, doesn't it Sean?"

"What do you mean Ben?"

"Well, as the Welshman said to you—here's a man in great need, he can't help himself, care for himself or change his situation. This fellow from yesterday is your man in need," Ben said with authority. "He's someone you could make a king."

Sean reined his horse to a stop and Ben turned around in his saddle but continued to ride on.

"Now, I'll agree that he has great need," Sean replied. "But if you think this fellow is someone that I can make a king—I'll tell you Ben Dixon that you're the one who's mad and I'd rather try to make a king of you."

They both laughed and Sean started forward again and they continued on together.

When they arrived at Dawn Light they saw a cart and horse near the house and as they drew nearer they recognized the captain seated on the porch steps.

"And where have you two been," the captain called. "Did you plead for Elizabeth to give you another meal today Sean?"

"There's where you're wrong, Captain," Sean replied. "At the Dixons one only must show up at the door and he'll be fed without having to plead or beg."

"I'm sure that's true, Sean. Now tell me what you two are about today?"

Sean explained to both men what he intended to do and within a few hours the three men were able to get the two new posts in place that supported the roof of the shed. During that time neither he nor Ben mentioned the strange fellow to the captain.

"I must get back home, Sean," Ben said. "Let me know if there are other repairs you'll need to be making that we can do together."

As Ben rode off the captain said: "I'd best be on my way as well. Why don't you come back home with me for a meal Sean and spend the night? It would make Nathan so happy of you'd spend the night and sleep with him."

"I'll delay that invitation for tonight, Captain. But I must speak to you about a matter."

"Aye, Sean, I'll be glad to oblige and was hoping you'd ask. I've been pondering the situation meself as well so let's sit awhile and talk."

Sean explained what happened the previous day when he encountered the strange fellow and the captain knew something of the man.

"He's likely the same that Fian told me of a few months ago," the captain began. "Some of the watermen told Fian that the man lost his mind over some tragedy when his wife died, but Fian thought he'd more likely been born that way. No one seems to know where he comes from or where he goes. Fian's heard it told that often he's gone for months at a time and I'm thinking that he's run off from one place to another and hides away so people don't bother him. What do you make of it, Sean?"

"Well, Ben and I've been talking and I'm thinking that this stranger may be the person in need that the Welshman told me would come into my acquaintance. I couldn't imagine anyone being more in need than a fellow like this, can you?"

"I could agree with that," the captain said. "But, Sean, you've got to take the rudder with a firm grip here. This man will never come about to become a king—as your Welshman says. You know that, don't you Sean?"

"And I could agree with that, Captain. Still, there's the chance that this is a charge that God's giving me that I can't refuse. I don't know what to think."

"Well, here's what I have to say, lad. Do what you will for this fellow—I can see you have your sails set to do so. But, I'll have to tell you right out, Sean, that it'll do no more good to try to make a king of that man than it would to float a rock out to sea. Oh, you can help him some—and I can see you're thinking it's your Christian charity that'll change him. But, Sean, you may be able to clean and fatten him, but he'll be the same deranged fellow he was before you began."

"You may be right, Captain, but try I must—I've given my pledge to the Welshman to do it."

"Well, I say that there's where you've lost your compass, Sean. And if the Welshman were here to give a response Sean, I'm telling you that he'd agree with me—I know it."

That ended the discussion. The captain had hoped that Sean wanted to speak to him about his niece. When he discovered that he was wrong he went his way. He left Sean determined to help the odd stranger, but more confused than ever about just what his duty to the Welshman should be.

Sean thought long and hard about the man and how he would be able to meet the requirement to fulfill his pledge to the Welshman. For several weeks he had neglected many of his responsibilities in caring for his son and maintaining Dawn Light, because he sought after the man. He went as far north as Kennett Village and traveled westward to Nottingham Lots. He asked strangers if they had seen the man or knew anything about him.

Everywhere he went he found those who knew something about the man, but no one seemed to know where he came from, where he might stay, or even if he had a family.

A man that Sean asked said: "Oh no, I've never seen him meself. But me father told me the man's been wandering the forests for fifty years. But he's quite harmless you know—but some do fear him because of his strange behavior."

When the man spoke of how the stranger had wandered the forests for more than fifty years, Sean thought *I'm thinking my fellow's a spry sort for someone that old.*

One woman told Sean: "He comes by quite regularly, you know. I suppose he comes round here about every six or eight months and we give him food and then he's off again. My husband doesn't like it one bit and he doesn't want the man about. But no, I don't know where you can find him. I know of no one who can tell us where he comes from or where he goes."

Another man said he knew a man who had been told by someone else that the odd fellow had been a well-respected, wealthy, scholarly barrister in Philadelphia. However, when his wife ran off to France with another man and she took their two children with her, he abandoned everything—his home and law practice—and simply disappeared.

Sean heard many stories about the man, but was discouraged for the lack of success in his quest for the unusual visitor.

One day he rode to North East to speak again with Fian regarding the man. However, when he arrived at the ship the captain was at the foot of the gangplank sitting on a barrel.

"Hello Sean, what brings you here today?" asked the captain.

"Hello to you Captain. I've come to question Fian about the strange fellow that came about. You told me that he seemed to know something about the man and maybe he'll remember more if I can talk with him."

"Here's what I have to say of that, Sean. Fian's gone to the smith with some iron that needed to be worked on and he'll be gone awhile. But I'm glad you came, because we need to talk "

"Talk?" asked Sean. "I'm thinking that I know where your conversation would be headed and I'm not willing Captain."

"Not willing Sean? That's just what you'll need to be willing to do. Sean, this isn't just about my niece, it's more about Nathan than anyone— Nathan and you Sean."

"Isn't that what I said Captain—that I know where you're headed? You're thinking to lay this burden of mine for caring for Nathan at the doorstep of your niece and show me how it all works together for the good of each of us. And I tell you Captain, I'll hold for none of that talk."

"And tell me, Sean, when did you learn to read my mind—or the mind of anyone? I'll tell you Sean, you can't deny that I'm right when I say that you don't even know your own mind."

Sean did not respond, but turned to walk away.

"Don't allow the truth to take the wind from your sails, lad," the captain said. "And don't leave the company of a friend who is only speaking the truth."

Sean stopped dead in his tracks and turned to glare at the captain.

"Am I wrong, Sean? If I'm wrong, all there is to do is tell me and I'll say no more."

Sean's look softened and after a few moments he responded.

"You aren't wrong, Captain. You're as right as the North Star. It's been four years, Captain, since I lost my Julia and . . ."

"Set it right, Sean," the captain interrupted. "Julia was lost to all of us, not only you. Her mother lost her daughter and your son lost his mother. Sean, you're not the only one with a sorrowful heart."

"I know that, Captain. That's a part of my confusion. I see everyone else going on with their lives and it has confused me. Why do I have such trouble going on with my life?"

"There's where you have to find your answer, Sean. You must find your answer for your life, but you cannot do so without including your son. I know you Sean, and you're not a man to abandon that responsibility to your son. I love Nathan as much as Cynthia does, but we're each day getting older. We cannot take responsibility for Nathan as you can Sean. And you need a woman's influence in your life and Nathan needs the love of a mother."

"All right, Captain. Stop it right where we are. You're coming around to your niece again."

"I can't deny that she's my niece, Sean. But would the oceans go dry if you were to but call her by her name? It's Sarah, Sean."

"I know her name, Captain. What I don't know is why everyone seems to be pushing me into a corner over this matter."

"Everyone Sean, and who might be pushing you lad? You know that's not my way, but I'm able to push if I need to and you know that as well. Here's all I'm asking—give Sarah the good manners of being kind. Acknowledge her when she's about, Sean. It'll do you no harm and it would do the rest of us a great deal of good."

"Then Captain, would this go well with you? I'll do as you ask, but first I must follow this belief I have that the odd stranger is the one I'm to help as the Welshman charged me to do."

"So, now it's a charge is it, Sean?" the captain asked smiling. "Follow it through then lad. I'm thinking that you'll soon see the right thing to do and I'll be pleased with that, knowing that it will satisfy you as well."

Sean mounted his horse he said, "And that's what I want Captain, to do the right thing."

As he rode slowly back toward Dawn Light he recalled those days long ago when the cousins, Ethan and Edward Tubbs, would sit on the porch in the dwindling evening light and read the Scriptures; and he remembered that one special night.

I long for the quiet counsel of those men. Ethan and Edward, such humble men. Never pushing themselves and almost hesitant to mention the importance of God lest I should be offended. Imagine—that I should become offended because they wanted me to know how God loved me. Oh Lord, what have I become that I would sit judging another such as Sarah? It's easier to say her name to you, Lord, than to speak her own name before the woman. What was it that Ethan read from the Bible that night I gave myself to you and you saved me Lord? It was something about how we're to give graciously just as you have provided for us—just as you've provided for me. Bu I've lost so much, I've lost my Julia. But, haven't I gained much as well? I have Nathan and Dawn Light and . . . oh Lord, you're so patient. Help me. Lord. I must find that Scripture in Julia's Bible.

That night Sean prayed as he had never prayed before. On his face he pled to God for forgiveness for every sin and shortcoming he could bring to his mind. Tears flowed from his eyes until none were left to fall upon the floor and still he prayed asking for God's leading in his life. He prayed even when the candle sputtered and there was no light—and he awoke with sun shining through the window and he stood to his feet.

Strangely he felt no stiffness or soreness from lying on the floor and he sensed a vitality he had not known for years. Without bothering to wash up or groom himself he went outside, saddled his horse and rode to the Murphy's.

Chapter Nineteen

Julia's Bible

"Oh, what a pleasant surprise, Sean," Cynthia said. "We didn't expect you this morning. Will you stay to eat?"

"And a very good morning to you, Cynthia—it's a fine morning indeed."

Missy and Sarah were outside in the summer kitchen. They had heard Sean's voice and Missy said, "Bes' be goin' inside, Miz Cynthia could be she need help."

"I'll stay with you," Sarah replied, blushing, "And we'll finish these cakes together."

Missy turned her back so Sarah couldn't see her smiling.

"Cynthia," Sean continued, "can you tell me where Julia's Bible is? I must have it."

"Certainly, Sean, I can get it for you. But can it wait until after we've shared a fine breakfast with you?"

Just then Nathan came bursting into the room.

"Daddy! I knew it was you, I heard you when you rode up."

Sean reached under Nathan's arms and lifted him into the air.

"How good it is to see you, Son. I can tell that your grandmother has been feeding you very well—far better than you've had when you stay with me at Dawn Light. You're getting as tall as a tree and as heavy as a barrel of rocks."

"A barrel of rocks? I'm not that heavy, Father—am I?"

"No," Sean laughed, "but a well-fed young seaman you are indeed."

Then, turning back to Cynthia Sean said, "Yes, of course, Cynthia. I'll be grateful for some good Murphy fare and I'll wait until you're able to get the Bible."

"What's all of this uproar about—have we been boarded by pirates?" the captain demanded as he strode into the room.

"There are no pirates, Grandfather—it's my father and we're the ones who are making so much noise."

"Oh well," said the captain, "then we've nothing to fear. But to be on the safe side, I'd say we'd do well to hide the food if your father's about."

"Now, Laird," chided Cynthia. "We've talked of this before. Young ears do not always know when we speak in jest."

"Oh, I have young ears Grandmother. And I know that we are simply having a good time together. Isn't that so Father?"

Before Sean could respond, Missy walked into the room followed by Sarah. They carried fried corn cakes that were still steaming and hot tea and Sean was sure he smelled ham as well.

"Bes' be eatin' 'fore cakes be getting' all cold an' greasy," Missy ordered.

"Ah yes, greasy," said the captain. "Just as a good seaman would have his cakes—cold and greasy."

Everyone laughed except Missy and Sarah as they sat down to eat. Before anyone had finished, Cynthia excused herself and the captain and Sean talked about the weather and how cold the next winter might be. Sarah chatted with Nathan and one time when she stole a quick glance at Sean their eyes met and both quickly looked away.

Cynthia walked back into the room and asked, "Has anyone seen Julia's Bible? I seem to have misplaced it.'

"Oh no, Aunt Cynthia," Sarah said. "Do you not recall? I asked if there was a Bible about, because I enjoy reading to Nathan from the Scriptures—and you gave me Julia's to read. It's in my room."

"You mean that it's in my mother's room, Miss Sarah," Nathan said, correcting her.

Sean smiled and Sarah corrected herself, "Of course, Nathan. It's in your mother's room, but it's the room where I have been sleeping and we've played together—isn't it?"

"Oh, thank you Sarah," Cynthia said relieved. "I had forgotten that I gave you the Bible—now—would you mind fetching the Bible for Sean? He wants to do some reading as well."

"Of course," Sarah replied. "I'll get it at once."

Sarah returned with the Bible and began to hand it to Cynthia.

"Oh, please dear," Cynthia said, "just give the Bible to Sean."

She walked to the other side of the table to give the Bible to Sean and almost dropped it in surprise when Sean smiled and said, "Thank you, Miss Sarah. It's good to know that Julia's Bible has been in good hands and has been used for such good purpose. Thank you."

"You're welcome, Sarah replied. "I am pleased that you were not offended by my use of her Bible. I know it must be a very precious remembrance to you."

"It is," Sean agreed, but not wishing to extend the dialogue further.

The conversation around the breakfast table suddenly ended with Missy's grumbling comment, "Not ever bodies gets to sits 'roun eatin' and talkin'—some uns bes' be cleanin' up." And the women began to clear the table.

Sean took Nathan back to Dawn Light and spent the day playing with him and looking for the passage of Scripture that Ethan Tubbs had used.

Later that morning Cynthia sat in her room sewing intricate flower patterns along the edges of a handkerchief, when there was a light knock on the door.

"Come in," she said.

The door opened, Sarah peered around it and said, "I wasn't sure if you were resting—may I come in?"

"Of course—come sit here next to me."

Sarah sat down and noticing the flowers that Cynthia was sewing said, "How beautiful. And your handwork is so particular and exact. The tiny flowers make one believe that they should have the beautiful aroma of a garden full of blooms."

"Why, thank you Sarah. I hadn't thought they were quite that beautiful, but it is pleasantly relaxing for me to sew this way. Even though I must concentrate, it somehow allows me to think matters through as well. I must teach you some of these stitches. Perhaps you would enjoy it as well. Julia appreciated the beauty of such handwork, but only if someone else did the sewing." Cynthia smiled as she spoke her daughter's name.

"Yes, perhaps one day you could teach me some of these petite stitches. One wonders how it can be done when the needle appears larger than the flowers you're stitching."

"You haven't come to learn of sewing today, have you Sarah?"

"No Aunt Cynthia. I have come seeking your guidance."

"Guidance—guidance in what matter, Sarah?"

"I am embarrassed to say it Aunt, but I am mortified concerning my very overt and forward actions yesterday with Sean."

"And when did that occur dear?"

"It was when I brought Julia's Bible to him. I was so unconcealed regarding the way I feel toward him. Didn't you notice?"

"Why yes, dear. Of course I noticed. But I'm a woman and I doubt that it was all that obvious to Sean—he's a man and they're not nearly as keen at making such observations."

"Oh please, Aunt, don't mock me in this way. You say you did notice how forward I was—then you did find it distasteful—didn't you?"

"I wouldn't mock you dear—and distasteful? My dear Sarah," Cynthia began as she lay her sewing aside. "However could such chaste and blameless manners be considered distasteful?"

"Is this true?" Sarah asked, shocked by Cynthia's response.

"Of course it's true. You've told me of your father's kindness and your husband's cruelty and you've become confused. You've been unable to know how you should regard someone like Sean. Although he's a kind and gentle man, somehow—for whatever reason—he seems to treat you more as an adversary than a friend. And Sarah, I think Sean doesn't know why this should be and I can only presume why he should behave in such a manner."

"Then what do you mean when you say 'he's a man'? Does that relieve me of my shame?"

"There's no shame in being a woman, dear Sarah. Quite the contrary is more the truth. God has blessed us beyond that which we sometimes care to accept. And Sarah, I must be very decided in advising you that you must shed this cloak of shame that you have placed on yourself and only you can truly remove. Sarah, I insist that you must take upon yourself the gift of womanhood that God has blessed you with. Accept that gift—that capacity for deep and abiding love—and live your life. Remember what I've told you before? You have a new life to live—now you must live it."

Elizabeth Dixon had sent Ben over to Dawn Light to invite Sean and Nathan for the evening meal.

"I know you'll think my mind is going awry again Ben," Sean said. "But I have an important task to complete today. Please give your wife my thanks, but we'll have to decline on this day."

"Can I go to Dixons to play with Annie, Daddy?"

"I think not, this isn't . . . ."

"Come now, Sean," Ben said. "Nathan can ride home with me and sleep with us, then you come by the house in the morning for a breakfast and you can fetch Nathan then."

"Will that suit Elizabeth?" Sean asked.

"It will go well with all of us. Come on Nathan, let's get back for supper," Ben said. Then he pulled Nathan up behind him.

Sean watched as they rode off and thought: *What provisions God has given me. A son, friends who hesitate at nothing just so they can care for us—how fortunate a man I am. Now I'll find those verses in the Bible I've searched for.*

He went inside, lit two candles, sat at the small eating table and opened Julia's Bible.

Lord, he prayed silently, *I have no idea where those verses are. But it's your word Lord, so please help me search out and find what I'm looking for. Thank you God, Amen.*

Sean sat there for several minutes with his eyes closed, remembering that night just a few short years ago with Ethan and Edward Tubbs when he had said something like:

> "Why haven't I seen this before? Why should God be so good to me? I've done so little for others. But I purpose in my heart to give just as the Bible says, because God has given me so much, including this very place of my birth, Dawn Light."

Oh my, reflected Sean, *when I purposed in my heart I was making a pledge to God, as much—no much more—than the promise I made to the Welshman. I've not done well at keeping the vows I've made.*

Sean flipped the pages of the Bible toward the New Testament when his eye suddenly fell on the words: *"He which soweth sparingly shall reap also sparingly; and he which soweth bountifully shall reap also bountifully."*

"This is it, then!" Sean shouted aloud. "This is it, let me see—certainly, this is it. Second Corinthians, chapter 9, beginning right here in verse 6."

151

Then Sean read on and when he came to verse 13 he could almost hear the voice of Ethan Tubbs saying: "They received the *'unspeakable gift'* God provided through His only Son, Jesus. And Sean, God has His hand upon you at this very time and wants you to receive His gift now, before it's eternally too late."

Sean thought, *My Lord, but haven't you been good to me? How could I be so neglectful of remembering how I prayed, confessed my sin and need for you, then confessed you as my Savior and from that very moment my life was changed for the good—forever.*

Sean reread the passage from 2 Corinthians several times. Then he prayed again and sat there alone thinking, until one of the candles began to sputter.

That candle's a sign for certain, Sean thought. *The life that God lit in me through Jesus Christ had surely begun to sputter—no, it's been sputtering for some time. And God's given me so many reminders to fan the flame and I've turned my back—oh, forgive me Lord. Help me relight this candle that's been all but snuffed out and give me a fresh start.*

Sean climbed the narrow stairs to his room. He chose the floor for sleeping instead of the bed. Somehow he felt that if he could but relive some of the discomfort of the wilderness that perhaps he would begin to understand how God wanted him to face his new candle-lit life.

As he laid himself down, he laughed out loud at the strange thoughts he'd had of discomfort somehow being able to help him continue on with his life.

The floor was hard and unyielding, but Sean spent the best night of sleep since returning home.

CHAPTER TWENTY

Will o' the Wisp

"Hello the house," Sean shouted as he approached the Dixons.

The words were barely out of Sean's mouth when Nathan came bounding from the house.

"Daddy? May I stay and spend the day?"

"Wait now, son," replied Sean as he dismounted. "Let's have me a hug and then I'll be deciding where we'll be spending this day."

"It's fine with us if you'd like him to stay the day, Sean," Elizabeth said as she stepped onto the porch. "But for now, come in and we'll have a good warm breakfast."

After visiting at the table for a while, Sean excused himself.

"I'll be riding to the Murphy's," Sean said, "to attend to an important matter and I'll return for Nathan before dark—and, no I'm not making a bad attempt to gain another meal."

They all laughed but Elizabeth said, "You know there's always a place at our table for you Sean. Then we'll see you later in the day."

Sean had decided to face things straightaway today. He felt that the night's sleep and thoughts he had been considering all morning had now materialized into a definite plan. However, the closer he came to the captain's house, the more he felt uncertain about his *definite* plan.

As the house came into view Sean reined the horse in and had decided to turn about and ride off when he heard Missy call out, "Mas' Sean be comin'."

It was too late to retreat now, because the captain came out to the porch and shouted, "Come sit, Sean. I'm in need of a man's talk, all I've heard this morning is the chatter of the hens."

"Be hens chatterin' cause don' be no rooster about," Missy said in her best loud mumble.

"You have work to do, Missy," the captain ordered. "Now go do it and leave us alone—but bring us water and some corn cakes before you get out of my sight."

Sean went to the side of the house and hobbled the horse so it could graze where it wanted. Then he went to the front porch and took a seat with the captain.

"It's good to see you this day, Sean." The captain offered. "I was wondering if the talk we had a few days back would keep us quiet for a time."

Sean grinned and said, "I don't think so, Captain. I think that even if we were to have a brawl it wouldn't much do anything to splinter our friendship. We're Irish and we benefit from a good fight now and again is what I say. Besides, we're not men that keep what we want to say locked away—are we?"

"Aye, Sean, agreed," the captain laughed. "That's the sort of friend that's for my liking."

"You know Captain, I've been puzzling over this matter of doing the bidding of the Welshman—or let me put it another way—because it's not the Welshman as much as it's me that made the vow to him."

"Your anchors dragging and you're drifting in circles, Sean. What are you saying? Make it plain for me."

"That's what I aim to do, and I'll make it as plain as I can say it for myself and that will have to do for you as well, Captain."

Just then Missy returned and placed two mugs of spring water and corn cakeson the small table next to the captain.

"Very well, Missy. And I do thank you from my seafaring rooster's heart."

Sean hadn't heard the earlier exchange about hens and roosters and he just smiled and continued while the captain bit into a corn cake.

Determining...

"You remember, Captain," Sean went on, "how you insisted that your niece . . . ."

"Her name's Sarah," the captain interrupted.

"Yes, yes," Sean replied in an annoyed tone, "I know that her name's Sarah. I explained what Morgan Glasfryn had explained to me about helping someone who was unable to help himself—the so-called person in need—and you insisted most fervidly that Sarah was that person in my life who was in need."

The captain took a long drink of water to wash his fried cake down and said, "The very words I used, Sean. Sarah is a person in great need, one of those who the Welshman would say was unable to help himself—or I should say herself."

"I didn't want to hear anything about tending to the needs of a woman and then, that very day, I came across the strange man—that odd sort who had been lurking about Dawn Light. I immediately took that as a notice—perhaps from God himself—that this fellow, who was unable to care for himself—couldn't even speak—that he was surely the person in need that I must help."

"Well then, Sean O'Connell, how would you say that pursuit has gone? What have you done with that poor soul?"

"You know the answer, Captain. He's like a *Will o' the Wisp*."

"I've heard tell of Will," the captain said thoughtfully. "Not a fellow you'd want as a friend, eh Sean?"

"You're right you are, Captain," agreed Sean. "As a lad, when my mother died and I went to live with my aunt, her maiden sister—there was a bog near her cottage. Her Scottish neighbor's child told me to never go near the bog. In the gloaming[16] if you would dare to walk near the bog, sometimes a dim and flickering light could be seen. It would seem to come close to you then flit away, darting from side to side and at times it appeared to beckon you. They called it *Will o' th' Wisp* and it was thought that Will would lead children off into the bog and they'd never be seen again."

"I've heard the very stories myself," repeated the captain, "and I've no reason to doubt those who've told me."

"What I've come to is this, Captain. This very strange man that I have sought so that I might fulfill his needs—well, I'd as soon be chasing after *Will o' th' Wisp*. Even those who have seen him most frequently have no plan for making a well man of him, and why should I think that I could?"

"Now I'm hearing some sense coming from you, Sean. I agree that you can't really help him."

"Well, maybe you're right—but maybe I could have been of some help to him. I did help him. But he was helped only long enough to need more help. All of his life, it seems to me, others have thought they've been helping him too, when all they've done is keep him living the same pitiful life he's always known."

"Aye, Sean," the captain agreed. "Pitiful it is, indeed."

"But Captain," Sean insisted, "more pitiable am I than that poor fellow. You see, Captain, I've used him as an excuse for refusing to give aid one that I can help—Sarah. So, Captain, I'm prepared to do something about it."

"I've known all along you'd see the light of day on this matter, Sean," the captain said emphatically. "Now, how is it that I can help with this—or should we talk to Cynthia about the matter. We both know that women have the mind for these matters of the heart."

"Matters of the heart?" Sean asked in unbelief. "I don't know what you have in mind, but I'm talking of asking Sarah to be a companion for Nathan. I'll pay her handsomely as soon as I'm able to secure some . . . ."

"Companion for Nathan?" the captain shouted as he stood. "Sean O'Connell, I thought we had an understanding in this matter."

The captain stormed into the house leaving Sean seated alone on the porch.

Much as I admire the man, thought Sean, *I'm not sure I'm able to understand him at all times.*

Then he recovered his horse and rode off.

"And what was the disturbance about Laird?" Cynthia asked as the captain strode into the kitchen.

"About? It's about that Sean of yours, that's what it's about."

"Oh dear," replied Cynthia in pretence of shock. "Then he's *my* Sean and not ours?"

"I'll not say I don't admire that man, but I'm not sure I understand him."

Cynthia smiled without even knowing that what the captain had said was almost exactly what Sean had been thinking of the captain.

"Now Laird," Cynthia began calmly, "I dare say that could be said of any of us, couldn't it? Although I'll admit that perhaps it's more often by some of us than others."

"Now, don't think I'm not understanding what you're about woman—but the man is hard as a barnacle at times."

"Yes dear, of course," Cynthia replied, smiling as she walked from the room. "Imagine that—someone being hard as a barnacle."

When Sean returned to Dawn Light he spent the remainder of the day busying himself with small tasks he had been forestalling. He was picking up small branches that had broken from trees during storms to use as kindling when he had a strangely familiar feeling—the sort of sensation that had often alerted him while in the wilderness.

Someone was watching him but he continued picking up branches until he came to a stout, straight stick that would do well as a shillelagh. He picked it up and struck the ground to test its soundness then stood upright and looked about.

At first, seeing nothing, he thought his imagination might be deceiving him. Then he saw him— the odd stranger stepped from the shadow of a large poplar.

Sean called, "Here now, you! What have I told you of skulking about?"

This time, rather than running off, the man began to walk toward Sean.

"Hold right there," Sean said as he raised the stick menacingly. He was now within ten feet and even from that distance the man's obnoxious odor was evident.

The man stopped and extended his hands to his sides with the palms up in a passive stance. Then he shocked Sean—"I saw you. You sought me."

Sean was certain that he was dreaming. The man had never spoken to him before, and from countless testimonies he had heard while searching for the man, no one else had ever heard him speak either.

Sean recovered and lowered the stick. "I thought you couldn't speak."

"I can, but I seldom do," the man said, "and only when I choose to do so.

"And what reason could you have for this silent way of yours?" Sean asked. "And why should you choose to speak to me?"

"My reason is my reason. I've neither need nor desire to express myself to others. And I care not to explain. Seldom have I encountered man or woman who sought my benefit as you have. I find that most simply chase me off—and that suits me you see, even if my presence and ways are not acceptable and perhaps disgusting to others."

"Very well, but why speak to me?"

"For this cause only, I've seen you about—no, I've seen you looking for me in many places. You seem driven to help me, but I tell you that you're released from whatever vow or promise you may have made to help such as me. Today I've come for this purpose only. I tell you that I choose my life, no one drives me to it and none is able to take it from me. I know you by your name, Sean O'Connell, and I thank you for your kind purpose. But understand this, if you tell anyone that we have spoken, no one would believe you so these things are best kept to ourselves. We'll never meet again."

The man turned and walked off in the direction from which he had arrived.

"Wait," Sean began, but as soon as he spoke the man started to run and was quickly out of sight in the forest.

What has happened? Sean asked himself as he looked about to be certain he was alone. *Am I bewitched? Others—no, everyone—agree that the man is unable to speak. And yet he has spoken to me. And he released me from a vow, by whose authority? And a vow of which he should have no knowledge. Was this something sinister Lord, or has this been a visitation from you?*

Sean went to the spring, rinsed his face and head with the cold water. He looked all about to see if the man could be seen, and seeing no one he then saddled the horse and rode to the Dixon house to fetch Nathan.

Along the way he tried his best to consider what to do. *Must I tell others of this experience, or take the advice of the nameless, strange, supposedly speechless fellow. He spoke as a well-educated, intelligent man. And I think that surely he was right. As he said, even if I were to tell someone—no one would believe this strange occurrence.*

Sean decided that for now silence would serve him best.

—— CHAPTER TWENTY-ONE ——

Sarah's Cottage

The following morning Sean awoke to the sound of Nathan's voice.

"Father, Father! Wake up, I'm hungry. Is there something to eat?"

Sean still had not accustomed himself to sleeping on a bed and as he rolled over toward the sound of his son's voice he stretched, then rubbed his eyes. The sun was just beginning to rise and light was drifting into the room.

"Not so loud son—I'm right here, not down the path somewhere. We've some jerky in the sideboard downstairs, but I'm thinking that we'll ride over to Grandmother's and have a good meal."

"All right, Daddy, but hurry, I'm hungry."

Sean grabbed Nathan by the arm and pulled him down to the floor where he had been sleeping, tickled him until Nathan squealed. Then hugging his son tightly, Sean wondered if Nathan knew how deeply he felt toward him.

"We'll go as soon as you help me with my boots, so be quick about it if you're so hungry."

Cynthia was returning from the summer kitchen and heard the horse coming. She stepped to the side of the house and saw Nathan just as he saw her.

Nathan waved, "Grandmother it's Father and me. We came to have breakfast."

"I'm not at all surprised to know that," Cynthia replied laughing. "You two seem to know when the food is ready here at the Murphy house."

Nathan jumped from the horse and took the reins. "I'll take him to the water, Daddy. Shall I hobble him? I can do it well, just as you've taught me."

"That would be fine, but be sure the hobble is secure so he doesn't wander off."

Everyone seemed in a pleasant mood and Sean was glad that the captain displayed no annoyance with having him at the table this morning.

Nathan had been right—he was hungry, very hungry, and had to be cautioned by his Grandmother to eat more slowly.

During a lull in the conversation, Sean blurted out, "I had an unusual surprise yesterday."

"A surprise Father, is it for me?"

"It wasn't that sort of surprise, Nathan."

"Well," Cynthia said, "I'm waiting to hear all about this unusual surprise."

"Aye, as we all are," added the captain.

Sean didn't know where to begin, because he recalled what the man had said about no one believing him, but felt that he had to risk telling them and was comfortable doing so with the captain and Cynthia.

"You'll find this a hard thing to believe," Sean began. "Yesterday, I had a visitor."

"A visitor, you didn't tell me you had a visitor, Daddy."

"Hush, now Nathan," Cynthia said. "Let your father tell us what he will."

Sean continued, "The visitor was the strange fellow I've been seeking."

"You mean he just showed up to visit you?" the captain asked.

"Just as you say, Captain," responded Sean. "Now here's that part of the visit that might cause you to think I'm mad—the man spoke to me."

A stunned silence filled the air.

Seeing the surprised looks, Sean continued. "I sense your astonishment, but no one was more amazed than I."

"Tell us, Sean," insisted the captain. "What in blazes is this all about?"

"Laird," admonished Cynthia, "don't be using such speech with Nathan present."

"It's all right, Grandmother. Sometimes Fian says 'blazes,' and some other words I don't know."

"Laird," Cynthia snapped as she glared at the captain, "I expect that you'll attend to this."

"Very well," the captain said, "but let's hear it now, Sean."

"I'll tell you this—it was a worrisome meeting. The man spoke like a person of high rank. I tell you it was a startling thing—not only to hear the man's voice—but the manner of his speech was a grand thing I tell you."

"No Sean," said the captain, "now don't be telling me that who you're mentioning is the filthy smelling man who's never spoke a word to you."

"The same, Captain. And you can be sure that I was more amazed than you that I'm telling it to. The man spoke with such high-tone speech that you might think you were in the presence of royalty—not that I've ever been. But, I tell you it was an experience I could never forget. I could smell the stench of him from 10 or 15 feet away—and I was upwind. But when he opened his mouth it was as though an angel from above spoke to me."

"Oh my, Cynthia said, "an angel—do you believe it Sean?"

"I wouldn't say that he wasn't, Cynthia. After he left I wondered as much. But I'll have to say I also wondered if he was a demon. He knew my name and called me by it."

"That's not a strange thing, Sean," said the captain. "You're well known about here."

"Aye, Captain. That's true enough—but . . ." Sean paused as if wondering whether to make his next statement.

"But Captain, he knew of my vow to the Welshman."

"Again, Sean, that's well-known enough."

"Captain, he then gave me permission to be released from the vow I've made to help such as him."

"Such nonsense and bilge water is what I'm hearing now, Sean," the captain declared.

"I think not. It's not idle talk Captain, not at all, for I've pondered this occurrence and I take it as a sign. Not that I would break my promise to the Welshman, but only as a sign to change my course. Somehow the man knew I was being driven to help someone and he saw the cut of my sail, as you would say. And, whether he knew it or not, he helped me to see more clearly the path I must follow."

"And what clear path might that be?" Cynthia asked.

"Trapped by my own words, I've been," Sean replied with a grin. "I should have been saying that it's only that I see there *is* a path. And maybe I see it a wee bit more clearly now than I had before."

Once again there was a pause in the conversation and that led Sean to continue.

"You know, the man also told me I'd do well to speak to no one of this. And with good reason, because he said that no one would believe me even if I did tell someone." Sean laughed at that and the others smiled politely.

Then Sean said, "I think he may have been right. I'll have to be thinking more on this—and Captain, you and I must continue our discussion."

Sarah, who had been sitting silently taking in the remarkable conversation and trying to understand then said: "But isn't it sad, that you won't see him again? And it does seem that he needs help—as many of us do." Then she looked down at her folded hands that lay in her lap.

Cynthia reached out and placed her hand on Sarah's.

"You're right dear," Cynthia began, "many of us need help. We need much help—oh we need so very much help. In fact, I dare say that no matter who we might be or what our circumstance, we all need assistance of one kind or another. Wouldn't you agree—Laird—Sean?"

"It's something to consider," said the captain. And Sean shook his head in affirmation.

Sean hadn't planned things this way, but it seemed to be an obvious time of transition that gave him a natural opportunity to present Sarah with his offer.

"Sarah, I trust that you'll excuse my boldness, but I wish to speak with you about an important matter. And, because we are all here together, I feel you may be more at ease in speaking with me in the presence of these. May I do so with your permission?"

Sarah looked at the captain and then at Cynthia as if expecting some sort of confirmation from them.

Understanding the expression of Sarah's face, Cynthia responded. "I've no idea what you may have in mind Sean, but I'm sure that Sarah will be free from anxiety to speak with you in our presence—am I right dear?" she asked, looking at Sarah.

"Why, yes. I imagine so, please do so Sean," Sarah replied.

With a glance at the captain, Sean began. "Sarah, I would begin by asking your forgiveness for the many times I have behaved rudely and in poor manner with you. When I returned from the wilderness and found you here with my son I was offended without reason. And I fear that lacking common sense I treated you as a foe rather than a friend and behaved more as a rogue animal than a man. Please forgive me."

Looking back into her lap Sarah answered, "Of course Sean, I understand. And yes, of course, I forgive you." Then looking directly at Sean she added, "And I am pleased to know that you no longer consider me an enemy." Then she looked back down into her lap.

"Well now, I'd say that clears the air for a good sail," the captain said.

"Laird," admonished Cynthia, "we're observers, not participants in this conversation."

"I thank you for your kindness in forgiving me," Sean continued, "and I must tell you how grateful I am that you and Nathan get on so well. You must know that I am not well suited to raise a young boy by myself. And while Cynthia and the Captain have provided a measureless and meaningful influence in Nathan's life, I cannot expect them to continue to disrupt their lives to accommodate me or relieve me of my responsibility to my son."

"Oh Sean, please don't think that . . ." Cynthia began.

"Observers, woman, we're observers," reproved the captain.

"So, here is what I would ask of you. Because you have developed a strong union with Nathan and because you already spend much time with him—would you be willing to consider serving as his companion, caregiver and teacher. Of course, for this I would expect to pay you a sum that we would agree upon."

The captain couldn't contain himself. "Look here, Sean, this is my brother's own daughter you're speaking to. Do you think she's for hire like a common laborer?"

Before Cynthia could add her perspective, Sarah answered.

"Please, Uncle, I take no offense in this at all—quite the contrary. And if I may say this intending no offense, I love young Nathan as if he were my own and would consider it an honor to care for Nathan as you ask, Sean. The only difficulty I would observe would be the matter of how this might come about."

"Come about?" asked Sean.

"Well yes," replied Sarah. "We are unmarried and it would serve propriety poorly if I were to live at Dawn Light." She paused to see the reaction of the others before continuing.

"And yet, if Nathan and I were to remain here with my aunt and uncle, it seems that you would remain in the same sort of situation with your son that you now find yourself. Have you considered such matters?"

Everyone but Nathan seemed shocked at the ready thoughtfulness of Sarah's response.

"I have, Sarah," Sean responded, "and I admit that I was only thinking of my convenience and had not given thought to your concerns. Again, I must apologize for lacking the good sense to consider you and your respectability."

"I'd say you lack more than sense, Sean O'Connell," the captain commented sarcastically.

"Now Laird," Cynthia said, "enough of such talk. Sarah and I will have many things to discuss concerning this matter, and she will make her own appropriate decision in her own time. Will that be suitable, Sean?"

"Oh yes," Sean responded. "And thank you—all of you. Yes, of course, an appropriate decision will have to be made, and in your time, Sarah. Now, if you'll excuse me I have some work needing my attention."

Sean left in a hurry, mainly because he was embarrassed over not considering the situation that Sarah had brought for their consideration.

Riding back to Dawn Light he thought: *She's a different woman than I've thought her to be, a woman who seems to have a very clear and clever means of observing things. Yes, a very quick wit and with deep understanding—a rather fine woman indeed. Strange it is that I should not have noticed that about her much earlier.*

For several days following, Sean made a point of visiting the Murphy home daily to see his son. Everyone agreed that until Sean could establish himself comfortably back into Dawn Light and some good plan might be determined for him and his son that it would be best for Nathan to stay with his grandparents. Sarah was pleased with this arrangement and so was Nathan—most of the time. However, every time Sean would leave the Murphy household Nathan wanted to return to Dawn Light with him.

Sean started his day before dawn because he was determined that some arrangement needed to be made other than the one that kept Nathan with the captain and Cynthia with him making daily trips to visit his son. He felt that if the Dixons would feed him this morning that he could also obtain some good advice on his next step.

"Hello the house," Sean shouted as he rode up to the Dixon's front porch.

Ben came from the house rubbing his eyes as though he had just gotten out of bed. "What time of day do you think we eat around here?" Ben said.

Sean laughed and pointed toward the east and said, "Well, it looks as though the sun knows it's time to arise, and I imagine that Elizabeth knows it as well."

Elizabeth walked up behind Ben. She was wiping her hands on her ever present apron and made an announcement. "Breakfast is just now ready for all within sound of my voice. That means you, Sean, and I'll even include this husband of mine who just now rolled from his bed."

Sean always enjoyed the table talk at the Dixons. Ben and Sean laughed and made good-natured, light complaints about one another, and Elizabeth served as a good mediator. Annie always had questions to ask about Nathan. "When will we be able to play riddles again, Mother? Could Nathan come to the house today?"

"We'll see, Annie," Elizabeth responded, "Now you eat your food."

"Sean," began Ben, "we both know how much you like Elizabeth's cooking, but I'm thinking that you have more than food on the mind this morning."

"You're right, Ben. It's about the matter of my son. Last week I had a discussion with Sarah about serving as a companion to Nathan and . . . ."

"Let me stop you there," Elizabeth interrupted. "Sean I've spoken with Cynthia and Sarah about this matter and I suggested an arrangement to them that seemed as though it might be acceptable—although they hadn't shared the matter with the captain."

"Seems that you were about to ask the wrong person's opinion about the matter, Sean," Ben added.

"What sort of arrangement did you suggest Elizabeth?" Sean asked.

"Well, we certainly agreed that it would be unacceptable for Sarah to live in the house with you and Nathan and that continuing on with the Murphy's would not be a suitable solution either."

"Yes, yes, wife," Ben prompted, "then what did you come to?"

"This may not strike you as a possibility Sean, but both Cynthia and Sarah thought that it could be done. It's a rather simple solution. If you were to make some improvements to the house where Samson and his family lived, that could provide Sarah with comfort, the ability to live separately from you and Nathan, and yet be conveniently close enough to perform the service you have requested of her in caring for and teaching Nathan."

"Oh, could he Mr. O'Connell," Annie squealed. "Could Nathan come and live close by?"

Sean sat silently for several seconds and then said, "I suppose that would be possible, but only if I were to alter that small structure and—and this could be the real difficulty—only if the captain would be in agreement."

Elizabeth smiled knowingly. "That," she said, "should be no problem at all, because both Cynthia and Sarah will have already spoken to the captain. I assure you that together they could prove to be very convincing and by now I would guess that the captain himself has found them quite persuasive as well."

Ben and Sean then spoke at length regarding what might be needed to repair the small home so that it would serve as an acceptable accommodation for Sarah.

"Seems quite suitable to me," Sean said. "But Ben, before you and I take hammer and nail to Samson's house, the first nail I need nail down is with the captain and then hope that he doesn't take the hammer to me."

They all laughed at that thought and then Sean excused himself and rode off to see the captain.

"It's as Cynthia and Sarah explained to me," Captain Murphy said, "there's nothing improper in that sort of arrangement. Mind you now Sean, I'll not say I was interested in their design and it's not my choosing. But if my niece can be satisfied by it then I'll have to agree with her—and Cynthia of course."

"Of course Captain," Sean smiled. "I understand—and I agree with them both as well. I think we've done a fine thing to come to such a grand decision in this agreement, don't you Captain?"

"Take care lad," the captain warned, then under his breath continued. "I've agreed to this for the sake of a peaceable home, but I'll have nothing unseemly being carried about with my own brother's daughter. And I'll not be made sport for ridicule by anyone and that means you as well Sean."

"And on that Captain you'll find we're agreed," Sean assured him. "Nothing of the kind was in my mind."

"Then it's done," Captain Murphy announced. "When will this take place, when will it begin?"

"Ben and I have plans for Samson's little house," Sean said, "but we've not started because we needed to know how you would consider the situation. Now that you have assured me of your agreement, we'll begin tomorrow. The building was well kept by Kezie and Samson and although it's been abandoned for quite some time, we hope to have the cottage comfortable and ready for Sarah by sometime next week."

"Aye, Sean," the captain sighed, "comfortable and ready for Sarah. And Sean, it's my expectation that this is what will be the right decision for all."

Two weeks later the Dixons, Murphy's and even Missy joined Sean and Nathan to see to it that Sarah was properly moved in and contented in her new home in what had once been slave quarters.

As the others returned to their homes Sean thought: *I'd say it's a tidy cottage now and I might have done the same for the comfort of Samson, Kezie and their brood too. But I did nothing more than grant them wood for their dirt floor. There's much inequality in life and who am I that I'm able to change that?*

CHAPTER TWENTY-TWO

Hurry Cane

During the first weeks after Sarah accepted her new responsibilities as Nathan's caregiver, she stayed to herself in her little cottage during mealtime and prepared her own food. At other times of the day she would have Nathan come to her cottage or if the weather was fair she would go the main house and there they might play a game on the porch or she would read to him and ask him questions about what she had read.

Sarah borrowed books from Cynthia and with these she helped Nathan become familiar with nature and Cynthia's poetry, which she also enjoyed. Sarah insisted that any time they spent for entertainment, whether it would be a board game, riddles or some other pastime such as story telling, had to be followed by a form of learning, usually by asking Nathan question. Of course many of the pastimes were in themselves intended to teach.

Elizabeth Dixon had been providing simple small meals every few days for Sean and Nathan and one day Ben brought over a particularly pleasant looking meal. So Sean asked Sarah if she would care to join them for supper.

"I'm not sure that would be proper," Sarah said, "and I am certain the captain would not approve."

"Sarah," Sean began, "Captain Murphy and I have been friends since I first came to Maryland many years ago. We agree on many things—no I must say that we agree on most things much of the time and only occasionally have I found myself at odds with him—and then for but a brief time. So, I believe I can say this with confident honesty—I don't know whether the captain would approve or not."

Sean paused and then laughed heartily. It took Sarah a few seconds before she saw the humor in his statement, but then she smiled modestly.

"But Sarah, this is my home. And you are a mature, refined woman and I assure you that the meal you have with us will be so proper that you will risk falling asleep while we're eating because of dullness of the company you will be keeping."

Sarah's face colored slightly but she managed to stammer, "Very well, uh, thank you Sean. I, uh, that is I, well I accept your kind invitation and I feel certain that I will not fall asleep because of taking a meal with you and Nathan. In fact I would venture that it would be anything but dreary."

When she said that, she blushed with a rosy glow, embarrassed by her own forwardness.

"Oh good," squealed Nathan, "then we can play riddles, can't we Father?"

"Riddles?" Sean responded absent-mindedly, somewhat taken aback by Sarah's bold response. "Riddles—no I think not son—not tonight."

The meal sent by Elizabeth was delicious as might be expected. Her salt pork always had something of a sweet flavor and the hard beans that Dixons grew themselves along with her delicious fried corn cakes made for an enjoyable meal.

Nathan chattered as they ate, Sean responded with brief grunts, and Sarah scarcely took her eyes from her plate. All in all the dinner was a striking success, even though no one may have realized it at the time.

The next day at mid-morning Sarah came to the house to see Nathan, who was seated on the steps with his father.

"No, you can't come with me today Nathan," Sean was saying. "I have many miles to travel and I can't have you bouncing around behind my saddle all day long. In fact I may not be home until after dark."

Then looking up when he heard Sarah clearing her throat as she came from around the house Sean said, "Oh, good morning Sarah."

"Good morning to you Sean—and as Aunt Cynthia would say, a very gracious good morning to you Nathan. It appears that this will be a pleasant day for us to sit on the porch for our lessons, don't you think?"

"I don't want to do lessons today," Nathan complained sullenly. "I want to go with you Father."

"That's already been settled, Nathan. You'll do as I've said and I'll expect to have Miss Sarah tell me how well you've done today. Sarah, please just get Nathan ready for bed, because I may be quite late returning tonight."

"Yes, of course," she replied, "we'll do just as you suggest and we'll get along splendidly—shan't we Nathan?"

"Yes Miss Sarah, we shall."

"And just look at the beautiful sky in the east," Sarah said, "the clouds are all shades of scarlet and pink and changing colors more quickly than your eye can capture. Isn't it lovely Nathan?"

"Yes, Miss Sarah—it's lovely," he replied disinterestedly. "But Father may I help put the bridle on the horse?"

"All right then," Sean responded, "let's find that lazy horse of mine and see if we can get it ready for riding."

Sarah sat down on one of the porch chairs gazed at the eastern sky and breathed deeply of the clear air thinking: *Sometimes—like this morning—I feel as though my life is no more than a dream, living safely in Maryland, free of the fear I've known during my harsh marriage, and now loved and cared for by Uncle Laird and Aunt Cynthia—and Nathan too. If only my little one had lived,* she thought, *wouldn't that have been a fine thing—oh, wouldn't that have been fine?*

A tear made its way slowly down her cheek and she wiped it dry with the back of her hand just as Sean and Nathan rode around the corner of the house, with Nathan on the horse's neck, holding the reins.

Giving Nathan his arm, Sean swung him carefully to the ground.

"Just as I said now son," Sean reminded him, "your best behavior for Miss Sarah today. I'll be late coming home, but I'll ask about your behavior in the morning."

"And, Sarah, I can't even know if I'll be home before midnight so I may not see either of you until the morning."

"He'll behave very well for me Sean, and we'll be just fine."

"Very well then, until later," Sean said as he turned the horse's head and rode toward the gate.

For some reason the loss of *Julia's Fairwinds* had been on his mind in recent days. He told no one of this, but had decided to visit the harbor in the hope that Fian might have heard some news about the sloop. He thought that perhaps someone might be aware of wreckage that may have been found. He had no plan for what he might do if remains of the sloop were reported. Nevertheless, he was compelled to search for possible information.

As he rode up to the *Southern Swallow* the crew was busily cleaning the top deck. Fian saw Sean coming and in a loud voice commanded, "Avast lads, Sean O'Connell be a'comin'—good reason for us rest ourselves."

Sean dismounted, allowed the horse to graze on the long grass along the quay and then made his way up the narrow gangplank to the deck.

"Fine morning to you Fian—and to you men," Sean said.

"Not so fine as it might appear, Sean," Fian replied. "What brings you aboard?"

"I've been wondering if you might have heard of some notice of wreckage from my sloop—some word that anyone came across any ruins or debris."

"Not one word, Sean." Fian responded. "Not that I've asked, you see. But this is the sort of thing seamen talk about, and we've heard nothing— am I right lads?"

The crew all agreed that no news of the sloop had been reported to any of them.

"Then why, Fian," Sean asked, "have you said it's not a fine morning?"

"It's the sky Sean, the sky. Red as a drunk man's nose it was earlier. And from reports we've been hearing from those who've come from Bermuda, we're wonderin' if this may be a year for a *hurry cane*."

Puzzled, Sean asked, "A 'hurry cane'?"

"Aye, Sean. A sloop from Bermuda just last week—was it last week?" he asked one of the crew who nodded affirmatively.

"Aye," Fian continued, "the first mate of a Bermuda sloop told of bad storms what they've been havin' in Bermuda. And not usual storms mind you, Sean. He told us water cut through into many inlets including probably the one at St. George. Aye, Sean, dreadful *hurry cane* it was he said, with tides much as 2 fathoms[17] more'n what they should be, broke down enormous amounts of trees and some houses. Aye, it's what he said Sean."

"I've never seen such, but I can believe it. After all, Fian, Bermuda's an island amidst the sea with no protection but its own rise from the sea. But, we're far inland here and no sea storm can be any worse than what sunk my sloop."

The moment Sean said that he began again to reflect on the tragic result of his unbridled anger when he chose to sail into the teeth of the storm that sank the *Julia's Fairwinds* and almost took Nathan's life and his.

"No, Fian, I believe we have nothing to fear here at Gunter's Harbour."

"Beggin' your pardon, sir," Fian said with a laugh, "don't you mean North East? That's as how Captain Murphy says we're to call it now— North East—wantin' to please them English."

"Sean laughed too, then said, "You're right, Fian, North East it is—and I say we have nothing to fear here at North East, for you'll not find me ever again taking a vessel to sea when a storm is brewing."

At that the crew joined Fian and Sean, laughing at the foolishness of what he had done when he lost the sloop.

"Maybe so, Sean. I'd not want to try me own gills stayin' afloat in a storm like that first mate from Bermuda told us of—not on your life."

Sean stayed aboard most of the morning and accepted Fian's offer to provide a place for him at the crew's table for an early noon meal.

"This meat's a bit more to my liking," Sean said. "Not nearly as green as the pork you had the last time I was here."

Fian laughed, but added, "Thought that was pork, did you Sean?"

The crew all laughed then and some bad remarks were made about all the food aboard the *Southern Swallow*.

"Enough of that blather," Fian said. "I'm not wantin' an unwilling crew. Now I'll say it this way—that if the food's not to your likin' aboard the *Southern Swallow* I'll do as the Royal Navy does and impress me some fine merchant sailors what would be glad to have a bite of Fian's food."

"Not hardly likely," responded an old grizzled seaman. "If you was to take others by impressment[18], why they'd die sure as they took their very first meal. We're the only ones what can survive this food, First-mate. It's a poor crew you'd get with your press."

Laughter followed and more crude remarks and banter about mutiny was offered up by the crew.

"Did you hear that?" Fian asked, holding his hand up to quiet the amused men. "Seems we've a strong wind comin'."

Sean joined the men as they left the table and as soon as they set foot on the upper deck they felt the force of a fresh easterly wind and as they looked eastward Fian said, "That rosy red sky from this mornin' has fled from those burly black clouds, eh Sean? Isn't it as I've said? Red sky in the mornin', sailors take warnin'."

"It appears so, Fian, and I think I'd best be riding back to Dawn Light."

No sooner had those words left his mouth than the air was filled with a surge that caused the hairs on their necks to bristle as the sky seemed to catch fire with lightning and that display was followed by what seemed the booming roar of dozens of murderous canon.

Sean had allowed his horse to graze freely along the quay, neglecting to tether or hobble it, so that when the thunder roared the startled horse ran off and was soon out of sight.

The skies were beginning to swirl with dark clouds that were so low that it appeared as if they wanted to touch the ground and then a fierce rain that felt like something shot from a gun began to pelt their faces.

Sean hurried down the gangplank in the hope of quickly recovering his horse, but he slipped and fell into the muddy water below. Undaunted, he decided that he could get no wetter than he was already, so he started after the horse hoping that it might find a place under some tree where it would try to escape the rain and he could recover it.

Fian called out to him to return to the shelter of the ship, but the roaring wind drowned out the sound of his voice and Sean didn't hear him.

As Sean trudged through what was quickly becoming more like a deepening shallow pond than the path back to Dawn Light, he noticed that the wind was beginning to shift in an irregular way as it moved from one side to the other and the rain seemed more like pebbles than water as it struck him in the face. One of those large "pebbles" struck his eye and it was then that he realized that the water had turned to ice—and hail was now mercilessly pounding down upon him.

He tried to look ahead for shelter, but he could see no more than a few yards because of the driving rain and hail. The ground at his feet began to have the appearance of clumped snow, and as the wind paused as it changed direction he was able to see a low growing pine tree that he thought might afford some protection.

Sean dropped to his knees and crawled under the lowest branches, close to the small trunk. He was satisfied that he would be protected from the hail and tried to relax and wait out the storm. However, the ever changing direction of the relentless wind, and his water soaked clothing caused him to begin to shiver. He tried to control his shaking, thinking that if he could but wait it out a little longer the storm would pass.

He was wrong and the howling wind and ferocity of the pelting rain and hail gave good cause for Sean to decide that he must get moving again.

He crawled from under the tree and as he stood a flash of lightning, accompanied by a deafening boom brought down a large tree behind him, tearing into the limbs of the small pine under which he had been hiding.

I've got to get back to Nathan, he thought as his mind reeled in panic over things that could happen in a storm like this. *I should have taken heed of Sarah's remarks when she told Nathan how beautiful the pink sky had been this morning—pink sky—'red sky in morning sailor take warning.' Fian knew that very well when he spoke of the coming storm. How long, Lord, before I learn. I'm so headstrong and ever wanting my way in all things.*

Coming to his senses he began a slow trot and went on until he was winded, then slowed to a walk and began his trot again when he was able. The time dragged by and he wondered: *Why hadn't I tethered the horse? I may have passed by the horse along the pathway without even seeing him. Has the storm been as fierce inland at Dawn Light as I've been seeing it?*

Suddenly he sensed something he couldn't explain. He stopped, looked around and then recognized that he had just passed the gate to Dawn Light, so he turned back to the entrance and ran as fast as he was able toward the house.

He climbed the steps onto the porch, saw that the front door was not closed and imagined that the wind must have blown it open. He stepped inside and as he struggled to shut and bolt the door he called out, "Nathan! Sarah! Are you here? Sara and Nathan, are you here?"

He went through the small winter kitchen into the hallway and up the narrow stairs, calling for them as he went. No one answered. He looked in every room. He had forgotten to close the window in his bedroom and the rain was blowing in, soaking the floor and walls. He tried to see Sarah's cottage through the widow but the rain, growing darkness and distance made it impossible to see. He went back downstairs, out the side entrance and ran toward the cottage.

Drawing close he thought he saw a dim light through the solitary window. Pounding on the door he shouted, "Sarah, Nathan—it's me. Open the door."

The door swung open and the gust of shifting wind that struck Sean in the back propelled him through the door knocking Nathan to the floor and Sean into the arms of Sarah. She tried to hold on to Sean but he released himself and struggled to close the small door, which was in danger of being blown off its cowhide hinges. At last he was able to straighten the door, get it in place and bolt it securely.

Nathan had gotten to his feet and was trying to tell his father something, but was sobbing so much that he was unable. Sarah drew Nathan to her and Sean saw that she was softly crying as well.

"Everything's all right now," Sean assured them. "It's very dark in here Sarah. Are there more candles?"

"I have more but I've been using them frugally."

"Get them," insisted Sean. "This is a time for brightness, not thrift."

She released Nathan to get the candles and he ran to his father, throwing his arms about Sean's waist.

"We were frightened, Father. I thought we were in danger—like it was when we were on mother's boat. But now everything's well, isn't it? We're safe now, aren't we Daddy?"

"Of course we're safe, son. And you were safe with Sarah too. But I know this must have been worrisome—it's been a very strong storm. I lost my horse and have been walking back from North East. And the rain has been a forceful thing to battle and I was pelted by hail. Do you know what hail is Nathan?"

"Oh, yes, Father. We had rain and hail too. And Sarah said that some of the hail was as large as a hen's egg. Isn't that what you said Sarah?"

"That is just what I said, Nathan—hen's eggs. And they were, Sean," she said as she handed him a lit candle. "Never had I experienced such in Ireland."

"Nor I, Sarah," Sean said then added, "and not here either."

As he took the candle from her she allowed her hand to linger on his and said, "We're both so pleased that you've returned Sean. Thank you for coming to us."

"I'm glad you have a small fire and some dry wood," Sean said, almost too urgently. "I see that there is much rain coming in through the roof and walls, so some heat from the fire will feel good. If you have a blanket that I might use to cover myself, I would like to remove some of these clothes and get them close to the fire so they will dry. And if you don't mind, Nathan could sleep with you and you'd both be warm. I'll stay by the fire and keep it going."

Sarah immediately responded to his request, gave the blanket to Sean and she and Nathan climbed into her small bed and covered themselves with a quilt. The air was not that cool, but the dampness caused them to feel chilled.

"This feels better Father. It's nice and warm with Sarah, why don't you come to the bed with us," Nathan offered.

The warmth Sean felt on his face did not come from the small fire. "I'll stay here Nathan and keep the small fire aglow. That way we'll each be warm."

"Your father's right Nathan. Now keep the quilt close to you and stay next to me and we'll be warm—very warm."

Even though Sean was exhausted from the day's ordeal he had no difficulty staying awake to tend the fire. The wind howled and whistled throughout the night. Sean knew that the storm had come from the east and so he thought it seemed very strange that the wind now appeared to be coming from the west. At times during the night Sean wondered if the small cottage would manage to hold together during the force of this gale.

He was glad that he had torn down the small shed years ago and used the wood to lay a wooden floor in the small cabin that had belonged to Samson and Kezie. But even with the wooden floor, ground water was seeping up through the separations in the floor and in the lower places of the floor, in the corners and along the wall's edges, puddles of water had formed.

Through the tiny window the sky began to lighten a bit and Sean sensed that it must be morning. The force of the wind had subsided so he quietly slipped into his damp outer clothes. Fortunately, being bundled in the blanket close to the fire during the night, his inner clothing was now dry. He unlatched the door and tried to open it quietly. However, it had been battered by the wind into a wedged position and Sean had to pound on the edge of the door with his fist and that disturbance wakened Sarah and Nathan.

"What are your doing Father?" Nathan asked as he rubbed the sleep from his eyes.

Sean struck the door once more with his fist, it flew open and Sean stepped outside.

"Oh, have you ever seen such as this?" Sean asked himself aloud.

"Seen what Daddy? What do you see?"

Come look, Sarah—Nathan, come look," he invited.

Still clothed from the night before they joined Sean at the muddy entrance to the cottage where they saw debris scattered all about. The air was eerily still, a soft rain continued to fall, and it was getting lighter by the minute, but a strange and sickly pale yellow colored the clouds above.

"I think we'd do well to get to the main house," said Sean. "The cottage is far to wet inside for it to be a healthy place to be right now. Gather what you need Sarah and then come to the house. Nathan you stay to help Sarah. I'll get a fire going and I have plenty of wood to keep us dry, because somehow I'm not convinced that this storm has gone for good."

Sean went to the house, started a fire in the winter kitchen then went upstairs to choose a room for Sarah that might still be dry, where she could have her privacy. Before long Nathan and Sarah came to the house with some necessary items that Sarah had decided upon.

Sean told Nathan, "Now take Miss Sarah upstairs to your room, it's very dry and very little water has been driven in through the window."

Then turning to Sarah he said, "We'll have to agree on this arrangement for now until I can see how to clean and dry your cottage. However, if you'd feel more comfortable going back to the Murphy's now, I would understand and we can manage that as well. What is your thinking?"

"This must be temporary of course," Sarah said, "but I think it best to stay here right now—would you agree?"

"Yes, I do agree and . . ." Sean paused as if he heard something and went to the door, opened it and stepped outside.

As if by signal, a fierce wind came roaring out of the west. Although Sean had no knowledge whatever of such occurrences, they had been experiencing the calm eye of a hurricane and were now being slammed by the backside of the eye as it passed overhead.

"Bolt the doors and close those on the front porch side," Sean shouted.

Sarah and Nathan went to bolt the other doors and Sean ran upstairs to be sure the windows were secure. As he went to the window in Nathan's room a tree branch came crashing through the window, followed by torrents of rain. He felt a sharp pain from a shard of glass that cut into his neck. He gingerly felt the area of pain and removed a long sliver of the window and when he looked at his hand it was full of blood.

He quickly checked the other rooms, and fortunately the lone window was on the leeward side of the wind. Then he ran downstairs and even above the din cause by the wind and the flying objects striking the house he heard Sarah screaming.

"Help, Sean! Help me I can't close the door!"

He went quickly into the hallway then into the winter kitchen and there was Sarah, unsuccessfully trying to close the door in order to bolt it. Despite the fact that the entrance was protected by the roof of the porch the rain was blowing in torrentially and Nathan had slipped and fallen to the floor as he attempted to help Sarah.

Nathan was crying and Sean pulled him out of the way then turned to help Sarah. As he did a particularly strong gust of wind blew the door completely open and threw Sarah backward into Sean's arms.

Still in Sean's arms she twisted herself about and saw the blood running down from the cut on his neck.

"You're bleeding Sean. What have you done?" she shouted above the clamor.

"It's nothing," he responded. "Here, take Nathan back into the hallway while I close this door."

"But Sean, you're bleeding and . . . ." she began.

"Do as I say Sarah, now! I must seal this door to give us some protection."

Sarah helped Nathan get up from the floor and they fled to the relative safety of the hallway. Sean struggled to get the door closed again, because the top hinge had been loosened and he had difficulty getting the door to fit back in its place. After what seemed a long time he was able to bolt the door, but as he turned to retreat to the hallway he felt himself becoming nauseated and disoriented, he lost his balance, fell slowly to the floor and his head hit the seat of a chair. He lay there unconscious.

"What—where am I?" Sean said as he regained consciousness. He tried to sit up but was again overcome by a wave of queasiness.

"Lie back down Sean, please," Sarah pled. "You've lost much blood and you must rest. Nathan and I have tried to make you comfortable, but you must rest."

"I'm all right," Sean responded somewhat perturbed. But as he tried to sit up, once again he became dizzy and realized that Sarah was right.

"You've been unconscious for some time and we were worried—weren't we Nathan?"

"Yes Daddy, we were very worried. Are you well now?"

"I feel much better and I thank you and Miss Sarah for caring for me."

Sean's neck felt restricted and when he placed his hand on it he winced with pain when he touched the place of the wound and realized that his neck had been covered to control the bleeding from the cut he had received.

"Yes Sean, I wrapped your neck, because you have bled much. But it seems to have stopped bleeding or at least it appears to have slowed greatly. You must forgive me, but I have used some of my garments to wrap your wound and . . ."

"Sarah" Sean said firmly. "You must not ask my forgiveness for treating my wounds. No, Sarah, I must thank you—you and your young helper for being so kind to me and caring for me."

"It was the only thing I could do Sean. And as you've said, Sean, this hallway seems a safe haven for us for now. Do you think we should remain here?"

"I do Sarah. And if you're able, one of you might go carefully up the stairs to see if there are any dry blankets, because we could use them to try and obtain some comfort during the night."

"I'll go Father. I know where the blankets are."

"Then you go son, what a brave man you are. I'm very proud of you and I know Miss Sarah is too."

When Nathan brought blankets to the hallway, Sarah made pallets for them to sleep upon. One was for Sean and the other for her and Nathan. She placed the pallets in the narrow passageway so that they lay head to head.

Even though the wind continued to howl through the night and no one was able to sleep peacefully, Sarah was comforted by the soft snoring of Sean and the close warmth of Nathan's body,

"It stopped," Nathan shouted. "Miss Sarah, Father, the wind has stopped blowing so loudly. Is it over now? Has the storm passed?"

Sarah jumped up quickly in response to Nathan's shouts, but Sean struggled to awaken and when he did his neck was throbbing and the pain seemed to have increased. However, his nausea had cleared and he sat upright and then carefully stood to his feet. When he did, he noticed the position of the sleeping pallets and smiled—but he wasn't sure why he smiled.

The gale force winds had diminished somewhat but the rain still pelted down as hard as Sean had ever experienced and he thought: *These have been the greatest gusts of wind—the most tremendous gales I've seen. And such great rainfall—would this have been the sort of storm the Bible speaks of when Noah was told to build the ark?*

Sean found that he was still somewhat dizzy, but he walked carefully to the door, almost tripping over the chair he had struck his head upon. He struggled to open the door, but found it was less difficult to open than it had been to close. He stepped out on the porch to survey the land and was shocked to see that the small creek that often ran almost dry had overcome its banks and was as wide as many rivers he had seen.

Then Sean heard a familiar voice shout, "Hello the house," and looking toward the gate he saw Ben Dixon coming down the muddy lane, leading Sean's horse.

— Chapter Twenty-Three —

Storm's Outcome

Sean, Ben, the captain, Fian and members of his crew spent weeks cleaning up the debris and repairing the damage cause by the storm. Even the captain's ship the *Southern Swallow* was damaged when water higher than anyone could remember accompanied the great gale and moved the ship onto the quay. Crews from other ships were solicited to help Captain Murphy get his ship back in the water and upright.

The sustained gale winds of the storm produced tides well over a fathom higher than the normal low water tides. For this reason, when high tides came in they brought as much as 10 feet of sea water extending well inland, flooding parts of North East and damaging most area crops.

Some seamen claimed that they had experienced a six to nine foot storm surge as it passed up the Chesapeake Bay. The combination of this tremendous rush of storm water and back-water flooding caused crests as high as two fathoms above low water. At least ten vessels met their fate in this fierce gale—this hurricane.

The Murphy's home withstood the effect of the storm much better than Dawn Light had and for this reason Sarah and Nathan moved back there for temporary accommodations. Sarah was delighted, because not only was it more pleasant and comfortable for her, but the move also allowed her to consider what had gone on during the storm. The two nights that she had spent so physically close to Sean had left her somewhat bewildered.

Nathan was outside playing and Sarah was resting in her room and thinking. *Strange how I find I have no misgivings whatever about what occurred during the storm. I'm seeing that my aversion to men was really no true dislike of men at all, it was no more than a loathing of Michael and his abuse. I felt so relaxed, safe and unafraid when I was with Sean. I should blush even for thinking this way, but—why should I? It's true. And it's proper as well, because I see that some of my comfort with Sean has to do with Nathan always having been present with us—and that was a good thing and as it should be. But I think that I would be very comfortable with Sean even if I were alone with him.*

"I hope you're not sleeping," Cynthia said as she knocked lightly on the bedroom door.

"No, I'm not sleeping, just resting—please come in," Sarah responded.

Cynthia entered the room and sat on the edge of the bed where Sarah rested on pillows she had propped under her head.

"Sean just stopped by for a moment," Cynthia said. "He asked to see you, but I thought you were asleep. He came to get some tools. The captain hasn't come back from the ship yet, but I expect him at any moment."

Sarah wasn't interested in the captain for the moment, but she did ask, "Did Sean say why he wanted to see me?"

"No," Cynthia replied, "but he sat and talked with Nathan for awhile."

"Did they speak of me?" Sarah asked and the moment the words left her mouth she wanted them back.

"Oh I wouldn't know that dear," Cynthia said with a puzzled expression on her face. "Could it be that there's something you'd want them to be speaking of?"

Sarah wanted desperately to audibly blurt out the feelings she had been relishing for those brief moments before Cynthia knocked on the door, but all she answered was, "Oh no, I simply thought it might be something he wanted of me."

"As I say," continued Cynthia, "I wouldn't know. He did look very well though. The wound on his neck looks to be sound indeed. There appears to be no infection and the cut is healing rapidly. He can thank you for giving such fine attention to that wound shortly after it happened. I understand that great blood loss, such as Sean's—especially when the loss occurs so rapidly—can cause death quite easily."

"So I've heard and I'm happy to know he's well, it makes me very happy indeed," Sarah acknowledged.

"I can tell by the pleasant look on your face that it makes you happy," Cynthia said smiling. Then she patted Sarah's hand, got up to leave the room and said, "Well, I must finish my tasks before the captain returns."

Ben and Sean had cleared off and burned most of the unusable debris they collected from the storm. They had repaired the cottage where Sarah stayed and made some improvements to things like the leather door hinges, which Sean had replaced with metal hinges from the blacksmith. The most difficult thing to replace was glass for the broken windows. It had to be obtained from Philadelphia and would take awhile before it could be delivered and replaced, because it required someone who was a craftsman with glass.

Sean ate most of his meals with the Dixons simply because their house was closer to Dawn Light than Murphy's and besides, Elizabeth expected him to join them for their meals. However, because he and Ben had completed the essential repairs that day he decided to ride to the Murphy's, because there was a matter that had been weighing on his mind.

After a good meal, Sean, Nathan and Sarah went to the parlor and listened as Sarah read from one of Cynthia's books of poetry.

"Father says that my mother liked to read poetry too—didn't she Daddy?"

"Yes, son, she loved poetry very much. And we can see that Miss Sarah enjoys poetry too, can't we?"

"Yes, Father, we can see that. But, I'd like to go try to trick Captain Murphy with some riddles I've made up. May I Father?"

"Yes, you go right ahead. Miss Sarah and I have something to talk about too."

Nathan left the parlor and ran upstairs to find the captain.

Sarah wondered what Sean had meant. Why did he have something to talk about with her?

"Sarah," Sean began, "I have many things on my mind and heart that I recently discovered that I've been concealing from others—but most importantly I've been concealing from myself. I tell you that I have nothing in mind that should embarrass you—at least not purposely so. But before I would begin I ask your permission to speak plainly and freely."

"Oh Sean, this is quite unexpected and makes me feel somewhat uneasy. Does this have to do with the way I have recently behaved, while we were in the throes of the storm?"

"Wait Sarah," Sean interrupted. "I think I've been extremely unfair in that I'm asking you to agree to something before you know what it is. I beg you this, allow me to begin anew. May I do so?"

Puzzled even more, Sarah sat there without responding for what seemed to Sean a very long time. Finally, she said, "Sean—you have my answer and it is this. I trust you and I believe that you will say nothing to me that would injure me in any way. I know this, because I have finally seen you, Sean, for the kind of man you really are. Please tell me what you will."

Sean stared at Sarah as if he was seeing her for the very first time. A few moments earlier, the situation would have made Sarah nervous and very uncomfortable, but now she felt completely at ease—eager to hear what Sean would say.

At last he began. "Sarah, I would say many things and perhaps some of what I tell you will make no sense at all. I may seem harsh at times, but I mean no disrespect or harm to you."

He paused and when he did, Sarah said, "I know this, Sean. I believe you, and I know this from my own heart."

"Sarah, I loved my wife Julia very much. If I had not had Julia's love for me I would be no man at all—I'd be made of straw. She loved our children—she loved Nathan dearly, the son God has allowed me to still have. Julia provided me with so much more than any wife should be expected to give her husband. We were very happy Sarah, and I loved her so very much."

Sean paused and looked down at the floor to hide the tears that formed in his eyes. He turned away and ran his hand across his eyes, then continued.

"I knew that Julia was the one who completed my life. Then I lost her. I was alone and no longer a man—at least not a complete man. I'm unable to tell you of the many things I've done and thought since her death, because I haven't the understanding myself to be able to explain them. When I returned from the wilderness and found you here, you immediately became my enemy—even though you had no reason to suspect that or to understand why. I was angry with the captain and Cynthia for allowing you to invade the room of my precious wife—a room I thought of as a sanctuary. I was angry with you, because I thought you had made Nathan your own."

"Oh Sean," Sarah interrupted, "I had no intent to do so. Of course I enjoy Nathan—and yes, I love Nathan—but he is your son and not mine. And yes Sean, I have a need, a great need for the love of someone such as Nathan. But I know that it is impossible for me; yet it is a need I cannot fulfill. It is something that . . ."

"Wait Sarah," Sean said almost shouting, "this is the very heart of the matter I'm trying to tell you."

Sean explained the meeting with Morgan Glasfryn. Sarah had known of the way the man helped Sean recover Dawn Light, but had never heard of the promise that the Welshman demanded of Sean. Sean explained how the vow had brought new meaning to his life and then continued.

"Sarah, I have a sense that you have great needs. I'm not able to know what they are, but I do know that they exist in your heart. I tell you truthfully that others have tried to force me to meet those unknown needs and I have refused. I'm not ashamed that I refused, because if I had done what they asked I might have ruined your life and mine entirely."

"Oh Sean, please don't say that, because I now know there is no way you would be able to disappoint me in life. So what then, Sean—what are you saying?"

"Here's what I must say, Sarah. To pay my debt to the Welshman, to fulfill my promise to him, I ask you, Sarah Fitzpatrick, to permit me to become a suitor for your love and your life. And, if you will allow me to do so I can promise you this—not only will I be able to complete my promise to Morgan Glasfryn, but you will fulfill the need of this man, a need that I now understand no one but you are able to fill—and Sarah, I intend to persuade you to become my wife."

Sean stood and stepped to where Sarah was seated. He held out his hands and she stared at his outstretched arms then looked up into his face. Smiling as tears ran from her eyes she took his hands and Sean pulled her gently to him and wrapped his arms about her.

"Daddy, Daddy," Nathan shouted as he ran into the parlor, "do you want to hear my riddle? Grandfather couldn't guess the answer—let's see if you or Miss Sarah can guess."

Then, realizing that Sean was holding Sarah he said, "Why are you crying Miss Sarah? Is that why you're hugging her Daddy—because she's sad and she's crying?"

"Well son," replied Sean, "that's exactly why I'm hugging Miss Sarah, but she's not crying because she's sad—are you Sarah?"

Sean gently released her and she turned to Nathan.

"No, Nathan. I'm not at all sad. I can't remember a time when I've been happier."

Then looking at Sean she said, "And we would both like to hear your riddle, wouldn't we? It must be a very clever riddle if your grandfather couldn't guess it."

"Oh, it is clever, Miss Sarah, it is. And I thought of it all by myself. Now, here's my riddle—what animal can jump higher than a house?"

"Jump higher than a house?" Sean asked, as if he were amazed with the thought. "How could any animal jump higher than a house? Oh, here—I know the answer. The answer to your riddle is this: that the house is very, very small—perhaps it's a toy house. Yes, that must be it—so an animal might jump higher than a toy house."

"No Father, no that's wrong. Now Miss Sarah—now you must guess."

"Nathan, I know of no animal that can jump higher than a house," she said.

"Then I'll tell you the answer to my riddle," Nathan said gleefully. "Any animal can jump higher than a house. And do you know why? It's because houses can't jump, so any animal can jump higher than a house."

Laughing, Sean said, "That is a very witty riddle son. It seems that you are much too clever for all of us. Now come, let's go speak to Captain Murphy, because I have something very important to ask of him."

Chapter Twenty-Four

Permission Granted

Sean spoke with confidence as he asked for Captain Murphy's agreement to court Sarah the only child of his brother in Ireland. Although there was a certain air of mild surprise—perhaps because of the timing—it was accompanied by a definite sense of approval on the part of both the captain and Cynthia—and by her appearance, Sarah was in agreement as well.

The captain gazed at each person in the room, including Nathan, as if demanding their attention before he began.

"I'm speaking for me own brother, Liam now," Captain Murphy said as he looked at Sarah and smiled. "It's my belief that your father would be pleased to have a man like Sean talking to you of marriage, Sarah."

He then turned to Sean and said, "I've known this man since he boarded the *Southern Swallow* in Southampton to come to Maryland and I've known him to be an honest and a trustworthy man. Through the years we've been through many a scrape and I could always count on Sean. I'm not telling you that we were always agreeing on everything, but I never had cause to doubt the uprightness of Sean."

The captain paused and looked about at the others as if trying to determine their thoughts in the matter.

"Now, what I have to say is this. There's no man I would choose—if choosing is what I'd have to do—than I would Sean. He's made of the same clay that God has made us all, but I'd say that he has more than clay in his soul."

"Did God really make you from clay Father—are we made of clay?" Nathan asked in amazement.

Everyone laughed but Nathan wasn't sure just what might have been funny just now.

"Aye, me little seaman," the captain responded to Nathan. "We're made of the clay the good Lord made us from, and that's why we return to the dust—the clay—the same way."

Nathan wanted to ask more but Sarah put her arm about him and hushed him.

"Now here's my answer to all. It's for Liam me brother I speak and I say that Sean O'Connell has the permission of Liam me brother to court Sarah his only daughter."

There was a stirring and Sean wanted to say something, but the captain continued.

"That's not all there is. There's a need to be proper in this courting, and Sarah will return to my house and I'll not permit her to spend time alone at Dawn Light."

"But Captain." Began Sean, "I'm in great need of Sarah's help with Nathan and . . . ."

"I stand by what I've said," the captain said firmly. "Nathan can continue on here with us, just as he did before you returned. And here he'll stay until this matter has been settled and agreed upon between you two—and that's the end of that."

"Now Laird," Cynthia began, "we're speaking of mature adults who I'm sure are completely trustworthy and I see no reason why . . . ."

"By all the saints above woman, did I not make meself clear enough for all to hear? All will be proper and it will be as I say. Can you agree with that Sarah?"

"Yes, Uncle, I do agree with your request."

"Ah but, Sarah, we'll not call it a request," the captain said. "And you, Sean, will you abide my demand?"

"Aye, Captain, that I will. And I thank you for your confidence in me to be a man of trust in this and in all matters."

Then the captain stood and said, "We'll begin just now with this matter of courtship. I'm off to me bed for now, and I'll bid you all a fair night."

He started from the room then turned about and said, "Sean, I'd not be askin' you to be in a rush about these important matters lad. And as for you Sarah, neither would I ask you to delay Sean in his pursuit of you. You both understand my meaning—am I right?"

"Yes Uncle," Sarah replied, "I fully understand and again I thank you for your counsel."

"Aye, Captain, your meaning is clear as the starriest night—couldn't be clearer Captain, not at all."

"All's well then," the captain said as he tried to appear as stern as possible when he left the room. But he was unable to hide the twinkle in his eye and his grunt, that all heard, was taken to be a sign of approval.

The weeks that followed passed quickly for Sean, because he had to balance the time he had to spend repairing the house, getting it in order for the possibility of a bride, and the pursuing of a bride to live in that house.

However, the time often seemed to stand still for Sarah. She had been released from the bitter memories that had plagued her marriage to Michael Fitzpatrick, and she was so very anxious for Sean to present himself to her as if she were a young maiden. And that he did—except that their opportunities for being together were very few and brief, because of Sean being consumed with the responsibilities of Dawn Light.

One day he and Ben were burning a large heap of odds and ends that had been destroyed in the storm. They stood close by the fire to be sure that the burning pile did not get out of control or throw sparks into the air that might fall on one of the buildings.

Nonchalantly Ben asked, "Sean, how much longer will it be before you'll be comfortable asking Sarah to be your wife?"

"How much longer?" Sean said as though puzzled. "I tell you Ben, the woman knows my plan to have her as my wife and I should think she would consider giving more of her energy to being available to me as her suitor."

"Oh, I see," responded Ben as if discovering a great truth. "Then you say that this commerce of courting lays more heavily on her than on you—do I understand you in this Sean?"

"I won't say that you're wrong, Ben. She knows how my time has been taken in getting Dawn Light ready for her and . . . ."

"A moment, Sean" Ben interrupted, "a moment if you would. I'm hearing a deaf man telling me that he's waiting until he hears—hears from a bride-to-be who isn't speaking. And all the while that he's preparing a home for her, a woman who has never said she would be his wife. She's waiting to be asked—do I understand this Sean?"

"No of course not, that is, I suppose . . . . that's not what I said. I said that—oh, I see what you're telling me. I've spent more time preparing a home for a woman who may not agree to live in it. Then what is it you think I should do?"

"Sean, you've become a bit dull-witted. You have a fine home and you'll be able to continue working on it. But first, find you this woman that you'll need to have live in it with you and ask her. If she'll agree, then is the time for carpentry. Get yourself to the Murphy's, Sean. Elizabeth says I'm to tell you that if you want to make both you and Sarah happy—stop delaying as you wait for a better time. This is when she needs to be asked."

"You're later than usual," Cynthia said as Sean walked up on the porch. "But we haven't eaten yet, so I know you'll want some supper with us."

"That would be fine. I am hungry, very hungry. And, Cynthia, I need to have some time alone with Sarah tonight—that is I would like to talk to her alone, just the two of us. Would you think the captain might approve of that?"

"Approve Sean?" Cynthia responded. "The captain's been ready to take you by the collar and present you before Sarah. Of course he'll approve. Sean, the captain and I have been wondering if you had changed your mind about courting Sarah, because it's been a time since you revealed your aspirations to us. And I'm sure that Sarah must have been wondering as well."

Sean sat in bewildered silence for several moments. "Cynthia, I'm finding all of this troublesome. You're the mother of my dear wife Julia, and now it seems that you must be a go-between, convincing me to ask another woman to be my wife. It's difficult for me to understand."

"Sean dear, there's nothing to understand. All that remains is what you must do. I love you and Nathan so very dearly, and now Sarah has found a most special place in my heart as well. What I am saying and doing now does nothing to diminish the love I have for Julia and it takes nothing from your love for her either. But Sean, Julia is gone. And you and I know very well that she would want nothing less than our happiness in a matter of the heart such as this."

"Ben called me dull-witted," Sean said pitifully, "and I believe he is right. But you've opened my eyes to this matter and I thank you for that. I'll go speak with the captain."

Sean thought the supper was especially tasty that evening and the conversation was open and flowed freely.

"With your permission," Sean began, "I would like to invite Sarah to join me on the front porch for a private discussion. It's a pleasant evening and the moon is bright."

"It is bright Father," Nathan agreed. "May I sit with you?"

Before Sean could respond, Sarah said, "I think not, Nathan. Tonight your father and I must speak of important matters, and we'll be sure to tell you all about it afterward."

Sean was taken aback by Sarah's ready and firm response and added, "Miss Sarah's right, son, we'll talk of it later."

Sarah and Sean sat on the top step of the porch. The moon was low above the horizon and the night was cloudless. The clear song of two nightingales sounded as though they were determined to outperform one another as they provided their beautiful musical accompaniment to the night.

"Aren't they lovely, Sean?"

"I agree they are. The stars are so brilliant even with such a bright moon," Sean replied.

"Yes, they are brilliant—but I meant the birds, the nightingales, their song is enchanting."

Sean turned to her and said, "Sarah, their singing is beautiful, but it is you who are enchanting. You have enchanted my heart and captivated my mind. For so long I was convinced that the true love of a woman would never again enter my life, but I was wrong. I am a fool—a fool to be pitied for being so unwise as to waste time trying to avoid being in your presence, when my time should have been spent adoring you."

He paused as he looked into her face and her eyes reflected the brightness of the moon. He took her hand in his and gently lifted and kissed it.

"Sarah, I refuse to dissipate more of our time—time that we could spend together. All that I want, all I know is to ask you this Sarah Fitzpatrick—would you accept my willingness to love you and would you honor me by being my wife?"

The words were scarcely out of his mouth when she responded, "Sean O'Connell, all that I know to answer is this—I would delight in being your wife. And Sean, in doing so I want you to understand this—that I will also receive your son Nathan as if he were ours, because I believe that a deep union has already occurred between us. I have supposed that the closeness I felt between Nathan and me may have been one of the things that kept you apart from me—that you may have thought I was stealing his love from you. But, now I see—and I'm sure you do as well—that we were meant to be together as a family. Oh yes, Sean. I am honored to accept you. I love you and wish to willing give myself to you."

Sean turned to embrace Sarah and lost his balance. Sarah screamed and they tumbled down the next two steps onto the ground with Sarah landing on top of Sean.

"What happened Daddy?" Nathan shouted as he ran from the house.

The captain followed Nathan and blustered, "What in the name of Neptune is going on out here?"

Sarah and Sean struggled to get to their feet when they heard the captain's voice, and Captain Murphy laughed with glee when he saw them.

—— CHAPTER TWENTY-FIVE ——

Annapolis Adventure

The idea was Cynthia's, but Sarah immediately agreed to the suggestion.

"Oh Aunt Cynthia, would he?" Sarah asked. "Do you believe the Reverend Sikes would be agreeable to our request for him to perform the marriage ceremony for Sean and me in Annapolis?"

"I'm quite sure that he would dear," Cynthia replied. "I'm not even certain that you're aware of this, but he married your Uncle Laird and me. I've known the Reverend and Mrs. Sikes for many years. Something else you probably weren't aware of is that my brother, the Reverend Jonathan Topping—may God rest his soul—was assigned by the church to Gunter's Harbour, or as they now say North East, by the authority of Reverend Sikes himself. Oh yes, my dear, I've known the Reverend and his wife Mary for many years, and I'm certain he would be willing."

"Then how shall we embark on this exciting escapade Aunt," she asked eagerly. "Do you think Sean will be agreeable?"

"Well, we certainly should expect that he will. However, I'll speak with your Uncle Laird and he'll then tell Sean what we have thought to be an excellent plan for the wedding. Your uncle can be very persuasive as you know. And besides, that would relieve you of any difficulties that you might fear."

"Oh, but Aunt Cynthia, I have no such fear. In fact I'm unable to explain to you how very courageous I have become—I can scarcely believe it myself. Still, I like the idea of Uncle and Sean being involved and at least making the plans to travel—don't you?"

"I do," Cynthia replied, "I do think I like that design very well."

Later that morning Cynthia presented the women's thoughts to the captain. He did not hesitate for a moment, but immediately took their proposal as his own.

"A more splendid idea I've not heard in awhile," the captain agreed. "And here's my suggestion about the matter. What might you think of this—we could also take guests to the wedding with us aboard the *Southern Swallow* and it would be a voyage none of us would soon forget."

The captain's plan was very agreeably received by Sarah and Cynthia. However, at first Sean was tentative about the thought of traveling to Annapolis for the marriage ceremony and even more hesitant about asking friends to join them in the journey.

Nevertheless, his uncertainty was soon broken and he was finally convinced—not by the persuasive Captain Murphy, but by the captain's niece. For some inexplicable reason Sarah seemed to have an unusual influence over Sean.

The wedding plans expanded until they almost developed a life of their own and nothing was able to stand in the way of the ideas that enlarged as time went along.

The captain had immediately sent a letter to the Reverend Sikes by the hand of a ship's captain that was sailing to Annapolis and within two weeks he had a positive response from Reverend Sikes who also sent along heartfelt best wishes to all from his wife, and he offered some proposed dates for the wedding.

Cynthia suggested that Julia's long-time friend Mary Davis be invited to come aboard the *Southern Swallow* to take the trip. But, her father Thomas Davis rejected the idea, saying "It would dishonor Julia's memory if Mary were to attend the ceremony of Sean's second marriage."

Isaac Newby the fisherman who had sold the small swampy piece of land to Sean where he built the Bermuda sloop was invited also. He declined the offer, but gave no reason.

They had even tried to find Maudie Hodge and her father Oswell, the man who had been innkeeper of the Crown Ordinary before the soldiers burned it to the ground. However, no one could be found who knew what had become of the Hodges once they arrived in Philadelphia.

Sean had spoken privately to Captain Murphy about a matter that weighed heavily on his mind and heart.

"Captain, I must speak with someone about this," Sean began somewhat tentatively, "and I'm thinking that you're the only one who would be able to understand this weight that troubles me so. And, Captain, I'm sure you'll try to prevent me before I say it all, but I'm asking you to hear me out in this matter."

"Have at it, Sean," the captain replied, "and I'll be after battening down my hatches."

"All right then, here's what it is. I've thought much of Samson and his family and I would wish they'd be able to know of my marriage. They were part of Julia's life and I somehow sense that I've a debt to them."

"Oh now, Sean," the captain interrupted, "that would be a mistake, because as we say, 'it's a good boat that finds the harbor it left.' You've come back Sean and those Blacks are better left where they are."

"I know that, Captain," Sean replied aggressively, "I'm only wanting to tell someone what it is here in my heart about the matter," He thumped his chest as he spoke.

"I'm not ashamed to say the same about Nokona," Sean continued. "And I'll include his sister Lomasi and even her heathen husband Bone Man. You see, Captain, just as with the Blacks, they have become such a part of who I am that it seems I'm deceiving them by leaving them from my life now."

"Aye, Sean," began the captain, "I do see your meaning. But you've missed mine. When I said 'a good boat finds the harbor it left' I spoke of you Sean. Do you see? It's a good thing to remember who we are and where we're from—our beginnings Sean, our beginnings, it's who we are."

"I know who I am Captain," replied Sean adamantly. "But I'm thinking that no one else really knows me—at least not the man I've become. I thank you for letting me trouble you with these matters, Captain. I thank you indeed, but believe I'll be alone with these feelings."

"Aye Sean," the captain began, "and it's no one can know where the boot pinches on another man's foot. I'm thinking that we're all alike in one way or another Sean, and still we can't fathom deep in a man's mind or heart. Let me say this though Sean, I can't promise slaves and savages for your wedding, but you might have a taste from days gone by if you decide to stay with us for a time."

Sean tried his best to pry the information mentioned from him, but the captain was determined that Sean would have to wait.

In less than a month an animated group of friends was at the quay in North East waiting to board the *Southern Swallow* for the wedding journey to Annapolis.

Captain Murphy wore the well-brushed uniform that he brought out only on special occasions—such as for his own wedding—and he deemed that the present circumstances were exceptional enough to have called for it as well.

Even though First-mate Fian O'Niall did not have what might be recognized as an authentic uniform of any sort, nevertheless he was well-bathed, shaved and smartly clad in an eclectic combination of some of the finest belongings that the crew had been able to put together for him to wear for this event.

The mood was festive and when the passengers carefully scaled the narrow gangplank, at times the atmosphere bordered on giddiness, because some lost their balance almost falling into the muddy quay below.

As the passengers boarded the *Southern Swallow*, Cynthia and Sarah moved among them chatting briefly with each in turn.

Nathan was delighted that the Dixons had chosen to bring their daughter Annie along, because she was his good friend and playmate. Francis Hough had accepted the invitation and came down from Nottingham Lots and Mrs. Hough accompanied him, expectantly eager to meet Sean's bride-to-be.

Unknown to the others Captain Murphy had contacted the Tubbs cousins with an invitation to the wedding. And even though Edward was unable to accept the invitation, because he had promised to complete unfinished work for a man in Philadelphia, Ethan was able to come.

Much to Sean's pleasure, when he saw Ethan Tubbs he understood the meaning of a "taste from days gone by" that the captain had mentioned.

—— CHAPTER TWENTY-SIX ——

The Pale

Francis Hough insisted that those who had traveled to Annapolis for the wedding should take rooms at the Eagle and Lamb Ordinary, the inn owned by his friend Stanley Shaw. Shaw was delighted to have that privilege, but the number of people in attendance for the wedding was more than the rooms he had available.

So, the night before the wedding, the Hough's, Ben, Elizabeth and Annie Dixon and Sean took rooms at the inn. Captain Murphy, Cynthia and Sarah stayed with the Sikes at the parish house, and the others, Nathan and Ethan stayed aboard the *Southern Swallow* with Fian and the crew.

Just before the wedding observance took place, Francis Hough called for silence and said that he had a singular disclosure to announce.

"Without permission, and asking your pardon for my forwardness in the matter, I have invited another guest to this occasion." He walked to the side of the parish house, opened a door and said, "May I introduce our good friend from the Isle of Anglesy in Wales."

Walking slowly from the house strode Barrister Morgan Glasfryn. Sean was delighted to see him. Of course, at first, most of the others did not realize who the man was.

"I see that you truly did understand, young Sean O'Connell," Glasfryn said as he walked toward Sean offering his outstretched hand. "And now our transaction is complete. You have compensated me for my fee—and a lovelier person in need I know you've never seen than your bride on this day. You'll not be able to make her a king, Sean lad, but a queen she'll be and you'll be her king."

Sarah was especially delighted to greet Glasfryn and the presence of this special guest hampered the ceremony somewhat while questions were asked and answered, but no one was concerned with the delay.

After a time the Reverend Sikes said, "Then shall we begin?"

The wedding was a brief ceremony held in the garden of the parish house in Annapolis and all who had traveled by ship to attend agreed that it was a trip worth taking and quite a grand event.

Rather than strictly following the common practice of the banns—the public church announcement that a marriage between a man and woman was to take place—the Reverend Sikes simply made extemporaneous comments, which he determined to be acceptable here in the colonies. And under these circumstances he took pleasure in granting himself this authority.

"As parish priest" the Reverend Sikes began, "I allow that, because there is no established parish in North East, let all hear that I shall here and now publish the banns of marriage between widower Sean Martin O'Connell of North East and widow Sarah Murphy Fitzpatrick recently of North East. If any here know of a cause or just impediment why these two persons should not be joined together in Holy Matrimony, you are to declare it now and so forth, and so forth. I add that this is the final time of asking."

Cynthia's thoughts went back to that day in the front garden of her home when Sean and her Julia had married. *What a happy day that was,* she reminisced. *I'm taken aback by this unexpected joy that I now sense as Sean takes another for his wife. Yet, Sarah has become as a daughter to me as well, and our Nathan needs a mother. And hasn't Sarah become the best sort of mother to Nathan—and we all know Sean needs a wife. Oh yes, this is a fine day and even with the sorrow of losing Julia this is a time for my heart to rejoice.*

"On this day and time appointed for the solemnization of Matrimony," the Reverend Sikes continued, "the persons to be married have joined with their family and friends, and I now read from *The Book of Common Prayer.*

'Dearly beloved, we are gathered together here in the sight of God, and in the face of this congregation . . .'"

As the ceremony continued, Sarah's mind recalled that day long ago when she had married Michael—and she dismissed the thought more quickly than it had appeared. At one point she felt as though she might faint as her wits went reeling, but she was able to recover, willed her mind to the present situation, and became alert to the words being spoken by the Reverend Sikes:

"Forasmuch as Sean Martin O'Connell and Sarah Murphy Fitzpatrick have consented together in Holy Wedlock, and have witnessed the same before God and this company, and thereto have given and pledged their troth either to other, and have declared the same by giving and receiving of a ring, and by joining of hands; I pronounce that they be Man and Wife together, In the Name of the Father, and of the Son, and of the Holy Ghost. Amen."

Because of the close relationship that the Sikes felt they had with Cynthia and the captain, Mary Sikes had determined that she would have her servant prepare a colonial version of high tea following the wedding. Everyone enjoyed the delicacies, but after tasting one of the offerings Fian slipped out and headed back to the ship to get something more substantial for his taste.

Mrs. Hough, being a Quaker and unaccustomed to practices of the Church of England, had been particularly awed by the proceedings and mentioned to Cynthia, "I do very much approve of the ceremony—although I would have to say that it was a bit pompous for the plain tastes of Mr. Hough and myself."

Cynthia, on the other hand, being of the Church of England and accustomed to high church services in England, was quick to correct Mrs. Hough.

"Oh no, Mrs. Hough," Cynthia said, "quite the contrary is true. The proceedings today—although quite lovely—were rather plain for the Church of England. And I most certainly must say that I thought the Reverend Sikes has outdone himself—quite lovely it was indeed."

The struggle for acceptance has existed ever since the Garden of Eden. In a symbolic sense there may be those who do not fit within the defensive borders we have built, perhaps because they do not share our beliefs, values, or social practices. We wrongfully banish people who are different from us to an existence outside of our conceptual *pale*—imagining that we will somehow protect ourselves. After all, we presume, our version of what is right, real, just and acceptable must be protected—perhaps by any means.

However, love, justice and even civilization itself cannot be confined within boundaries whether literal or figurative—because these are provided by God for the benefit of mankind.

Whether being *beyond the pale* is only an expression of one's figurative place in a family or society, or it is an actual physical, geographical location, this much is true: Sarah Murphy O'Connell will never again be considered an outsider, and Sean Martin O'Connell has returned from beyond the pale to be rightfully reunited among his own.

As the *Southern Swallow* made its way toward North East on the calm swells of Chesapeake Bay, Sean and Sarah stood holding hands, looking eastward.

"Sean," Sarah began, "there's a surprise that I have been preparing for you."

"A surprise?" he asked.

"Yes, and although it was Cynthia's suggestion she assured me that you would not be offended by it."

"Offended?" Sean said, taken aback. "Why might I be offended—what is it then?"

"It's a portion of a poem that has long been her favorite and she told me that it was a favorite of Julia's as well. At first I refused to consider it, but she seemed to believe that you would understand—and I must tell you Sean, since she taught me the verse it has become very significant to me as well. May I?"

"Of course you may and I do know the very poem of which you speak, even though there was a day when the only verses I knew came from the inns of Ireland and weren't fit for the delicate ears of gentle women. It's the poem by Anne Bradstreet I'll wager. Please recite it and I'll tell you this—even though I've known it as Cynthia's and Julia's verse, I'll now hear it as if for the first time. I'll hear it as yours alone. Please recite it Sarah."

"Very well then, but please don't expect that I will have the same sense of the . . . ."

"As I've said, I make no comparison, the verse is yours alone and I will hear it as such as if it were the first time I've heard."

Sarah's eyes grew moist as she looked into Sean's and began:

> *If ever two were one, then surely we.*
> *If ever man were lov'd by wife, then thee.*

If ever wife was happy in a man,
Compare with me, ye women, if you can
I prize thy love more than whole mines of gold,
Or all the riches that the East doth hold.
My love is such that rivers cannot quench,
Nor aught but love from thee, give recompense.
Thy love is such I can no way repay,
The heavens reward thee manifold, I pray.
Then while we live, in love so persevere
That, when we live no more, we may live ever.

Sean repeated what he had said earlier, "Sarah, the verse is yours alone and I have heard it as such."

They embraced again, and those passengers who had been watching the newly married couple smiled their approvals.

They stood in their silent embrace for awhile and then Sean began pensively: "Sarah, when we consider all that represents our past, in the end we can either allow others to control us until we become who they want us to be—or else we can decide for ourselves who we really are."

"I think I understand, Sean," Sarah said, "but I'm not certain so please tell me more."

"I have been considering how others estimate me," Sean said and then paused in reflection. "At one time in my life some thought of me as no more than an orphan living with a maiden aunt in Dublin—and later others thought me a wastrel and a rogue." Again he hesitated as if he had lost his thought, but then continued.

"Yet, in the midst of that, while others may have thought little of me, my Aunt Elayne considered me quite capable of directing the family's affairs and holdings here in Maryland. And yet, coming here I proved myself inept in so many ways at endeavors such as tobacco growing, printing, and boat building."

"Oh, but Sean dear," Sarah pleaded, "you're not inept, nor are you what others may have said."

"Perhaps you do understand," Sean responded. "Yes—that's what I'm trying to express. You see, some may have seen me as the man who married Julia out of guilt. After all, they knew that in some ways I felt that I was responsible for the death of her uncle the Reverend Topping. But, Sarah, they were wrong. I married Julia because of her love for me and my love for her—I plead your pardon for speaking my love for her when you and I have just married."

"Sean, please go on," Sarah said confidently. "I do understand what you're saying and you have offended me in no way. Expressing love for your departed Julia does not in any way make me doubt your love for me."

Somewhat dumfounded, Sean simply stared at Sarah and then said, "You have the heart of a truly honest woman Sarah, and God certainly has blessed me greatly by permitting you to give me your love."

Sean drew her close in an embrace and there they stood for several minutes.

"Allow me to say more," Sean continued. "I could never be able to understand what you have gone through in your violent marriage to Fitzpatrick or know what you've gone through in the loss of your child. Even though I too have lost children, I am aware of the dreadful difference when such a loss must be faced by a mother."

"No one can measure grief, Sean," she responded, "mine or yours."

"And that's my meaning, Sarah. No one knows about us except you and me. This is a new beginning for us both—and I say it's a fine beginning. Just as some thought I married Julia because of my guilt—there may be those now who consider ours a marriage of convenience with you having your needs and I having mine. Sarah I know this, we can never control the expectations others may have for us or what they may want us to be or become."

Sean paused as if in deep thought then claimed, "Yet, this is what we do have power over—to decide that we will become who we desire to be. We will not allow others—whether for our benefit or harm—to direct our lives. Do you understand what I'm saying?"

"Oh yes, Sean," Sarah replied with a smile, "I do understand indeed. And you have given me such fresh hope and a new heart for life, because I know that I can depend on your love and kindness to provide for me—for us—for Nathan, you and me. And, Sean, you must know—I pledge that you can depend on my love for you as well."

"Indeed I do my wife Sarah, and what a great outlook I see for our future. I never really knew why our family manor had been called Dawn Light and never thought to ask why that name was chosen. But I do know this—what it signifies for us Sarah is that today is the beginning of our new days together and the dawn light of every day of our lives together will announce an unblemished prospect for us to be able to choose who we are. No matter whether within the pale or beyond the pale, we shall be together."

DREAM IF YOU MUST

By Harv Nowland

Once upon a life a man should be
the person he always dreams of being

Once upon a dream a man should see
the person he actually is

Once upon a reality a dreamer
becomes what his dreams have been
and the practical man is forgotten

Where are the dreamers
who dream dreams and become men?

Endnotes

[1] *Honniasont* – An Iroquois term that means: "Wearing something round the neck", they belonged to the Iroquoian linguistic family. Also called Black Minqua, a reference to the black badge they wore on their breast, Minqua indicated their relationship to the White Minqua, or Susquehanna. Sean's friend Nokona was a Honniasont. In the 1600s the Honniasont assisted the Susquehanna in war and traded with the Dutch, but eventually were betrayed and destroyed by the Susquehanna and Seneca.

[2] *Shawnee* – From the Algonquin word *shawun* or *shawunogi* meaning southerner, a reference to their original location in the Ohio Valley, south of the Great Lakes, southern Ohio, West Virginia, and western Pennsylvania. They were driven from this area by the Iroquois in the 1660s and scattered to South Carolina, Tennessee's Cumberland Basin, eastern Pennsylvania, and southern Illinois. By 1730 most Shawnee had returned to their homeland but were forced to leave once again—this time by the westward settlement of whites.

[3] *Tuscarora* – *Hemp gatherers*. The hemp plant had many uses among the Carolina Tuscarora. The Tuscarora language is from the northern branch of the Iroquoian languages. Encroachment of Tuscarora lands and the kidnapping and selling their young in Pennsylvania as slave by the whites—caused the so-called Tuscarora war in 1711-13. During the war

an act was passed on June 7, 1712, forbidding the importation of Indians, but allowing their sale as slaves in case any *should* be imported for that purpose. [The white man's version of: "how to make friends and influence people."] After the war most Tuscarora aligned with the Iroquois in New York, especially with the Oneida.

[4] *Quay* (pronounced *key* or *kay*) – A wharf constructed parallel to the bank of a waterway where ships and other vessels are loaded.

[5] *Lenni Lenapi* – The Lenni Lenape (*true people*) spoke *unami*, a dialect of the Algonquian family. They were the Delaware, for which the river that runs through their territory was named. Most Lenni Lenape were driven from their Mid-Atlantic homeland by the English. They would not reveal their true names to those outside of their clan fearing that their name and spirit would be stolen. When forced to fight they were fierce warriors, but their pleasant nature led other tribes to respect them as the *Grandfather* tribe, and they often settled disputes among rivals. The Delaware signed the very first Indian treaty with the newly formed United States Government on September 17, 1778. Nevertheless, just as the English had, this new government forced most Lenni Lenape to give up their lands and move westward to Ohio, then Indiana, Missouri, Kansas and finally Indian Territory, now Oklahoma.

[6] *Yardarm* – Either end of the yard, the spar on a mast from which sails are set.

[7] *Sean anákawa sheénay kawa* = "I (Nokona) will always be Sean's friend" [An alleged Indian phrase, which was passed down from Harvey L. Nowland, Sr. and has become a Nowland family tradition.]

[8] *Pale* –Used in this sense the term *pale* dates back at least to the 15th Century. The *English Pale* was a barrier of posts, ditches and fences that protected an area that included the Irish Counties of Dublin, Meath, Louth, and Kildare. Gradually fortified to prevent attacks by the Irish, it was never completed by the English. To travel outside of that boundary, *beyond the pale*, meant the law and institutions of English culture were left behind. The English, in their estimable humility, considered their society synonymous with civilization itself. To them, *beyond the pale* meant being

outside of the boundaries of civilization where no expectation of civilized treatment existed.

[9] *Perch* – A variable measure used for stonework. One perch is approximately two rods. A rod equals 16.5 feet, making a perch equal to 33 feet. Dawn Light would have been 4,000 acres, which would be approximately 6.25 square miles.

[10] *Socage* – Middle English word meaning: "A tenure of land by agricultural service fixed in amount and kind or by payment of money rent only and not burdened with any military service." *Webster's Ninth New Collegiate Dictionary.*

[11] *Fealty* – Middle English word meaning: "The fidelity of a vassal or feudal tenant to his lord." *Webster's Ninth New Collegiate Dictionary.*

[12] *Toe Toaster* – Tool used to toast bread in the fireplace. The toaster turned on a pivot using one's foot in order to protect the hand from getting burned.

[13] *Sheets* – Landlubbers (like me) might incorrectly think that "sheets" are the sails. However, sheets are rope lines used to adjust or control (trim) sail and the rope lines that are used to raise sails are called halyards.

[14] *Whipstaff*–The ship's wheel did not appear until the mid-to-late 1700s. Ships were steered by a vertical shaft called a whipstaff, found aft usually on the starboard side of the ship. The whipstaff was attached to the rudder bar and when pivoted it moved the rudder to turn the ship.

[15] *Nine Men's Morrice* – A game played on a board, a piece of paper, or even drawn in the dirt. Simple markers of corn, stones, or beans were used for play. A game for two, each player selects nine markers of corn, coins, stones, beans, or whatever they chose just so the markers are different from the opponent's. The object of the game is to make rows of three markers on a line and to prevent the other player from doing the same.

[16] *Gloaming* – Dusk or twilight, after the sun sets but before darkness settles on the land. (p. 84)

[17] *Fathom* – Unit of water-depth measurement that was originally the length of a man's outstretched arms; now the fathom is six feet or 1.83 meters.

[18] *Impressment* – The act of compelling men to serve aboard a ship by force and without notice. Once used extensively by the British Royal Navy.

stonetracebooks
5548 Stone Trace
Gainesville GA 30504-8151
www.stonetracebooks.com

Other books by Harv Nowland

Dawn Light: On the Chesapeake (Xulon Press)
Dark Shadows at Dawn Light (Xulon Press)

Chapbooks from *stonetracebooks*

The Husbandman
(A 14-strophe poetic biblical narrative)

The Way We Tell a Story
(Collection of short stories)

Letter to Flavius
(About the world's only living man)

I Don't Speak Irish
(Poetry)

Books, new and gently read—Original Artwork
Writing—Research—and much more at

www.stonetracebooks.com